THE LAW OF THE GUN

Smoke Jensen checked his guns. He filled both cylinders and every loop on his gunbelt, then checked the short-barreled pistol he carried in his shoulder holster. Breaking open the sawed-off shotgun, he filled both barrels with buckshot loads. Smoke looked on with approval as York pulled two spare .44s out of his warbag and loaded them full. The Arizona Ranger tucked them behind his belt and picked up a Henry repeating rifle, loading it full and levering in a round.

"I'll tell you how I see this thing," Smoke said. "I'm not taking any prisoners."

"I hadn't planned on it myself, Smoke."

"You ready to strike up the band, Ranger?"

"Damn right!" York said with a grin.

"Let's do it!"

BOOK YOUR PLACE ON OUR WEBSITE AND MAKE THE READING CONNECTION!

We've created a customized website just for our very special readers, where you can get the inside scoop on everything that's going on with Zebra, Pinnacle and Kensington books.

When you come online, you'll have the exciting opportunity to:

- View covers of upcoming books
- Read sample chapters
- Learn about our future publishing schedule (listed by publication month *and author*)
- Find out when your favorite authors will be visiting a city near you
- Search for and order backlist books from our online catalog
- Check out author bios and background information
- Send e-mail to your favorite authors
- Meet the Kensington staff online
- Join us in weekly chats with authors, readers and other guests
- Get writing guidelines
- AND MUCH MORE!

**Visit our website at
http://www.kensingtonbooks.com**

WILLIAM W. JOHNSTONE

REVENGE OF THE MOUNTAIN MAN

Pinnacle Books
Kensington Publishing Corp.

http://www.pinnaclebooks.com

PINNACLE BOOKS are published by

Kensington Publishing Corp.
850 Third Avenue
New York, NY 10022

Copyright © 1988 by William W. Johnstone

All rights reserved. No part of this book may be reproduced in any form or by any means without the prior written consent of the Publisher, excepting brief quotes used in reviews.

If you purchased this book without a cover you should be aware that this book is stolen property. It was reported as "unsold and destroyed" to the Publisher and neither the Author nor the Publisher has received any payment for this "stripped book."

Pinnacle and the P logo Reg. U.S. Pat. & TM Off.

First Printing: March, 1988
First Pinnacle Printing: October, 2000
20 19 18 17 16 15

Printed in the United States of America

This book is pure Western fiction. Any resemblance to actual persons, living or dead, is purely coincidental. To the best of my knowledge, there are no towns in Colorado named Big Rock or Dead River.

I am the wound and the knife!
I am the blow and the cheek!
I am the limbs and the wheel
—the victim and the executioner.

Baudelaire

1

They had struck as cowards usually do, in a pack and at night. And when the man of the house was not at home. They had come skulking like thieving foot-padders; but instead of robbery on their minds, their thoughts were of a much darker nature.

Murder.

And they had tried to kill Smoke Jensen's wife, Sally. When Smoke and Sally had married, just after Smoke almost totally wiped out the small town of Bury, Idaho, Smoke had used another name; but later, during the valley war around Big Rock and Fontana, he had once more picked up his real name, and be damned to all who didn't like the fact that he had once been a gunfighter.

It had never been a reputation that he had sought out; rather, it had seemed to seek him out. Left alone as a boy, raised by an old mountain man called Preacher, the young man had become one of the most feared and legended gunslingers in all the West. Some say he was the fastest gun alive. Some say that Smoke Jensen had killed fifty, one hundred, two hundred men.

No one really knew for certain.

All anyone really knew was that Smoke had never been an outlaw, never ridden the hoot-owl trail, had no warrants out on him, and was a quiet sort of man. Now married, for several years he had been a farmer/rancher/horse breeder. A peaceful man who got along well with his neighbors and wished only to be left alone.

The night riders had shattered all that.

Smoke had been a hundred miles away, buying cattle, just starting the drive back to his ranch, called the Sugarloaf, when he heard the news. He had cut two horses out of his remuda and tossed a saddle on one. He would ride one, change saddles, and ride the other. They were mountain horses, tough as leather, and they stood up to the hard test.

Smoke did not ruin his horses on the long lonely ride back to the Sugarloaf, did not destroy them as some men might. But he rode steadily. He was torn inside, but above it all Smoke remained a realist, as old Preacher had taught him to be. He knew he would either make it in time, or he would not.

When he saw the snug little cabin in the valley of the high lonesome, the vastness of the high mountains all around it, Smoke knew, somehow, he had made it in time.

Smoke was just swinging down from the saddle when Dr. Colton Spalding stepped out of the cabin, smiling broadly when he spied Smoke. The doctor stopped the gunfighter before Smoke could push open the cabin door.

"She's going to make it, Smoke. But it was a close thing. If Bountiful had not awakened when she did and convinced Ralph that something was the matter . . ." The doctor shrugged his shoulders. "Well, it would have been all over here."

"I'm in their debt. But Sally is going to make it?"

"Yes. I have her sedated heavily with laudanum, to help her cope with the pain."

"Is she awake?"

"No. Smoke, they shot her three times. Shoulder, chest, and side. They left her for dead. She was not raped."

"Why did they do it? And who were they?"

"No one knows, except possibly Sally. And so far, the sheriff has not been able to question her about it."

"Bounty hunters, maybe. But there is no bounty on my head. I'm not wanted anywhere that I'm aware of."

"Nevertheless, Sheriff Carson believes it was bounty hunters. Someone paid to kill you. Or to draw you out, to come after them. The sheriff is with the posse now, trying to track the men."

"I'll just look in on her, Colton."

The doctor nodded and pushed open the cabin door. Smoke stepped past him.

The doctor's wife, Mona, a nurse, was sitting with several other women in the big main room of the cabin. They smiled at Smoke as he removed his hat and hung it on a peg by the door. He took off his gunbelt and hung it on another peg.

"Doc said it was all right for me to look in on her."

Mona nodded her head.

Smoke pushed open the bedroom door and stepped quietly inside, his spurs jingling faintly with each step. A big man, with a massive barrel chest and arms and shoulders packed with muscle, he could move as silently as his nickname implied.

Smoke felt a dozen different emotions as he looked at the pale face of his wife. Her dark hair seemed to make her face look paler. In his mind, there was love and hate and fury and black-tinged thoughts of revenge, all intermingled with sorrow and compassion. Darker emotions filled the tall young man as he sat down in a chair beside the bed and gently placed one big rough hand on his wife's smaller and softer hand.

Did she stir slightly under his touch? Smoke could not be sure. But he was sure that somehow, in her pain-filled mind, Sally knew that he was there, beside her.

Now, alone, Smoke could allow emotions to change his usually stoic expression. His eyes mirrored his emotions. He wished he could somehow take her pain and let it fill his own body. He took the damp cloth from her head, refreshed it with water, wrung it out, and softly replaced it on her brow.

All through the rest of that day and the long, lonely night that followed, the young man sat by his wife's bed. Mona Spalding would enter hourly, sometimes shooing Smoke out of the room, tending to Sally's needs. Doc Spalding slept in a chair, the two other women, Belle North and Bountiful Morrow, Smoke and Sally's closest

11

neighbors, sleeping in the spare bedroom.

Outside, the foreman, Pearlie, and the other hands had gathered, war talk on their lips and in the way they stood. Bothering a woman, good or bad, in this time in the West, was a hangin' matter . . . or just an outright killin'.

Little Billy, Smoke and Sally's adopted son, sat on a bench outside the house.

Just as the dawn was breaking golden over the high mountains around the Sugarloaf, Sally opened her eyes and smiled at her husband.

"You look tired," she said. "Have you had anything to eat?"

"No."

"Have you been here long?"

"Stop worrying about me. How do you feel?"

"Washed out."

He smiled at her. "I don't know what I'm going to do with you," he said gently. "I go off for a time and you get into a gunfight. That isn't very ladylike, you know? What would your folks back east think?"

She winked at him.

"Doc says you're going to be all right, Sally. But you're going to need lots of rest."

"Three of them," she whispered. "I heard them talking. I guess they thought I was dead. One was called Dagget . . ."

"Hush now."

"No. Let me say it while I still remember it. I heard one call another Lapeer. He said that if this doesn't bring you out, nothing will."

She closed her eyes. Smoke waited while she gathered strength.

Doc Spalding had entered the room, standing in the doorway, listening.

He met Smoke's eyes and inwardly cringed at the raw savagery he witnessed in the young man's cold gaze. Spalding had seen firsthand the lightning speed of Smoke's draw. Had witnessed the coldness of the man when angered. Fresh from the ordered world back east, the

12

doctor was still somewhat appalled at the swiftness of frontier justice. But deep inside him, he would reluctantly agree that it was oftentimes better than the ponderousness of lawyers jabbering and arguing.

Sally said, "The third one was called Moore. Glen Moore. South Colorado, I think. I'm tired, honey."

Spalding stepped forward. "That's all, Smoke. Let her sleep. I want to show you something out in the living room."

In the big room that served as kitchen, dining, and sitting area, the doctor dropped three slugs into Smoke's callused palm.

He had dug enough lead out of men since his arrival to be able to tell one slug from another. ".44's, aren't they?"

"Two of them," Smoke said, fingering the off-slug. "This is a .44-40, I believe."

"The one that isn't mangled up?"

"Yes."

"That's the one I dug out of her chest. It came close to killing her, Smoke." He opened his mouth to say something, sighed, and then obviously thought better of it.

"You got something else to say, Doc?"

He shook his head. "Later. Perhaps Sally will tell you herself; that would be better, I'm thinking. And no, she isn't going to die. Smoke, you haven't eaten and you need rest. Mona agrees. She's fixing you something now. Please. You've got to eat."

"You will eat, and then you will rest," Belle said, a note of command in her voice. "Johnny is with the posse, Smoke. Velvet is looking after the kids. You'll eat, and then sleep. So come sit down at the table, Smoke Jensen."

"Yes, ma'am," Smoke said with a smile.

"I was waiting to be certain," Sally told him the next morning. "Dr. Spalding confirmed it the day before those men came. I'm pregnant, Smoke."

A smile creased his lips. He waited, knowing, sensing

13

there was more to come.

Sally's eyes were serious. "Colton is leaving it all up to me, isn't he?"

"I reckon, Sally. I don't know. I do know that your voice is much stronger."

"I feel much better."

Smoke waited.

"You're not going to like what I have to say, Smoke. Not . . . in one way, that is."

"No way of knowing that, Sally. Not until you say what's on your mind."

She sighed, and the movement hurt her; pain crossed her face. "I'm probably going to have to go back east, Smoke."

Smoke's expression did not change. "I think that might be best, Sally. For a time."

She visibly relaxed. She did not ask why he had said that. She knew. He was going after the men who attacked her. She expected that of him. "You're not even going to ask why I might have to go back east?"

"I would think it's because the doctor told you to. But you won't be going anywhere for weeks. You were hard hit." He smiled. "I've been there, too." He kissed her mouth. "Now, you rest."

Mona and Belle stayed for three days; Bountiful lived just over the hill and could come and go with ease. On the morning of the fourth day, Sally was sitting up in bed, her color back. She was still in some pain and very weak, and would be for several more weeks.

Smoke finally brought up the subject. "The Doc is sure that you're with child?"

"Both of us are," she smiled with her reply. "I knew before the doctor."

Discussion of women's inner workings embarrassed Smoke. He dropped that part of it. "Now tell me why you think you might have to go back east."

"I have several pieces of lead in me, Smoke. Colton could not get them all. And he does not have the expertise nor the facilities to perform the next operation. And also, I have a small pelvis; the birth might be a difficult one. There is a new—well, a more highly refined procedure that is being used back east. I won't go into detail about that."

"Thank you," Smoke said dryly. "Cause so far I don't have much idea of what you're talking about."

She laughed softly at her husband. A loving laugh and a knowing laugh. Smoke knew perfectly well what she was saying. He was, for the most part, until they had married, a self-taught man. And over the past few years, she had been tutoring him. He was widely read, and to her delight and surprise, although few others knew it, Smoke was a very good actor, with a surprising range of voices and inflections. She was continually drawing out that side of him.

"Mona's from back east, isn't she?"

"I'm way ahead of you, Smoke. Yes, she is. And if I have to go—and I'm thinking it might be best, and you know why, and it doesn't have anything to do with the baby or the operation—Mona will make all the arrangements and travel most of the way with me."

"That'll be good, Sally. Yes. I think you should plan on traveling east." She knew the set of that chin. Her leaving was settled; her husband had things to do. "You haven't seen your folks in almost five years. It's time to visit. Tell you what I'll do. I'll come out for you when it's time for you and the baby to return."

This time her laugh was hearty, despite her injuries. "Smoke, do you know the furor your presence would arouse in Keene, New Hampshire?"

"If *fu-ror* means what I think it does, why should people get all in a sweat about me coming east?"

"For sure, bands would play, you would be a celebrity, and the police would be upset."

"Why? I ain't wanted back there, or anywhere else for that matter."

She could but smile at him. If he knew, he had dismissed the fact that he was the most famous gunfighter in all of the West; that books—penny dreadfuls—had been and still were being written about his exploits—some of them fact, many of them fiction. That he had been written up in tabloids all over the world, and not just in the English-speaking countries. Her mother and father had sent Sally articles about her husband from all over the world. To say that they had been a little concerned about her safety—for a while—would be putting it mildly.

"People don't really believe all that crap that's been written about me, do they? Hell, Sally, I've been reported at fourteen different places at once, according to those stories."

"If they just believed the real things you've done, Smoke, that is enough to make people very afraid of you."

"That's silly! I never hurt anybody who wasn't trying to hurt me. People don't have any reason to be afraid of me."

"Well, I'm not afraid of you, Smoke. You're sort of special to me."

He smiled. "Oh, yeah? Well, I'd have to give it a lot of thought if someone was to offer to trade me a spotted pony for you, Sally."

2

Smoke Jensen and Sally Reynolds, gunfighter and schoolteacher, had met several years back, in Idaho. Just before Smoke had very nearly wiped out a town and all the people in it for killing his first wife and their child, Nicole and Baby Arthur; the boy named after Smoke's friend and mentor, the old mountain man, Preacher.

Smoke and Sally had married, living in peace for several years in the high lonesome, vast and beautiful mountains of Colorado. Then a man named Tilden Franklin had wanted to be king of the entire valley . . . and he had coveted Smoke's wife, making it public news.

Gold had been discovered in the valley, and a bitter, bloody war had ensued.

And in the end, all Tilden Franklin got was a half-a-dozen slugs in the belly, from the guns of Smoke Jensen, and six feet of hard cold ground.

That had been almost two years back; two years of peace in the valley and in Smoke and Sally's high-up ranch called the Sugarloaf.

Now that had been shattered.

On the morning of the first full week after the assault on Sally, Smoke sat on the bench outside the snug cabin and sipped his coffee.

Late spring in the mountains.

1880, and the West was slowly changing. There would be another full decade of lawlessness, of wild and woolly days and nights; but the law was making its mark felt all over the area. And Smoke, like so many other western men, knew that was both good and bad. For years, a common-sense type of justice had prevailed, for the most part, in the West, and usually—not always, but usually—it worked. Swiftly and oftentimes brutally, but it worked. Now, things were changing. Lawyers with big words and fancy tongues were twisting facts, hiding the guilt to win a case. And Smoke, like most thinking people, thought that to be wrong.

The coming of courts and laws and lawyers would prove to be both a blessing and a curse.

Smoke, like most western men, just figured that if someone tried to do you a harm or a meanness, just shoot the son of a bitch and have done with it. Cause odds were, the guilty party wasn't worth a damn to begin with. And damn few were ever going to miss them.

Smoke, like so many western men, judged other men by what they gave to society as opposed to what they took away from it. If your neighbor's house or barn burned down or was blown down in a storm, you helped him rebuild. If his crops were bad or his herd destroyed, you helped him out until next season or loaned him some cows and a few bulls. If he and his family were hungry through no fault of their own, you helped out with food and clothing.

And so on down the line of doing things right.

And if a man wouldn't help out, chances were he was trash, and the sooner you got rid of him, the better.

Western justice and common sense.

And if people back east couldn't see that—well, Smoke thought . . . Well, he really didn't know what to think about people like that. He'd reserve judgment until he got to know a few of them.

He sipped his coffee and let his eyes drift over that part of his land that he could see from his front yard. And that was a lot of land, but just a small portion of all that he and Sally owned . . . free and clear.

There was a lot to do before Smoke put Sally on the steam trains and saw her off to the East—and before he started after those who had attacked her like rabid human beasts in the night.

And there was only one thing you could do with a rabid beast.

Kill it.

Billy stepped out of the house and took a seat on the bench beside his adopted father. The boy had been legally adopted by the Jensens; Judge Proctor had seen to that. Billy was pushing hard at his teen years, soon turning thirteen. Already he was a top hand and, even though Smoke discouraged it, a good hand with a gun. Uncommon quick. Smoke and Sally had adopted the boy shortly after the shoot-out in Fontana, and now Billy pulled his weight and then some around the Sugarloaf.

"You and Miss Sally both gonna go away?" Billy asked, his voice full of gloom.

"For a time, Billy. Sally thought about taking you back east with her, but you're in school here, and doing well. So Reverend Ralph and Bountiful are going to look after you. You'll stay here at the ranch with Pearlie and the hands. We might be gone for the better part of a year, Billy, so it's going to be up to you to be the man around the place."

Pearlie was leaning up against a hitch rail and Smoke winked at his friend and foreman.

"If I hadn't a-been out with the hands the other night . . ." Billy said.

Smoke cut him off. "And if your aunt had wheels, she'd have been a tea cart, Billy. You and the hands were doing what I asked you to do—pushing cattle up to the high grass. Can't any of you blame yourselves for what happened."

"I don't think my aunt had no wheels, Smoke," Billy said solemnly. Then he realized that Smoke was funning with him and he smiled. "That would be a sight to see though, wouldn't it?"

Pearlie walked up to the man and boy. "We'll be all right here, Billy. I don't know what I'd do without you. You're a top hand."

Billy grinned at the high compliment.

When the foreman and the boy had walked away, Smoke

stepped back into the house and fixed breakfast for Sally, taking it to her on a tray. He positioned pillows behind her shoulders and gently eased her to an upright position in the bed.

He sat by the bed and watched her eat; slowly she was regaining her strength and appetite. But she was still very weak and had to be handled with caution.

She would eat a few bites and then rest for a moment, gathering strength.

"I'm getting better, Smoke," she told him with a smile. "And the food is beginning to taste good."

"I can tell. At first I thought it was my cooking," he kidded her. "Your color is almost back to normal. Feel like telling me more about what happened?"

She ate a few more bites and then pushed the tray from her. "It's all come back to me. The doctor said it would. He said that sometimes severe traumas can produce temporary memory loss."

Colton had told Smoke the same thing.

She looked at him. "It was close, wasn't it?"

"You almost died, honey."

She closed her eyes for a moment and then opened them, saying, "I remember the time. Nine o'clock. I was just getting ready for bed. I remember glancing at the clock. I was in my gown." Her brow furrowed in painful remembrance, physically and mentally. "I heard a noise outside, or so I thought. But when it wasn't repeated, I ignored it. I walked in here, to the bedroom, and then I heard the noise again. I remember feeling a bit frightened. . . ."

"Why?" he interrupted. He was curious, for Sally was not the spooky or flighty kind. She had used a rifle and pistol several times since settling here, and had killed or wounded several outlaws.

"Because it was not a natural sound. It was raining, and I had asked Billy, when he came in to get lunch packets for the crew, to move the horses into the barn, to their stalls for the night. Bad move, I guess. If Seven or Drifter had been in the corral, they would have warned me."

"I would have done the same thing, Sally. Stop blaming yourself. Too much of that going on around here. It was nobody's fault. It happened, it's over, and it's not going to happen again. Believe me, I will see to that."

And she knew he would.

"When the noise came again, it was much closer, like someone brushing up against the side of the house. I was just reaching for a pistol when the front door burst open. Three men; at least three men. I got the impression there was more, but I saw only three. I heard three names. I did tell you the names, didn't I? That part is hazy."

"Yes."

"Dagget, Lapeer, and Moore. Yes. Now I remember telling you. The one called Dagget smiled at me. Then he said"—she struggled to remember—"'Too bad we don't have more time. I'd like to see what's under that gown.' Then he lifted his pistol and shot me. No warning. No time at all to do anything. He just lifted his gun and shot me. As I was falling, the other two shot me."

Smoke waited, his face expressionless. But his inner thoughts were murderous.

Sally closed her eyes, resting for a moment before once more reliving the horrible night. "Just as I was falling into darkness, losing consciousness, I heard one say, 'Now the son of a bitch has us all to deal with.'"

And I will deal with you, Smoke thought. One by one, on a very personal basis. I will be the judge, the jury, and the executioner.

Smoke started to roll and light one of his rare cigarettes, then thought better of it. The smoke might cause Sally to cough and he knew that would be harmful.

"Do you know any of the men I mentioned, Smoke?"

"No. I can't say that I've even heard of them." There was a deep and dangerous anger within him. But he kept his voice and his emotions well in check. He hated night riders, of any kind. He knew those types of people were, basically, cowards.

He kept his face bland. He did not want Sally to get alarmed, although he knew that she knew exactly what he was going to do once she was safely on the train heading east. He also knew that when she did mention it—probably only one time—she would not attempt to stop him.

That was not her way. She had known the kind of man he was when she married him.

He met her eyes, conscious of her staring at him, and smiled at her. She held out a hand and Smoke took it, holding it gently.

"It's a mystery to me, honey," she said. "I just don't understand it. The valley has been so peaceful for so many months. Not a shot fired in anger. Now this."

Smoke hushed her, taking the lap tray. He had never even heard of a lap tray until Sally had sent off for one from somewhere back east. "You rest now. Sleep. You want some more laudanum?"

She minutely shook her head. "No. Not now. The pain's not too bad. That stuff makes my head feel funny."

She was sleeping even before Smoke had closed the door.

He scraped the dishes and washed them in hot water taken from the stove, then pumped a pot full of fresh water and put that on the stove, checking the wood level that heated the back plate and checking the draft. He peeled potatoes for lunch and dropped them into cold water. Then he swept the floor and tidied up the main room, opening all the windows to let the house cool.

Then the most famous and feared gunfighter in all the west washed clothes, wrung them out, and hung them up to dry on the clothesline out back, the slight breeze and the warm sun freshening them naturally.

He walked around to the front of the cabin and sat beside the bedroom window, open just a crack, so he could hear Sally if she needed anything.

Lapeer, Moore, and Dagget. He rolled those names around in his mind as his fingers skillfully rolled a cigarette. He had never heard of any of them. But he knew one thing for certain.

They were damn sure going to hear from him.

3

Smoke did not leave the Sugarloaf range for weeks. If supplies were needed, one of the hands went into town for them. Smoke did not want to stray very far from Sally's side.

The days passed slowly, each one bringing another hint of the summer that lay lazily before them. And Sally grew stronger. Two weeks after the shooting, she was able to walk outside, with help, and sit for a time, taking the sun, taking it easy, growing stronger each day.

Smoke had spoken with Sheriff Monte Carson several times since the posse's return from a frustrating and fruitless pursuit. But Monte was just as baffled as Smoke as to the why of Sally's attack and the identity of the attackers.

Judge Proctor had been queried, as well as most of the other people around the valley. No one had ever heard of the men.

It was baffling and irritating.

Not even the legended Smoke could fight an enemy he could not name and did not know and could not find.

Yet.

But he was going to find them, and when he did, he was going to make some sense out of this.

Then he would kill them.

It was midsummer before Dr. Colton Spalding finally gave Sally the okay to travel. During that time, he had wired the hospital in Boston several times, setting up Sally's operation. The doctor would use a rather risky procedure called caesarean to take the baby—if it came to that. But the Boston doctor wanted to examine Sally himself before he elected to use that drastic a procedure. And according to Dr. Spalding, the Boston doctor was convinced a caesarean was necessary.

"What's this operation all about?" Smoke asked Dr. Spalding.

"It's a surgical procedure used to take the baby if the mother can't deliver normally."

"I don't understand, but I'll take your word for it. Is it dangerous?"

Colton hesitated. With Smoke, it was hard to tell exactly what he knew about any given topic. When they had first met, the doctor thought the young man to be no more than an ignorant brute, a cold-blooded killer. It didn't take Colton long to realize that while Smoke had little formal education, he was widely read and quite knowledgeable.

And Colton also knew that Smoke was one of those rare individuals one simply could not lie to. Smoke's unblinking eyes never left the face of the person who was speaking. Until you grew accustomed to it, it was quite unnerving.

Before Colton could speak, Smoke said, "Caesar's mother died from this sort of thing, didn't she?"

The doctor smiled, shaking his head. Many of the men of the West were fascinating with what they knew and how they had learned it. It never ceased to amaze the man to see some down-at-the-heels puncher, standing up in a barroom quoting Shakespeare or dissertating on some subject as outrageous as astrology.

And knowing what he was talking about!

"Yes, it is dangerous, Smoke. But not nearly so dangerous as when Caesar was born."

"Let's hope not. What happens if Sally decides not to have this operation?"

"One of two things, Smoke. You will decide whether you want Sally saved, or the baby."

"I won't be there, Doc. So I'm telling you now—save my

wife. You pass the word along to this doctor friend of yours in Boston town. Save Sally at all costs. You'll do that, right?''

"You know I will. I'll wire him first thing in the morning.''

"Thank you.''

Colton watched as Smoke helped Sally back to bed. He had not fully leveled with the young man about the surgical procedure. Colton knew that sometimes the attending physician had very little choice as to who would be saved. And sometimes, mother and child both died.

He sighed. They had come so far in medicine, soaring as high as eagles in such a short time. But doctors still knew so very little . . . and were expected to perform miracles at all times.

"Would that it were so,'' Colton muttered, getting into his buggy and clucking at the mare.

As the weather grew warmer and the days grew longer, Sally grew stronger . . . and was beginning to show her pregnancy. Several of the women who lived nearby would come over almost daily, to sew and talk and giggle about the damndest things.

Smoke left the scene when all that gabble commenced.

And he was still no closer to finding out anything about the men who attacked his wife.

Leaving Sally and the women, with two hands always on guard near the cabin, Smoke saddled the midnight-black horse with the cold killer eyes, and he and Drifter went to town.

The town of Fontana, once called No Name, which had been Tilden Franklin's town, was dying just as surely as Tilden had died under Smoke's guns. Only a few stores remained open, and they did very little business.

It was to the town of Big Rock that Smoke rode, his .44's belted around his lean waist and tied down, the Henry rifle in his saddle boot.

Big Rock was growing as Fontana was dying. A couple

of nice cafés, a small hotel, one saloon, with no games and no hurdy-gurdy girls. There was a lawyer, Hunt Brook, and his wife, Willow, and a newspaper, the *Big Rock Guardian*, run by Haywood and Dana Arden. Judge Proctor, the reformed wino, was the district judge and he made his home in Big Rock, taking his supper at the hotel every evening he was in town. Big Rock had a church and a schoolhouse.

It was a nice quiet little town; but as some men who had tried to tree it once found out, Big Rock was best left alone.

Johnny North, who had married the widow Belle Colby after her husband's death, was—or had been—one of the West's more feared and notorious gunfighters. A farmer/rancher now, Johnny would, if the situation called for it, strap on and tie down his guns and step back into his gunfighter's boots. Sheriff Monte Carson, another ex-gunfighter, was yet another gunhawk to marry a grass-widow and settle in Big Rock. Pearlie, Smoke's foreman, had married and settled down; but Pearlie had also been, at one point in his young life, a much-feared and respected fast gun. The minister, Ralph Morrow, was an ex-prizefighter from back east, having entered the ministry after killing a man with his fists. Ralph preached on Sundays and farmed and ranched during the week. Ralph would also pick up a gun and fight, although most would rather he wouldn't. Ralph couldn't shoot a short gun worth a damn!

Big Rock and the area surrounding it was filled with men and women who would fight for their families, their homes, and their lands.

The dozen or so outlaws who rode into town with the thought of taking over and having their way with the women some months back soon found that they had made a horrible and deadly mistake. At least half of them died in their saddles, their guns in their hands. Two more were shot down in the street. Two died in the town's small clinic. The rest were hanged.

The word soon went out along the hoot-owl trail: Stay away from Big Rock. The town is pure poison. Folks there will shoot you quicker than a cat can scat.

Smoke caught up with Johnny North, who was in town for supplies. The two of them found Sheriff Carson and went to the Big Rock saloon for a couple of beers and some conversation. The men sipped their beers in silence for a time. Finally, after their mugs had been refilled, Johnny broke the silence.

"I been thinkin' on it some, Smoke. I knew I'd heard that name Dagget somewheres before, but I couldn't drag it out of my head and catch no handle on it. It come to me last night. I come up on that name down near the Sangre de Cristo range a few years back. It might not be the same fellow, but I'm bettin' it is. Sally's description of him fits what I heard. If it is, he's a bad one. Bounty hunter and bodyguard to somebody. I don't know who. I ain't never heard of the two other men with him."

"I ain't never heard of any of them," Monte said sourly. "And I thought I knew ever gunslick west of the Big Muddy. That was any good, that is."

"Dagget don't ride the rim much," Johnny explained. "And he only takes jobs his boss wants him to take. If this is the same fellow, he's from back east somewheres. Came out here about ten years ago. Supposed to be from a real good family back there. Got in trouble with the law and had to run. But his family seen to it that he had plenty of money. What he done, so I'm told, is link up with some other fellow and set them up an outlaw stronghold; sort of like the Hole-In-The-Wall. All this is just talk; I ain't never been there."

Smoke nodded his head. Something else had jumped into his mind; something the old mountain man, Preacher, had said one time. Something about the time he'd had to put lead into a fellow who lived down near the Sangre de Cristo range. But what was the man's name? Was it Davidson? Yes. Rex Davidson.

"Rex Davidson," Smoke said it aloud.

Both Monte and Johnny stiffened at the name, both men turning their heads to look at Smoke.

When Johnny spoke, his voice was soft. "What'd you

say, Smoke?''

Smoke repeated the name.

Monte whistled softly. "I really hope he ain't got nothing to do with the attack agin Sally.''

Smoke looked at him. "Why?''

Monte finished his beer and motioned the two men outside, to the boardwalk. He looked up and down the street and then sat down on the wooden bench in front of the saloon, off to the side from the batwing entrance. Johnny and Smoke joined him.

"That name you just mentioned, Smoke . . . what do you know about him?''

"Absolutely nothing. I heard Preacher mention it one time, and one time only. That was years back, when I was just a kid. The name is all I know except that Preacher told me he had to put lead into him one time.''

Monte nodded his head. "So that's it. Well, that clears it up right smart. Finishes the tale I been hearin' for years. I'll just be damned, boys!''

The men waited until Monte had rolled and licked a cigarette into shape and lighted it.

"Must have been . . . oh, at least twenty years back, so the story goes. Rex Davidson was about twenty, I guess. Might have been a year or two younger than that. I don't know the whole story; just bits and pieces. But this Davidson had just come into the area from somewheres. California, I think it was. And he thought he was castin' a mighty big shadow wherever it was he walked. He was good with a gun, and a mighty handsome man, too. I seen him once, and he is a lady killer. What's the word I'm lookin' for? Vain, that's it. Pretties himself up all the time.

"There was a tradin' post down on the Purgatoire called Slim's. Run by a Frenchman. It's still there, and the same guy runs it. Only now it's a general store. It sits east and some north of Trinidad, where the Francisco branches off from the Purgatoire.

"This Davidson was there, braggin' about how he was gettin' rich diggin' gold and running cattle up between the Isabel and the Sangre de Cristos. Said he was gonna build hisself a town. Done it, too."

Monte dragged on his cigarette and Johnny said, "Dead River."

"You got it."

"Damn good place to stay shut of."

"Sure is," Monte ground out his smoke under the heel of his boot. "Whole damn town is owned by this Davidson and maybe by this Dagget, too. Anyways, this was back . . . oh, 'bout '60, I reckon, and this mountain man come into the tradin' post with some pelts he'd taken up near the Apishapa and the Arkansas. Him and Slim was jawin' over the price when this Rex Davidson decided he'd stick his nose into the affair. He made some crack about the mountain man's weapons and the way he was talkin'. This mountain man wasn't no big fellow; but size don't amount to a hill of beans when you start gettin' smart-lipped with them people—as you well know, Smoke."

Smoke nodded his head. He knew all too well the truth in that statement. Mountain men, for the most part, stayed away from people and civilization, keeping mostly to themselves, but God have mercy on your soul if you started trouble with them.

Oh, yes, Smoke knew. He had been raised up during his formative years by the most legended of all mountain men—old Preacher.

"Well, that mountain man's name was Preacher," Monte continued. "Slim told me that Preacher didn't say nothin' to Davidson; just ignored him. And that made Davidson hot under the collar. He called out, 'Hey, you greasy old bastard. I'm talking to you, old man!'"

"He shouldn't have done that," Smoke said softly.

And in his mind's eye, as Monte told his tale, Smoke could see what had happened. Smoke smiled as he visualized the long-ago day. . . .

Preacher turned slowly, looking at the young man with the twin Colt Navy .36's belted around his waist and tied down low. The fast draw was new to the West, and some that thought they were fast weren't. The mountain man, slim and lean-waisted, had a faint smile on his lips.

"What'd you want, Tadpole?"

Davidson flushed red, hot and unreasonable anger flashing in his eyes.

The kid is crazy, Preacher guessed accurately. And he's a killer.

"The name is Rex Davidson, old man."

"Do tell? Is that 'pposed to mean something to me, Tadpole?"

"Yeah. I'm a gunfighter."

"Is that right?" Preacher drawled. "Well, now, how come it is I ain't never seen none of your graveyards, Tadpole?"

"Well, old man, maybe you just haven't been in the right towns, standing in the right boot hill. I got 'em scattered around, here and there."

"My, my! I 'spect I should be im-pressed." He smiled. "But I ain't," he added softly.

"I thought you mountain men was supposed to be so damn tough!" Rex sneered. "You sound like you're scared to visit a graveyard."

"Oh . . . well, now, I tend to shy away from graveyards, Tadpole. They can be mighty spooky places. Some Injuns believe a man can lose his soul by wanderin' around in a graveyard. Mayhaps that's what happened to you, Tadpole."

"What the hell are you babbling about, you old bastard? I think you're silly!"

"Tadpole, I think you've prowled around so many old boneyards, lookin' up names on markers so's you could lie about how bad you want people to think you is . . . why, hell, Tadpole, I think you lost your soul."

"You calling me a liar, old man?" Rex fairly screamed the question, his hands dropping to his sides to hover over the butts of his Navy Colts.

"Could be, Tadpole," Preacher spoke softly. "But if I was you, I wouldn't take no of-fense. Not if you want to go

on livin' healthy."

Slim Dugas got the hell out of the line of fire. He didn't know this punk-faced kid from Adam's Off Ox, but he sure as hell knew all about Preacher and that wild breed of men called mountain men. There just wasn't no back-up in a mountain man. Not none at all.

"No man calls me a liar and lives, you greasy old fart!" Rex screamed.

"Well, now, Tadpole. It shore 'ppears like I done it, though, don't it?"

"Damn your eyes! Draw!" Davidson shouted, his palms slapping the butts of his guns.

Preacher lifted his Sharps and pulled the trigger. He had cocked it while Davidson was running off at the mouth about how bad he was. The .52 slug struck the young man in the side, exactly where Preacher intended it to go; he didn't want to kill the punk. But in later years he would realize that he should have. The force of the slug turned Davidson around and spun him like a top, knocking him against a wall and to the floor. He had not even cleared leather.

Monte chuckled and that brought Smoke back from years past in his mind.

"Slim told me that Preacher collected his money for his pelts, picked up his bacon and beans, and walked out the door; didn't even look at Davidson. There was four or five others in the room, drinking rotgut, and they spread the story around about Davidson. Smoke, Davidson has hated Preacher and anyone connected with him for years. And one more thing: All them men in that room, they was all back-shot, one at a time over the years. Only one left alive was Slim."

"That tells me that this Davidson is crazy as a bessie-bug."

"Damn shore is," Johnny agreed. "What kind of man would hate like that, and for so long? It ain't as if Smoke was any actual kin of Preacher's. Why wait this long to do something about it?"

"You askin' me questions I ain't got no answers for," Monte replied.

Smoke stood up. "Well, you can all bet one thing. I'm damn sure going to find out!"

4

Smoke could tell that Sally was getting anxious to travel east and see her folks. She tried to hide her growing excitement, but finally she gave in and admitted she was ready to go.

Some men—perhaps many men—would have been reluctant to let their wives travel so far away from the hearth of home, especially when taking into consideration the often terrible hardships that the women of the West had to endure when compared with the life-style of women comfortably back east, with their orderly, structured society and policemen walking the beat.

Why, Sally had even told of indoor plumbing, complete with relief stations, not just bathing tubs. Smoke couldn't even imagine how something like that might work. He reckoned it would take a hell of a lot of digging, but it sure would be smelly if the pipes were to clog.

"You real sure you're up to this thing?" Smoke asked her.

"I feel fine, honey. And the doctor says I'm one hundred percent healed."

He patted her swelling belly and grinned. "Getting a little chubby, though."

She playfully slapped at his hand. "What are you going to do if it's twins?"

He put a fake serious look on his face. "Well, I might just take off for the mountains!"

She put her arms around him. "Mona says all the travel arrangements are complete. She says we'll be leaving the last part of next week."

"She told me. The Doc and me will ride down to Denver with you and see you both off."

"I'll like that. And then, Smoke? . . ."

"You know what I have to do, Sally. And it isn't a question of wanting to do it. It's something I have to do."

She lay her head on his chest. "I know. When will they ever leave us alone?"

"Maybe never, honey. Accept that. Not as long as there is some punk kid who fancies himself a gun-slick and is looking to make a rep for himself. Not as long as there are bounty hunters who work for jackasses like this Rex Davidson and his kind. And not as long as there are Rex Davidsons in the world."

"It's all so simple for you, isn't it, Smoke?"

He knew what she was talking about. "Yes. If we could get rid of the scum of the earth, it would be such a very nice place to live."

With her arms still around him, feeling the awesome physical strength of the man, she said, "Didn't you tell me that this Dagget person came from back east?"

"Yeah. That's what Johnny told me and the sheriff. Came out here about ten years ago. Are you thinking that you know this fellow?"

"It might be the same person. Maybe. It was a long time ago, Smoke. And not an experience that I wanted to remember. I've tried very hard to put it out of my mind."

"Put what out of your mind?"

She pulled away from him and walked to the open window, the curtains ruffling with the slight breeze. "It was a long time ago. I was . . . oh, I guess nine or ten." She paused for a time, Smoke waiting patiently. "I finally forced myself to remember something else Dagget said that night. He said that he . . . had wanted to see me naked for a long time. Then he grinned. Nasty. Evil. Perverted. Then I recalled that . . . experience so long ago."

She turned to face him.

"I was . . . molested as a child. I was not raped, but molested. By a man whom I believe to be this Dagget

34

person. I screamed and it frightened him away. But before he left me, he slapped me and told me that if I ever told, he would kill my parents." She shrugged her shoulders. "I never told anyone before this."

"And you believe this Dagget is the same man?"

"I'm sure of it now. Shortly after my . . . incident, the man was forced to leave town; he killed a man in a lover's quarrel."

"All the more reason to kill the man."

"I was not the only little girl he molested. Some were actually raped. It's the same man," she said flatly. "That is not something a woman ever forgets."

"They still have warrants out for him in New Hampshire, you reckon?"

"I'm sure they do. Why do you ask?"

"Maybe I'll bring his head back in a bag. Give it to the police."

She shuddered. "Smoke, you don't do things like that in New Hampshire."

"Why? He's worse than a rabid beast. What's the matter with the people back east?"

"It's called civilization, honey."

"Is that right? Sounds to me like they got a yellow streak running up their backs."

She shook her head and fought to hide a smile.

"If I take him alive, you want me to wrap him up in a fresh deer hide and stake him out in the sun?"

Sally sighed and looked at her man. "Smoke . . . no! How gruesome! What would that accomplish?"

"Pay back, Sally. Sun dries the hide around them; kills them slow. Helps to tie a fresh cut strip of green rawhide around their heads. That really lets them know they've done wrong; that someone is right displeased with them."

She shuddered. "I think they would get that message, all right."

"Almost always, Sally. Your folks back east, Sally, they've got this notion about treating bad men humanely. That's what I've been reading. But the bad men don't treat their victims humanely. Seems like to me, your folks got things all screwed up in their heads. You won't have crime, Sally, if you don't have criminals."

She sighed, knowing there was really no argument against what he was saying. It was a hard land, this frontier, and it took a hard breed to survive. They were good to good people. Terribly brutal to those who sought the evil way.

And who was to say that the hard way was not the right way?

She smiled at her man. "I guess that's why I love you so much, Smoke. You are so direct and straightforward in your thinking. I think you are going to be a most refreshing cool breeze to my family and friends back in New Hampshire."

"Maybe."

"Smoke, I am going to say this once, and I will not bring it up again. I married you, knowing full well what kind of man you are. And you are a good man, but hard. I have never tried to change you. I don't believe that is what marriage is all about."

"And I thank you for that, Sally."

"I know you are going man-hunting, Smoke. And I know, like you, that it is something you have to do. I don't always understand; but in this case, I do. My parents and brothers and sisters will not. Nor will my friends. But I do."

"And you're going to tell them what I'm doing?"

"Certainly. And you'll probably be written up in the local newspaper."

"Seems to me they ought to have more important things to write about than that."

Sally laughed at his expression. How could she explain to him that the people back in Keene didn't carry guns; that most had never seen a fast draw; that many of them didn't believe high noon shoot-outs ever occurred?

He probably wouldn't believe her. He'd have to see for himself.

"Smoke, I know that you take chances that many other men would not take. You're a special breed. I learned early on why many people call you the last mountain man. Perhaps that is yet another of the many reasons I love you like I do. So do this for me: When you put me on that train and see me off, put me out of your mind. Concentrate solely on the job facing you. I know you have that quality about you; you do it. I will leave messages at the wire offices for you, telling you how I am and where I can be reached at all times. You try to do the same for me, whenever you can."

"I will, Sally. And that's a promise. But I'm going to be out-of-pocket for a couple of months, maybe longer."

"I know. That's all I ask, Smoke. We'll say no more about it." She came to him and pulled his head down, kissing him.

"I have an idea, Sally."

"What?"

"All the hands are gone. The place is all ours. But it might hurt the baby."

"I bet it won't." She smiled impishly at him.

She was right.

Smoke stood watching until the caboose was out of sight. Dr. Spalding had walked back into the station house. Spalding and his wife, Mona, along with Sally, had ridden the stage into Denver. Smoke had ridden Drifter. He had not brought a pack animal; he'd buy one in the city.

There were already laws in parts of Denver about carrying guns, so Smoke had left his twin Colts back in the hotel room. He carried a short-barreled Colt, tucked behind his belt, covered by his coat.

Smoke turned away from the now-silent twin ribbons of steel that linked the nation. "See you soon, Sally," he muttered. He walked back into the station house.

"Are you going to stay in town for a time and see some of the shows?" Colton asked.

Smoke shook his head. "No. I'm going to gear up and pull out." He held out his right hand and Colton shook it.

"You'll stay in touch with the doctors in Boston?"

"Yes. I'll have progress reports for you whenever you wire Big Rock."

"Check on Billy every now and then."

Colton nodded. "Don't worry about him. He'll be fine. You take care, Smoke."

"I'll be in touch." Smoke turned and walked away.

He bought three hundred rounds of .44's. The ammo was interchangeable between rifle and pistols. He bought a tent and a ground sheet, a coffee pot and a skillet. Coffee and beans and flour and a small jug of lard. Bacon. He walked around the store, carefully selecting his articles, choosing ones he felt a back-east dandy come west might pick up to take on his first excursion into the wilds.

He bought lace-up boots and a cap, not a hat. He bought a shoulder holster for his short-barreled Colt. He bought a sawed-off 12-gauge shotgun and several boxes of buckshot shells.

"Have this gear out back on the loading dock in two hours," Smoke instructed the clerk. "That's when I'll be coming for it. And I'll pay you then."

"Yes, sir. That will be satisfactory. I shall see you in two hours."

"Fine."

Smoke inspected several packhorses and chose one that seemed to have a lot of bottom. Then he took a hansom to a fancy art-house and bought a dozen sketch pads and several boxes of charcoal pencils.

He had not shaved that morning at the hotel and did not plan on doing anything other than trimming his beard for a long time to come.

At a hardware store, he picked up a pair of scissors to keep his beard neat. An artist's beard. He would cut off his beard when it came time to reveal his true identity.

When it came time for the killing.

Smoke had a natural talent for drawing, although he had never done much with it. Now, he thought with a smile, it was going to come in handy.

At the art store, the clerk was a dandy if Smoke had ever seen one, prissing around like a peacock, fussing about this and that and prancing up one aisle and down the other.

Smoke told him what he wanted and let the prissy little feller fill the bill.

Smoke studied the way the clerk walked. Wasn't no damn way in hell he was gonna try to walk like that. Some bear might think he was in heat.

He went to a barbershop and told the barber he wanted his hair cut just like the dandies back east were wearing theirs. Just like he'd seen in a magazine. Parted down the middle and all greased back. The barber looked at him like he thought Smoke had lost his mind, but other than to give him a queer look, he made no comment. Just commenced to whacking and shaping.

Smoke did feel rather like a fop when he left the barber chair, and he hoped that he would not run into anyone he knew until his beard grew out. But in a big city like Denver—must have been four or five thousand people in the city—that was unlikely.

Smoke checked out of the hotel and got Drifter and his packhorse from the stable, riding around to the rear of the store, picking up and lashing down his supplies. His guns were rolled up and stored in a spare blanket, along with the sawed-off express gun.

He was ready.

But he waited until he got outside of the city before he stuck that damn cap on his head.

He rode southeast out of Denver, taking his time, seeing the country—again. He and old Preacher had ridden these trails, back when Smoke was just a boy. There were mighty few trails and places in Colorado that Smoke had not been; but oddly enough, down south of Canon City, down between the Isabels and the Sangre de Cristo range, was one area where Preacher had not taken him.

And now Smoke knew why that was: The old man had been protecting him.

But why so much hate on the part of this Rex Davidson? And was Sally right? Was this Dagget the same man who had molested her as a child? And how were he and Davidson connected—and why?

He didn't know.

But he was sure going to find out.

And then he would kill them.

Smoke spent a week camped along the West Bijou, letting his beard grow out and sketching various scenes, improving upon his natural talent. He still didn't like the silly cap he was wearing, but he stuck with it, getting used to the damned thing. And each day he combed and brushed his hair, slicking it down with goop, retraining it.

Damned if he really wasn't beginning to look like a dandy. Except for his eyes; those cold, expressionless, and emotionless eyes. And there wasn't a damn thing he could do about that.

Or was there? he pondered, smiling.

"Oh, yes, there was.

Allowing himself a chuckle, he swiftly broke camp and packed it all up, carefully dousing his fire and then scattering the ashes and dousing them again. He mounted up and swung Drifter's head toward the south and slightly west. If he couldn't find what he was looking for in Colorado City, he'd head on down to Jim Beckworth's town of Pueblo—although some folks tended to spell it Beckwourth.

Smoke stopped in at the fanciest store in town and browsed some, feeling silly and foppish in his high-top lace-up boots and his city britches tucked into the tops like some of them explorer people he'd seen pictures of. But if he was gonna act and look like a sissy, he might as well learn the part—except for the walk—cause he damn sure was gonna look mighty funny if he could find him a pair of those tinted eyeglasses.

He found several pairs—one blue-tinted, one yellow-tinted, and one rose-tinted.

"Oh, what the hell," he muttered.

He bought all three pairs and a little hard case to hold them in, to keep them from getting broken.

Smoke put on his red-tinted eyeglasses and walked outside, thinking that they sure gave a fellow a different outlook on things.

"Well, well," a cowboy said, stepping back and eye-balling Smoke and his fancy getup. "If you jist ain't the purtiest thing I ever did see." Then he started laughing.

Smoke gritted his teeth and started to brush past the half-drunk puncher.

The puncher grabbed Smoke by the upper arm and spun him around, a startled look on his face as his fingers gripped the thick powerful muscles of Smoke's upper arm.

Smoke shook his hand loose. Remembering all the grammar lessons Sally had given him, and the lessons that the urbane and highly educated gambler, Louis Longmont, had taught him, Smoke said, "I say, my good fellow, unhand me, please!"

The cowboy wasn't quite sure just exactly what he'd grabbed hold of. That arm felt like it was made of pure oak, but the speech sounded plumb goofy.

"What the hell is you, anyways?"

Smoke drew himself erect and looked down at the smaller man. "I, my good man, am an ar-tist!"

"Ar-tist? You paint pitchers?"

"I sketch pic-tures!" Smoke said haughtily.

"Do tell? How much you charge for one of them sketchies?"

"Of whom?"

"Huh?"

Smoke sighed. "Whom do you wish me to sketch?"

"Why, hell . . . me, o' course!"

"I'm really in a hurry, my good fellow. Perhaps some other time."

"I'll give you twenty dollars."

That brought Smoke up short. Twenty dollars was just about two thirds of what the average puncher made a month, and it was hard-earned wages. Smoke stepped back, taking a closer look at the man. This was no puncher. His boots were too fancy and too highly shined. His dress was too neat and too expensive. And his guns—two of them, worn low and tied down—marked him.

"Well . . . I might be persuaded to do a quick sketch. But not here in the middle of the street, for goodness sake!"

"Which way you headin', pardner?"

Smoke gestured with his arm, taking in the entire expanse. "I am but a free spirit, a wanderer, traveling where the wind takes me, enjoying the blessing of this wild and magnificent land."

Preacher, Smoke thought, wherever you are, you are probably rolling on the ground, cackling at this performance.

Smoke had no idea if Preacher were dead or alive; but he preferred to believe him alive, although he would be a very old man by now. But still? . . .

The gunfighter looked at Smoke, squinting his eyes. "You shore do talk funny. I'm camped on the edge of town. You kin sketch me there."

"Certainly, my good man. Let us be off."

Before leaving town, Smoke bought a jug of whiskey and gave it to the man, explaining, "Sometimes subjects tend to get a bit stiff and they appear unnatural on the paper. For the money, I want to do this right."

The man was falling-down drunk by the time they got to his campsite.

Smoke helped him off his horse and propped him up against a tree. Then he began to sketch and chat as he worked.

"I am very interested in the range of mountains known as the Sangre de Cristos. Are you familiar with them?"

"Damn sure am. What you wanna know about them? You just ax me and I'll tell you."

"I am told there is a plethora of unsurpassed beauty in the range."

"Huh?"

"Lots of pretty sights."

"Oh. Why didn't you say so in the first place? Damn shore is that."

"My cousin came through here several years ago, on his way to California. Maurice DeBeers. Perhaps you've heard of him?"

"Cain't say as I have, pardner."

"He stopped by a quaint little place for a moment or two. In the Sangre de Cristos. He didn't stay, but he said it was . . . well, odd."

"A town?"

"That's what he said."

"There ain't no towns in there."

"Oh, but I beg to differ. My cousin wrote me about it. Oh . . . pity! What was the name? Dead something-or-the-other.

The man looked at him, an odd shift to his eyes. "Dead River?"

"Yes! That's it! Thank you!"

Drunk as he was, the man was quick in snaking out a pistol. He eased back the hammer and pointed the muzzle at Smoke's belly.

5

Smoke dropped his sketch pad and threw his hands into the air. He started running around and around in a little circle. "Oh, my heavens!" he screamed, putting as much fright in his voice as he could. Then he started making little whimpering sounds.

The outlaw—and Smoke was now sure that he was—smiled and lowered his gun, easing down the hammer. "All right, all right! Calm down 'fore you have a heart attack, pilgrim. Hell, I ain't gonna shoot you."

Smoke kept his hands high in the air and forced his knees to shake. He felt like a total fool but knew his life depended on his making the act real. And so far, it was working.

"Take all my possessions! Take all my meager earnings! But please don't shoot me, mister. Please. I simply abhor guns and violence."

The outlaw blinked. "You does what to 'em?"

"I hate them!"

"Why didn't you just say that? Well, hell, relax. Don't pee your fancy britches, sissy-boy. I ain't gonna shoot you. I just had to check you out, that's all."

"I'm terribly sorry, but I don't understand. May I please lower my hands?"

"Yeah, yeah. Don't start beggin'. You really is who you say you is, ain't you?" His brow furrowed in whiskey-soaked rumination. "Come to think of it, just who in the hell is you, anyways?"

"I am an artist."

"Not that! What's your name, sissy-britches?" He lifted the jug and took a long, deep pull, then opened his throat to swallow.

"Shirley DeBeers," Smoke said.

The outlaw spat out the rotgut and coughed for several minutes. He pounded his chest and lifted red-rimmed eyes, disbelieving eyes to Smoke.

"Shirley! That there ain't no real man's name!"

Smoke managed to look offended. What he really wanted to do was take the jerk's guns away from him and shove both of them down his throat. Or into another part of the outlaw's anatomy.

"I will have you know, sir, that Shirley is really a very distinguished name."

"I'll take your word for that. Get to sketching, Shirley."

"Oh, I simply couldn't!" Smoke fanned his face with both hands. "I feel flushed. I'm so distraught!"

"Shore named you right," the outlaw muttered. "All right, Shirley. If you ain't gonna draw my pitcher, sit down and lets us palaver."

Smoke sat down. "I've never played palaver; you'll have to teach me."

The outlaw put his forehead into a hand and muttered under his breath for a moment. "It means we'll talk, Shirley."

"Very well. What do you wish to talk about?"

"You. I can't figure you. You big as a house and strong as a mule. But if you're a pansy, you keep your hands to yourself, you understand that?"

"Unwashed boorish types have never appealed to me," Smoke said stiffly.

"Whatever that means," the gunhawk said. "My name's Cahoon."

"Pleased, I'm sure."

"What's your interest in Dead River, Shirley?"

"I really have no interest there, as I told you, other than to sketch the scenery, which I was told was simply breathtakingly lovely."

Cahoon stared at him. "You got to be tellin' the truth.

You the goofiest-lookin' and the silliest-talkin' person I ever did see. What I can't figure out is how you got this far west without somebody pluggin' you full of holes."

"Why should they do that? I hold no malice toward anyone who treats me with any respect at all."

"You been lucky, boy, I shore tell you that. You been lucky. Now then, you over the vapors yet?"

"I am calmed somewhat, yes."

"Git to sketchin', Shirley."

When Smoke tossed off his blankets the next morning, the outlaw, Cahoon, was gone. Smoke had pretended sleep during the night as the outlaw had swiftly gone through his pack, finding nothing that seemed to interest him. Cahoon had searched one side of the pack carefully, then only glanced at the other side, which held supplies. Had he searched a bit closer and longer, he would have found Smoke's twin Colts and the shotgun.

Smoke felt he had passed inspection. At least for this time. But he was going to have to come up with some plan for stashing his weapons close to Dead River.

And so far, he hadn't worked that out.

Cahoon had left the coffee pot on the blackened stones around the fire and Smoke poured a cup. He was careful in his movements, not knowing how far Cahoon might have gone; he might well be laying out a few hundred yards, watching to see what Smoke did next.

Smoke cut strips of bacon from the slab and peeled and cut up a large potato, dropping the slices into the bacon grease as it fried. He cut off several slices of bread from the thick loaf and then settled down to eat.

He cut his eyes to a large stone and saw his sketch pad, a double eagle on the top page, shining in the rays of the early morning sun.

Cahoon had printed him a note: YOU DO FARLY GOOD DRAWINS. I PASS THE WORD THAT YOU OK. MAYBE SEE YOU IN DEAD RIVER. KEEP THIS NOTE TO HEP YOU GIT IN. CAHOON.

Smoke smiled. Yes, he thought, he had indeed passed the first hurdle.

Smoke drifted south, taking his time and riding easy. He had stopped at a general store and bought a bonnet for Drifter and the packhorse. The packhorse didn't seem to mind. Drifter didn't like it worth a damn. The big yellow-eyed devil horse finally accepted the bonnet, but only after biting Smoke twice and kicking him once. Hard.

Smoke's beard was now fully grown out, carefully trimmed into a fuller Vandyke but not as pointed. The beard had completely altered his appearance. And the news was spreading throughout the region about the goofy-talking and sissy-acting fellow who rode a horse with a bonnet and drew pictures. The rider, not the horse. The word was, so Smoke had overheard, that Shirley DeBeers was sorta silly, but harmless. And done right good drawin's, too.

And Cahoon, so Smoke had learned by listening and mostly keeping his mouth shut, was an outlaw of the worst kind. He fronted a gang that would do anything, including murder for hire and kidnapping—mostly women, to sell to whoremongers.

And they lived in Dead River, paying a man called Rex Davidson for security and sanctuary. And he learned that a man named Danvers was the Sheriff of Dead River. Smoke had heard of Danvers, but their trails had never crossed. The title of Sheriff was a figurehead title, for outside of Dead River he had no authority and would have been arrested on the spot.

Or shot.

And if Smoke had his way, it was going to be the latter.

Smoke and Drifter went from town to town, community to community, always drifting south toward the southern-most bend of the Purgatoire.

Smoke continued to play his part as the city fop, getting it down so well it now was second nature for him to act the fool.

At a general store not far from Quarreling Creek—so named because a band of Cheyenne had quarreled violently over the election of a new chief—Smoke picked up a few dollars by sketching a man and his wife and child, also picking up yet more information about Dead River and its outlaw inhabitants.

"Outlaws hit the stage outside Walensburg last week," he heard the rancher say to the clerk. "Beat it back past Old Tom's place and then cut up into the Sangre de Cristos."

The clerk looked up. There was no malice in his voice when he said, "And the posse stopped right there, hey?"

"Shore did. I reckon it's gonna take the Army to clean out that den of outlaws at Dead River. The law just don't wanna head up in there. Not that I blame them a bit for that," he was quick to add.

"Nobody wants to die," the clerk said, in a matter of agreeing.

"I have heard so much about this Dead River place," Smoke said, handing the finished sketch to the woman, who looked at it and smiled.

"You do very nice work, young man," she complimented him.

"Thank you. And I have also heard that around Dead River is some of the most beautiful scenery to be found anywhere."

The rancher put a couple of dollars into Smoke's hand and said, "You stay out of that place, mister. It just ain't no place for any decent person. And you seem to be a nice sort of person."

"Surely they wouldn't harm an unarmed man?" Smoke asked, holding on to his act. He managed to look offended at the thought. "I am an artist, not a troublemaker."

The clerk and the rancher exchanged knowing glances and smiles, the clerk saying, "Mister, them are bad apples in that place. They'd as soon shoot you as look at you. And that's just if you're lucky. I'd tell you more, but not in front of the woman and child."

"Mabel," the rancher spoke to his wife. "You take Jenny and wait outside on the boardwalk. We got some man-talking to do." He glanced at Smoke. "Well . . . some talking to do, at least."

Smoke contained his smile. He could just imagine Sally's reaction if he were to tell her to leave the room so the men could talk. A lady through and through, she would have nevertheless told Smoke where to put his suggestion.

Sideways.

The woman and child waiting on the boardwalk of the store, under the awning, the rancher looked at Smoke and shook his head in disbelief. Smoke was wearing a ruffle-front shirt, pink in color, tight-fitting lavender britches—he had paid a rancher's wife to make him several pairs in various colors—tucked into the tops of his lace-up hiking boots, tinted eyeglasses, and that silly cap on his head.

Foppish was not the word.

"Mr. DeBeers," the rancher said, "Dead River is the dumping grounds for all the scum and trash and bad hombres in the West. Some of the best and the bravest lawmen anywhere won't go in there, no matter how big the posse. And for good reason. The town of Dead River sits in a valley between two of the biggest mountains in the range. Only one way in and one way out."

The clerk said, "And the east pass—the only way in—is always guarded. Three men with rifles and plenty of ammunition could stand off an army forever."

Smoke knew that one-way-in and one-way-out business was nonsense. If he could find some Indians, he'd discover a dozen ways in and out. When he got close to the range of mountains, he'd seek out some band and talk with them.

The rancher said, "There've been reports of them outlaws gettin' all drunked up and draggin' people to death just for the fun of doin' it, up and down the main street. Some men from the Pinkerton agency, I think it was, got in there a couple of years ago, disguised as outlaws. When it was discovered what they really was, the outlaws stripped 'em nekkid and nailed 'em up on crosses, left the men there to die, and they died hard."

"Sometimes," the clerk added, "they'll hang people up

on meathooks and leave them to die slow. Takes 'em days. And it just ain't fittin' to speak aloud what they do to women they kidnap and haul in there. Makes me sick to just think about it."

"Barbaric!" Smoke said.

"So you just stay out of that place, mister," the rancher said.

"But Mr. Cahoon said I would be welcome," Smoke dropped that in.

"You know Cahoon?" The clerk was bug-eyed.

"I sketched him once."

"You must have done it right. Cause if you hadn't, Cahoon would have sure killed you. He's one of the worst. Likes to torture people—especially Indians and women; he ain't got no use for neither of them."

"Well, why doesn't someone do something about it?" Smoke demanded. "They sound like perfectly horrid people to me."

"It'd take the Army to get them out," the rancher explained. "At least five hundred men—maybe more than that; probably more than that. But here's the rub, mister: No one has ever come out of there to file no complaints. When a prisoner goes in there, he or she is dead. And dead people don't file no legal complaints. So look, buddy . . . eh, fellow, whatever, the day'll come when the Army goes in. But that day ain't here yet. So you best keep your butt outta there."

Smoke drifted on, and his reputation as a good artist went before him. He cut east, until he found a town with a telegraph office and sent a wire to Boston. He and Sally had worked out a code. He was S.B. and she was S.J. He waited in the town for a night and a day before receiving a reply.

Sally was fine. The doctors had removed the lead from her and her doctor in Boston did not think an operation would be necessary for child-birthing.

Smoke drifted on, crossing the Timpas and then following the Purgatoire down to Slim's General Store. A little settlement had been built around the old trading post, but it was fast dying, with only a few ramshackle buildings remaining. Smoke stabled his horses and stepped into the old store.

An old man sat on a stool behind the article-littered counter. He lifted his eyes as Smoke walked in.

"I ain't real sure just perxactly what you might be, son," the old man said, taking in Smoke's wild get-up. "But if you got any fresh news worth talkin' 'bout, you shore welcome, whether you buy anything or not."

Smoke looked around him. The store was empty of customers. Silent, except for what must have been years of memories, crouching in every corner. "Your name Slim?"

"Has been for nigh on seventy years. Kinda late to be changin' it now. What can I do you out of, stranger?"

Smoke bought some supplies, chatting with Slim while he shopped. He then sat down at the offer of a cup of coffee.

"I am an artist," he announced. "I have traveled all the way from New York City, wandering the West, recreating famous gunfights on paper. For posterity. I intend to become quite famous through my sketchings."

Slim looked at the outfit that Smoke had selected for that morning. It was all the old man could do to keep a straight face. Purple britches and flame-red silk shirt and colored glasses.

"Is that right?" Slim asked.

"It certainly is. And I would just imagine that you are a veritable well of knowledge concerning famous gunfighters and mountain men, are you not?"

Slim nodded his head. "I ain't real sure what it is you just said, partner. Are you askin' me if I knowed any gunfighters or mountain men?"

"That is quite correct, Mr. Slim."

"And your name be? . . ."

"Shirley DeBeers."

"Lord have mercy. Well, Shirley, yeah, I've seen my share of gunfights. I personal planted six or eight right back yonder." He pointed. "What is it you want to know about, pilgrim?"

Smoke got the impression that he wasn't fooling this old man, not one little bit. And he was curious as to the why of that.

"I have come from New York," he said. "In search of any information about the most famous mountain man of all time. And I was told in Denver that you, and you alone, could give me some information about him. Can you?"

Slim looked at Smoke, then his eyes began to twinkle. "Boy, I come out here in '35, and I knowed 'em all. Little Kit Carson—you know he wasn't much over five feet tall—Fremont, Smith, Big Jim, Caleb Greenwood, John Jacobs; hell, son, you just name some and I bet I knew 'em and traded with 'em."

"But from what I have learned, you did not name the most famous of them all!"

Slim smiled. "Yeah, that's right. I sure didn't—Mr. Smoke Jensen."

6

Over a lunch of beef and beans and canned peaches, Smoke and Slim sat and talked.

"How'd you know me, Slim? I've never laid eyes on you in my life."

"Just a guess. I'd heard people describe you 'fore. And I knowed what went on up on the Sugarloaf, with them gunnies an your wife; I figured you'd be comin' on along 'fore long. But what give you away was your accent. I've had folks from New York town in here 'fore. Your accent is all wrong."

"Then I guess I'd better start working on that, right?"

"Wrong. What you'd better do is shift locations. You ain't never gonna talk like them folks. You best say you're from Pennsylvannie. From a little farm outside Pittsburgh on the river. That ought to do it. If you're just bounded and swore to go off and get shot full of holes."

Smoke let that last bit slide. "How's Preacher?" He dropped that in without warning.

Slim studied him for a moment, then nodded his head. "Gettin' on in years. But he's all right, last I heard. He's livin' with some half-breed kids of hisn up in Wyoming. Up close to the Montanie line."

"It's good to know that he's still alive. But I can't figure why he won't come live with me and Sally up on the Sugarloaf."

"That ain't his way, Smoke, and you know it. He's happy, boy. That's what's important. Why, hell, Smoke!" he grinned, exposing nearly toothless gums. "They's a

55

whole passel of them ol' boys up yonder. They's Phew, Lobo, Audie, Nighthawk, Dupre, Greybull—two/three more. Couple of 'em has died since they hepped you out three/four years back."

Smoke remembered them all and smiled with that remembrance.

"Yeah," Slim said. "I'm thinkin' hard on sellin' out and headin' up that way to join them. Gettin' on in years myself. I'd like to have me a woman to rub my back ever now and then. But," he sighed, "I prob'ly won't do that. Stay right here until I keel over daid. But Preacher and them? They happy, boy. They got their memories and they got each other. And when it's time for them to go, they'll turn their faces to the sky and sing their death songs. Don't worry none 'bout Preacher, Smoke. He raised you better than that."

"You're right, Slim." Smoke grinned. "As much as I'd like to see him, I'm glad he can't see me in this get-up today."

Slim laughed and slapped his knee. "He'd prob'ly laugh so hard he'd have a heart attack, for sure. I got to tell you, Smoke, you do look . . . well . . . odd!"

"But it's working."

"So far, I reckon it is. Let's talk about that. You got a plan, Smoke?"

"About getting into Dead River?" Slim nodded. "No. Not really. But for sure, I'm going in like this."

Smoke did not hesitate about talking about his plans to Slim. He could be trusted. Preacher had told him that.

"Might work," Slim said.

"The outlaws think they've got everybody convinced there is only one way in and one way out. I don't believe that."

"That's a pile of buffalo chips! You get on with the Utes, don't you?"

"Stayed with them many times."

"White Wolf and a bunch of his people is camped over just west of Cordova Pass. The word is, from old-timers that I talked to, White Wolf's braves make a game out of slippin' in and out of Dead River. White Wolf ain't got no use for none of them people in there. They been hard on Injuns. You talk to White Wolf. He's an old friend and enemy of Preacher."

Smoke knew what he meant. You might spend a summer with the Indians and the winter fighting them. That's just the way it was. Nearly anyone could ride into an Indian camp and eat and spend the night and not be bothered. 'Course they might kill you when you tried to leave. But at least you'd die after a good night's sleep and a full stomach.

Indians were notional folks.

"I did meet and sketch and convince some outlaw name of Cahoon." He showed Slim the note.

The old man whistled. "He's a bad one; 'bout half crazy. Hates Injuns and women; ain't got but one use for a woman and you know what that is. Then he tortures them to death. How'd you meet him?"

Smoke told him, leaving nothing out. Slim laughed and wiped his eyes.

"Well, you can bet that Cahoon has told his buddies 'bout you plannin' on comin' in. And you can bet somebody is right now checkin' on your back trail. And they'll be here 'fore long. So you best draw me two or three of them pitchers of yourn and I'll stick 'em up on the wall."

Smoke spent several days at Slim's, relaxing and learning all that the old man knew about Dead River, Rex Davidson, and the man who called himself Dagget.

And Slim knew plenty.

They were the scum of the earth, Slim said, reenforcing what Smoke had already guessed. There was nothing they would not do for money, or had not already done. Every man in Dead River had at least one murder warrant out on his head.

That was going to make Smoke's job a lot easier.

"Smoke, if you do get inside that outlaw stronghold,"

Slim warned him, "don't you for one second ever drop that act of yourn. 'Cause ifn you do, sure as hell, someone'll pick up on it and you'll be a long time dyin'.

"Now, listen to me, boy: Don't trust nobody in there. Not one solitary soul. You cain't afford to do that.

"Now personal, Smoke, I think you're a damn fool for tryin' this. But I can see Preacher's invisible hand writ all over you. He'd do the same thing." He eyeballed Smoke's foppish get-up and grinned. "Well, he'd go in there; let's put it that way! I ain't gonna try to turn you around. You a growed-up man."

"But they have people being held as slaves in there, or so I'm told."

"Yeah, that's right. But some of them would just as soon turn you in as look at you, for favor's sake. You know what I mean?"

Smoke knew. It sickened him, but he knew. "How many you figure are in there, Slim? Or do you have any way of knowing that?"

"Ain't no way of really tellin' 'til you git in there," Slim said. "Them outlaws come and go so much. Might be as many as three hundred. Might be as low as fifty. But that's just the real bad ones, Smoke. That ain't countin' the shop owners and clerks and whores and sich. Like the minister."

"Minister! Wait a minute. We'll get back to him. What about the clerks and shop owners and those types of people?"

"What about them? Oh, I get you. Don't concern yourself with them. They're just as bad, in their own way, as them that ride out, robbin' and killin'. The clerks and shopkeepers are all on the run for crimes they done. There ain't no decent people in that town. Let me tell you something, boy: When a baby is borned to them shady gals in there, they either kill it outright or tote it into the closest town and toss it in the street."

Smoke grimaced in disgust. "I can't understand why this town hasn't attracted more attention."

"It has, boy! But lak I done tole you, can't no legal thing

be done 'cause no decent person that goes in there ever comes out. Now, I hear tell there's a federal marshal over to Trinidad that might be convinced to git a posse together if somebody would go in and clear a path for them. His name's Wilde."

Smoke made a mental note of that. "Tell me about this so-called minister in Dead River."

"Name is Tustin. And he's a real college-educated minister, too. Got him a church and all that goes with it."

"But you said there wasn't any decent people in the town!"

"There ain't, boy. Tustin is on the run jist lak all the rest. Killed his wife and kids back east somewheres. He's also a horse thief, a bank robber, and a whoremonger. But he still claims to be a Christian. Damndest thing I ever did hear of."

"And he has a church and preaches?"

"Damn shore does. And don't go to sleep durin' his sermons, neither. If you do, he'll shoot you!"

Smoke leaned back in his chair and stared at Slim. "You're really serious!"

"You bet your boots I am. You git in that place, Smoke, and you're gonna see sights like the which you ain't never seen."

"And you've never been in there?"

"Hell, no!"

Smoke rose from his chair to walk around the table a few times, stretching his legs. "It's time to put an end to Dead River."

"Way past time, boy."

"You think my wife was attacked just because of a twenty-year-old hate this Davidson has for Preacher?"

"I'd bet on it. Davidson lay right over there in that corner," he pointed, "and swore he'd get Preacher and anyone else who was a friend of hisn. That's why them outlaws is so hard on Injuns. 'Specially the Utes. Preacher was adopted into the Ute tribe, you know."

Smoke nodded. "Yeah. So was I."

"All the more reason for him to hate you. Law and order

is closin' in on the West, Smoke. And," he sighed, "I reckon, for the most part, that's a good thing. Them lak that scum that's over to Dead River don't have that many more places to run to . . . and it's time to wipe that rattler's nest out. Sam Bass was killed 'bout two years ago. Billy the Kid's 'bout run out his string, so I hear. John Wesley Hardin is in jail down in Texas. The law is hot on the trail of the James gang. Bill Longley was hanged a couple of years back. The list is just gettin' longer and longer of so-called bad men that finally got they due. You know what I mean, Smoke?"

"Yes. And I can add some to the list you just named. You heard about Clay Allison?"

"Different stories about how he died. You know the truth of it?"

"Louis Longmont told me that Clay got drunk and fell out of his wagon back in '77. A wheel ran over his head and killed him."

Slim laughed and refilled their coffee cups. "I hear Curly Bill is goin' 'round talkin' bad about the Earp boys. He don't close that mouth, he's gonna join that list, too, and you can believe that."

Smoke sipped his coffee. "Three hundred bad ones," he said softly. "Looks like I just may have bitten off more than I can chew up and spit out."

"That's one of the few things you've said about this adventure of yourn that makes any sense, boy."

Smoke smiled at the old man. "But don't mean I'm gonna give it up, Slim."

"I's afeared you'd say that. Boy, I don't lak that grin on your face. Now, what the hell have you got up that sleeve of yourn?"

"Where is the nearest wire office, Slim?"

"Trinidad. It's a real big city. Near'bouts three thousand people in there. All jammed up lak apples in a crate. Gives me the willies."

"That U.S. Marshal might be in town."

"Could be. I know he comes and goes out of there a whole lot. What's on your mind, boy?"

60

Smoke just grinned at him. "Can you get a message to Preacher?"

"Shore. Good God, boy! You ain't figurin' on dealing Preacher in on this, are you?"

"Oh, no. Just tell him I'm all right and I'm glad to hear that he's doing okay."

"I'll do it. You keep in touch, boy."

Smoke rose to leave. "See you around, Slim."

"Luck to you, boy."

After the U.S. Marshal got over his initial shock of seeing the red and lavender-clad Shirley DeBeers introduce himself, he looked at the young man as if he had taken leave of his senses.

He finally said, "Have you got a death wish, boy? Or are you as goofy as you look?"

"My name is not really Shirley DeBeers, Marshal."

"That's a relief. I think. What is your handle—Sue?"

"Smoke Jensen."

The U.S. Marshal fell out of his chair.

7

"The reason I wanted us to talk out here," Marshal Jim Wilde said, standing with Smoke in the livery stable, "is 'cause I don't trust nobody when it comes to that lousy damn bunch of crud over at Dead River."

Smoke nodded his agreement. "You don't suspect the sheriff of this county of being in cahoots with them, do you?"

"Oh, no. Not at all. He's a good man. We've been working together, trying to come up with a plan to clean out that mess for months. It's just that you never really know who might be listening. Are you really Smoke Jensen?" He looked at Smoke's outfit and shuddered.

Smoke assured him that he was, despite the way he was dressed.

"And you want to be a U.S. Marshal?"

"Yes. To protect myself legally."

"That's good thinkin'. But this plan of yours ain't too bright, the way I see it. Let me get this straight. You're goin' to act as point man for a posse to clean up Dead River?"

"That is my intention. At my signal, the posse will come in."

"Uh-huh."

"You, of course, will lead the posse."

"Uh-huh." The marshal's expression was hound-dog mournful. "I was just afraid you was gonna say something 'bout like that."

*   *   *

U.S. Marshal Wilde checked his dodgers to see if there were any wanted flyers out on Smoke. There were not. Then he sent some wires out to get approval on Smoke's federal commission. Smoke lounged around the town, waiting for the marshal's reply wires.

Trinidad was built at the foot of Raton Pass, on a foothill chain of the Culebra Range. The streets of the town twisted and turned deviously, giving it a curiously foreign look. The Purgatoire River separated the residential area from the business district.

Trinidad was known as a tough place, full of rowdies, and due to its relative closeness to Dead River, Smoke kept a close eye on his back trail.

On his third day in town, sensing someone was following him, he picked up his pursuers. They were three rough-looking men. Inwardly, he sighed, wanting nothing so much as to shed his role as Shirley DeBeers, foppish artist, and strap on his guns.

But he knew he had to endure what he'd started for a while longer.

He had deliberately avoided any contact with any lawmen, especially Jim Wilde. He had spent his time sketching various buildings of the town and some of the more colorfully dressed Mexicans.

But the three hard-looking gunhawks who were always following him began to get on his nerves. He decided to bring it to a head, but to do it in such a way as to reenforce his sissy, foppish act.

With his sketch pad in hand, Smoke turned to face the three men, who were standing across a plaza from him. He began sketching them.

And he could tell very quickly that his actions were not being received good-naturedly. One of the men made that perfectly clear in a hurry.

The man, wearing his guns low and tied down, walked across the plaza and jerked the sketch pad out of Smoke's hands, throwing it to the street.

"Jist what in the hell do you think you're doin', boy?"

Smoke put a frightened look on his face. "I was

64

sketching you and your friends. I didn't think you would mind. I'm sorry if I offended you."

Smoke was conscious of the sheriff of the county and of Jim Wilde watching from across the plaza, standing under the awning of a cantina.

The outlaw—Smoke assumed he was an outlaw—pointed to the sketch pad on the ground and grinned at Smoke. "Well, you shore did o-fend me, sissy-pants. Now pick that there pitcher book up offen the ground and gimmie that drawin' you just done of us."

Smoke drew himself up. "I most certainly will do no such thing . . . you ruffian."

The man slapped him.

It was all Smoke could do to contain his wild urge to tear the man's head off and hand it to him.

Smoke fought back his urge and put a hand to his reddened cheek. "You struck me!" he cried. "How dare you strike me, you—you animal!"

The man laughed as his friends walked across the plaza to join him. "What you got here, Jake?" one of them asked. "Looks to me like you done treed a girl dressed up in britches."

"I don't know what the hell it is, Red. But he shore talks funny."

"Le's see if he'll fight, Shorty," Jake said.

The three of them began pushing Smoke back and forth between them, roughing him up but doing no real physical damage; just bruising his dignity some. A crowd had gathered around, most of the men drinking, and they were getting a big laugh out of the sissy being shoved back and forth.

"Now, you all stop this immediately!" Smoke protested, putting a high note of fear into his voice. "I want you to stop this now . . . you hooligans!"

"Oh, my!" the outlaw called Red said, prancing around, one hand on his hip. "We hooligans, boys!"

Shorty reached out and, with a hard jerk, sent Smoke's trousers down around his ankles. Red shoved Smoke, who hit the ground hard and stayed there.

"I guess Cahoon was right, Shorty," Red said. "He ain't got a bit of sand in him." Then he turned and gave Smoke a vicious kick in the side, bringing a grunt of pain from him.

Forcing himself to do it, Smoke rolled himself up in a ball and hid his face in his hands. "Oh, don't hurt me anymore. I can't stand pain."

The crowd laughed. "Hell, Jake," Red said. "We wastin' our time. Sissy-boy ain't gonna fight."

Not yet, Smoke thought.

"Le's make him eat some horseshit!" Shorty suggested.

"Naw, I got a better idee. 'Sides, there ain't fresh piles around. We done found out what we come to find out: He's yeller."

"That shore was funny the time we made that drummer eat a pile of it, though!"

Shorty then unbuttoned his pants and urinated on Smoke's legs. The crowd fell silent; only Jake and Red thought that was funny.

Smoke's thoughts were savage.

The three hardcases then left and the crowd broke up, with no one offering to help Smoke to his feet.

Smoke hauled up his britches, found his sketch pad, and brushed himself off, then, with as much dignity as he could muster, he walked across the plaza. As he passed by the sheriff and the U.S. Marshal, Smoke whispered, "I think I'm in."

He stopped to brush dirt off his shirt.

"Picked a hard way to do it," the sheriff said. "I'd a never been able to lay there and take that."

"Let's just say it's going to be interesting when I come out of this costume," Smoke whispered.

"We'll be there," Wilde whispered. "There is a packet for you in your room. Good luck."

The packet contained a U.S. Marshal's badge, his written federal commission, and a letter.

On the night of Smoke's seventh day in Trinidad, two

hours after dusk, unless Smoke could get a signal out to tell them differently, the U.S. Marshals, and various sheriffs and deputies from a four county area, beefed up with volunteers from throughout the area, would strike at Dead River. They would begin getting into position just at dusk. It would be up to Smoke to take out the guards at the pass. Do it any way he saw fit.

And to Smoke's surprise, the marshal had a plant inside Dead River, one that had been there for about six months.

A woman. Hope Farris.

It would be up to Smoke to contact her. The marshal had no way of knowing whether she was dead or alive; they had received no word from her in several months.

They feared she might have been taken prisoner. Or worse.

Good luck.

"Yeah," Smoke muttered, burning the note in the cut-off tin can that served as an ashtray. "I am sure going to need that."

He pulled out of Trinidad before dawn the next morning, after resupplying the night before. He headed west, avoiding the tiny settlements for the most part. But a threatening storm forced him to pull up and seek shelter in the small town of Stonewall.

And Stonewall was not a place Smoke cared to linger long. The town and the area around it was torn in a bitter war between cattlemen and the lumber industry on one side and the homesteaders on the other side, over grazing and lumber interests.

Smoke knew he would have to be very careful which saloon he entered that night, if any, for each side would have their own watering holes in this war. Finally he said to hell with having a drink and sketching anyone. He got him a room and stayed put.

He pulled out before daylight, before the café even opened, and made his way to Lost Lake. There he caught some trout for breakfast, broiling them. Looking around, far above the timberline, Smoke could see the tough and hardy alpine vegetation: kinnikinnick, creeping phlox, and stunted grass.

After a tasty breakfast and several cups of strong hot coffee, Smoke bathed quickly—very quickly—in the cold blue waters of Lost Lake.

Shivering, even though it was the middle of summer, he dressed and had one more cup of coffee. He was still a good three days hard ride from the outlaw town, but he wanted to sort out all his options, and considering where he was going, they were damn few.

And once again, the question entered his mind: Was he being a fool for doing this?

And the answer was still the same: Yes, he was. But if he didn't settle it now, it would just happen again and again, and with a child coming, Smoke did not want to run the risk of losing another family.

So it had to be settled now; there was no question about that.

And, if the truth be told—and Smoke was a truthful man—there was yet another reason for his challenging the seemingly impossible: He wanted to do it.

He followed an old Indian trail that cut between Cordova Pass to the east and Cucharas Pass to the west. He found what he hoped was White Wolf's Ute camp and approached it cautiously. They seemed curious about this big strong-looking white man who dressed and behaved like a fool.

Smoke asked them if they would like to share his food in return for his spending the night. They agreed, and over the meal, he explained where he was going but not why.

The Ute chief, White Wolf, told him he was a silly man to even consider going into the outlaw town.

And Smoke could not understand the twinkle in the chief's eyes.

He asked them what they could tell him about the town called Dead River.

Smoke was stunned when White Wolf said, "What does the adopted son of my brother Preacher wish to know about that evil place?"

When he again found his voice, Smoke said, "For one thing, how did you know I was not who I claimed to be, White Wolf?"

Dark eyes twinkling, the chief of the small band of Utes said, "Many things give you away, to us, but probably not to the white man. The white man looks at many things but sees little. Your hands are as hard as stones. And while you draw well, that is not what you are."

Smoke did not offer to sketch the Indians, for many tribes believe it is not good medicine to have their pictures taken or their images recreated.

Smoke told them of his true plans.

They told him he was a very brave man, like Preacher.

"Few are as brave and noble as Preacher."

"That is true," White Wolf agreed. "And is my brother well?"

"Slim Dugas just told me that Preacher and a few other mountain men are well and living up near Montana."

"Thank you. That is also truth. Preacher is living with the children of my sister, Woman-Who-Speaks-With-Soft-Voice. Because she married Preacher, the children are recognized as pure and are not called Apples."

Red on the outside, white on the inside. Indians practiced their own form of discrimination.

"It is good to know they are true Human Beings."

"As you are, Smoke Jensen."

"Thank you. I have a joke for you."

"A good laugh makes a good meal even better."

"I was told that most people believe there is but one way in and one way out of Dead River."

The Indians, including the squaws, all found that richly amusing. After the laughter, White Wolf said, "There are many ways in and out of that evil place. There are ways in and out that the white man have not now and never will know, not in our lifetime."

Smoke agreed and finished his meal, belching loudly

and patting his full belly. The Indians all belched loudly and smiled, the sign of a good meal. And the squaws were very pleased.

Smoke passed around several tobacco sacks, and the Indians packed small clay pipes and smoked in contentment. Smoke rolled a cigarette and joined them.

"You still have not told me how you knew I was the adopted son of Preacher, White Wolf."

The chief thought on that for a moment. "If I told you that, Smoke, then you would know as much as I know, and I think that would not be a good thing for one as young as you."

"It is true that too much knowledge, learned before one is ready, is not a good thing."

White Wolf smiled and agreed.

Smoke waited. The chief would get to the matter of Dead River when he was damn good and ready.

White Wolf smoked his pipe down to coals and carefully tapped out the ashes, then handed the pipe to his woman. "It has been a fine game for us to slip up on the outlaw town and watch them. All without their knowing, of course," he added proudly.

"Of course," Smoke agreed. "Anyone who does not know the Ute is as brave as the bear, cunning as the wolf, and sharp-eyed as the eagle is ignorant."

The braves all nodded their heads in agreement. This white man was no fool. But they all wished he would do something about his manner of dress.

"A plan has come to me, White Wolf. But it is a very dangerous plan, if you and your braves agree to it."

"I am listening, Smoke."

"I met with a man in Trinidad. I believe he can be trusted. He is a government man. His name is Jim Wilde."

"I know this man Wilde," White Wolf said. "He carries Indian blood in his veins. Co-manche from Texas place. He is to be trusted."

"I think so, too. Could you get a message to him?"

"Does the wind sigh?"

Smoke smiled. Getting his sketch pad, he sketched the

campfire scene, leaving the faces of the Utes blank but drawing himself whole. On the bottom of the sketch, he wrote a note to Wilde.

"If you agree to my plan, have this delivered to Wilde, White Wolf."

"If we agree, it will be done. What is this thing that you have planned?"

"Times have not been good for you and your people."

"They have been both good and bad."

"Winter is not that far away."

"It is closer tonight than it was last night, but not as close as it will be in the morning."

"There are guns and much food and clothing and warm blankets in the outlaw town."

"But not as many as in the town of Trinidad."

"But the people in Trinidad are better than the people in Dead River."

"A matter of opinion. But I see your point. I think that I also see what you have in mind."

"If you agree, some of your people will surely die, White Wolf."

"Far better to die fighting like a man than to grovel and beg for scraps of food from a nonperson."

Only the Indians felt they were real people. Most whites had no soul. That is the best way they could find to explain it.

"I know some of how you feel. I do not think you want the buildings of the town."

White Wolf made an obscene gesture. "I spit on the buildings of the outlaw town."

"When the battle is over, you may do with them as you see fit."

"Wait by the fire," Smoke was told. "I will talk this over with my people."

Smoke sat alone for more than an hour. Then White Wolf returned with his braves and they took their places.

"We have agreed to your plan, Smoke."

They shook hands solemnly.

"Now it depends on the government man, Jim Wilde."

"I will send a brave to see him at first light. Once he has agreed, then we will make our final plans."

"Agreed."

They once more stuffed their pipes and smoked, with no one talking.

White Wolf finally said, "There is a young squaw, Rising Star. She does not have a man. She is very hard to please. I have thought of beating her for her stubbornness. Do you want her to share your robes this night?"

"I am honored, White Wolf, but I have a woman and I am faithful to her only."

"That is good. You are an honorable man."

"I'll pull out at first light. I'll be camped at the head of Sangre de Cristo creek, waiting to hear from you."

White Wolf smiled. "It will be interesting to see if the white men at the outlaw town die well."

"I think they will not."

"I think you are right," White Wolf agreed.

8

Smoke angled down the slopes and onto the flats, then cut northwest, reaching his campsite by late afternoon. He made his camp and waited.

And waited.

It was three full days before a brave from White Wolf's band made an appearance.

He handed Smoke a note, on U.S. Marshal's stationery. Jim Wilde had agreed to the plan and complimented Smoke on enlisting the Utes.

He told the brave what the scratchings on the paper meant.

"Yes," the brave said. "The Co-manche lawman told me the same thing. All the rest of your plan is to remain the same. Now I must return and tell him when you plan to enter the outlaw town."

Smoke had calculated the distance; about a day and a half of riding over rough country. "Tell Wilde I will enter the town day after tomorrow, at late afternoon. Do you know a place near the town where you could hide some guns for me?"

The brave thought for a moment, and then smiled. "Yes. Behind the saloon with an ugly picture of a bucket on the front of it. The bucket is filled with what I think is supposed to be blood."

"The bloody bucket?" Smoke guessed.

"Yes! Behind the little building where the men go to relieve themselves there is a rotting pile of lumber. I will put them under the lumber."

"Good. What is your name?"

"Lone Eagle."

"Be very careful, Lone Eagle. If you're caught, you will die hard."

The Ute nodded. "I know. The Co-manche lawman says that two hours after dark, on the seventh day of your entering the outlaw place, we shall attack. And White Wolf says that you need not worry about the guards. Concern yourself only with the town. It might take the main body of men an hour to fight their way to your location."

"Tell White Wolf thank you. It will be a good coup for you all."

The brave nodded. "The outlaws in the town have not been kind to my people. They have seized and raped some of our young girls. Twice, they have taken young braves and have been cruel beyond any reason. One they cut off his feet and left him to die, slowly. They called it sport. On the night of the seventh day, we shall have our sport with the outlaws."

Smoke nodded, repeating what he had said to the chief, "They shall not die well, I am thinking."

The Ute smiled, very unpleasantly. "We are counting on that."

Then he was gone, back to his pony hidden in the deep timber.

The outlaws of Dead River had had their way for years, torturing, raping, robbing and looting, enslaving the innocent and ravaging the unsuspecting for several hundred miles, or more, in any direction. Now they were about to have the tables turned on them. And Smoke knew the more fortunate ones would die under his guns or the guns of the posse.

It would be very unpleasant for those taken alive by the Utes.

For the Utes knew ways of torture that would make the Spanish Inquisitioners green with envy. Dying well was an honor for the Indians, and if a prisoner died well, enduring hours and sometimes days of torture, they would

74

sing songs about that person for years, praising his courage. That person who died well would not be forgotten.

The Indians had nothing but contempt for a man who begged and cried and died in dishonor.

They had their own code of honor and justice, and the whites had theirs. There were those who said the red man was nothing but a barbaric savage. But he had learned to scalp from the European white man. The Indians were different; but they would not steal from within their own tribe. The white man could not say that. War was a game to the Indians—until the white man entered the picture and began killing in war. For the Indians, for centuries, counting coup by striking with a club or stick was preferable to killing.

So it is very questionable who was the savage and who was the instructor in barbarism.

Smoke had lived with the Indians and, in many ways, preferred their life-style to the white ways. Smoke, as did nearly anyone who learned their ways, found the Indians to be honest, extremely gentle, and patient with their children or any captured children, of any color. The Indians lived a hard life in a hard land, so it was foolish to think their ways to be barbaric. They were, Smoke felt, just different.

Smoke felt nothing for the outlaws in the town. He knew the truth in the statement that whatever befalls a man, that man usually brought the bad onto himself. Every person comes, eventually, to a fork in the road. The direction that person takes comes from within, not from without, as many uninformed choose to believe when slavering pity on some criminal. The outlaw trail is one that a person can leave at any time; they are not chained to it.

An outlaw is, in many ways, like an ignorant person, who knows he is ignorant and is proud of it, enjoying wallowing in blind unenlightenment, knowing what he is is wrong but too lazy to climb the ladder of knowledge. Too inwardly slovenly to make the effort of reaching out and working to better himself.

To hell with them!

"It's a different world for me," Sally said, sitting in her parents' fine home in New Hampshire. "And a world, I fear, that I no longer belong in."

"What an odd thing to say, dear," her mother said, looking up from her knitting.

Sally smiled, glancing at her. She shifted her gaze to her brothers and sisters and father, all of them seated in the elegant sitting room of the mansion. And all of them, including her father, not quite sure they believed anything their sister had told them about her husband, this seemingly wild man called Smoke.

"Odd, Mother? Oh, I think not. It's just what a person wants; what that person becomes accustomed to, that's all. You would consider our life hard; we just consider it living free."

"Dear," her father spoke, "I am sure you find it quite amusing to entertain us with your wild stories about the West and this . . . person you married. But really now, Sally, don't you think it a bit much to ask us to believe all these wild yarns?"

"Wild yarns, Father?"

Jordan, Sally's oldest brother, and a bore and stuffed shirt if there ever were one, took some snuff gentlemanly and said, "All that dribble-drabble about the wild West is just a bunch of flapdoodle as far as I'm concerned."

Sally laughed at him. She had not, as yet, shown her family the many newspapers she had brought back to New Hampshire with her; but that time was not far off.

"Oh, Jordan! You'll never change. And don't ever come west to where I live. You wouldn't last fifteen minutes before someone would slap you flat on your backside!"

Jordan scowled at her but kept his mouth closed.

For a change.

Sally said, "You're all so safe and secure and comfortable here in Keene, in all your nice homes. If you had trouble,

76

you'd shout for a constable to handle it. There must be more than a dozen police officers here in this town alone. Where I live in Colorado, there aren't a dozen deputies within a two-thousand-square-mile radius."

"I will accept that, Sally," her father, John, said. "I have heard the horror stories about law and order in the West. But what amazes me is how you handle the business of law and order."

"We handle it, Father, usually ourselves."

"I don't understand, Sally," her sister Penny said. "Do you mean that where you live women are allowed to sit on juries?"

Sally laughed merrily. "No, you silly goose!" She kidded her sister. "Most of the time there isn't even any trial."

Her mother, Abigal, put her knitting aside and looked at her daughter. "Dear, now I'm confused. All civilized places have due process. Don't you have due process where you live?"

"We damn sure do!" Sally shocked them all into silence with the cuss word.

Her mother began fanning herself vigorously. Her sisters momentarily swooned. Her brothers looked shocked, as did her brothers-in-law, Chris and Robert. Her father frowned.

"Whatever in the world do you mean, dear?" Abigal asked.

"Most of the time it's from a Henry," Sally attempted to explain, but only added to the confusion.

"Ah-hah!" John exclaimed. "Now we're getting to it. This Henry person—he's a judge, I gather."

"No, a Henry is a rifle. Why, last year, when those TF riders roped and dragged Pearlie and then attacked the house, I knocked two of them out of the saddle from the front window of the house."

"You struck two men?" Betsy asked, shocked. "While they were stealing your pearls?"

Sally sighed. "Pearlie is our foreman at the ranch. Some TF riders slung a loop on him and tried to drag him to death. And, hell, no, I didn't strike them. When they attacked the house, I shot them!''

"Good Lord," Chris blurted. "Where was your husband while this tragedy was unfolding?''

Sally thought about that. "Well, I think he was in Fontana, in the middle of a gunfight. I believe that's where he was.''

They all looked at her as if she had suddenly grown horns and a tail.

Smiling, Sally reached into her bag and brought out a newspaper, a copy of Haywood's paper, which detailed the incident at the Sugarloaf, where she and young Bob Colby had fought off the attackers.

"Incredible!" her father muttered. "My own daughter in a gunfight. And at the trial, dear, you were, of course, acquitted, were you not?''

Sally laughed and shook her head. They still did not understand. "Father, there was no trial.''

"An inquest, then?" John asked hopefully, leaning forward in his chair.

Sally shook her head. "No, we just hauled off the bodies and buried them on the range.''

John blinked. He was speechless. And for an attorney, as he and his sons were, that was tantamount to a phenomenon.

"Hauled off the . . . bodies," Robert spoke slowly. "How utterly grotesque.''

"What would you have us do?" Sally asked him. "Leave them in the front yard? They would have attracted coyotes and wolves and buzzards. And smelled bad, too.'' Might as well have a little fun with them, she concluded.

Robert turned an ill-looking shade of green.

And Sally was shocked to find herself thinking: what a lily-livered bunch of pansies.

Abigal covered her mouth with a handkerchief.

"Did the sheriff even come out to the house?" Walter inquired.

"No. If he had, we'd have shot him. At that time, he was in Tilden Franklin's pocket.''

John sighed with a parent's patience.

Penny was reading another copy of Haywood's newspaper. "My God!" she suddenly shrieked in horror. "According to this account, there were ten people shot down in the streets of Fontana in one week."

"Yes, Sister. Fontana was rather a rowdy place until Smoke and the gunfighters cleaned it up. You've heard of Louis Longmont, Father?"

He nodded numbly, not trusting his voice to speak. He wondered if, twenty-odd years ago, the doctor had handed him the wrong baby. Sally had always been a bit . . . well, free-spirited.

"Louis was there, his hands full of Colts."

Sally's nieces and nephews were standing in the archway, listening, their mouths open in fascination. This was stuff you only read about in the dime novels. But Aunt Sally—and this was the first time most of them could remember seeing her—had actually lived it! This was exciting stuff.

Sally grinned, knowing she had a captive audience. "There was Charlie Starr, Luke Nations, Dan Greentree, Leo Wood, Cary Webb, Pistol LeRoux, Bill Foley, Sunset Hatfield, Toot Tooner, Sutter Cordova, Red Shingletown, Bill Flagler, Ol' Buttermilk, Jay Church, The Apache Kid, Silver Jim, Dad Weaver, Hardrock, Linch—they all stayed at our ranch, the Sugarloaf. They were really very nice gentlemen. Courtly in manner."

"But those men you just named!" Jordan said, his voice filled with shock and indignation. "I've read about them all. They're killers!"

"No, Jordan," Sally tried to patiently explain, all the while knowing that he, and the rest of her family, would never truly understand. "They're gunfighters. Like my Smoke. A gunfighter. They have killed, yes; but always because they were pushed into it, or they killed for right and reason and law and order."

"Killed for right and reason," John muttered. His attorney's mind was having a most difficult time comprehending that last bit.

Abigal looked like she might, at any moment, fall over from a case of the vapors. "And . . . your husband, this Smoke person, he's killed men?"

"Oh, yes. About a hundred or so. That's not counting Indians on the warpath. But not very many of them. You see, Smoke was raised by the mountain man, Preacher. And we get along well with the Indians."

"Preacher," John murmured. "The most famous, or infamous, mountain man of the West."

"That's him!" Sally said cheerfully. "And," she pulled an old wanted poster out of her bag and passed it over to her father, "that's my Smoke. Handsome, isn't he?"

Under the drawing of Smoke's likeness, was the lettering:

WANTED
DEAD OR ALIVE
THE OUTLAW AND MURDERER
SMOKE JENSEN
$10,000.00 REWARD

"Ye, Gods!" her father yelled, "the man is wanted by the authorities!"

Sally laughed at his expression. "No, Father, That was a put-up job. Smoke is not wanted by the law. He never has been on the dodge."

"Thank God for small favors." John wiped his sweaty face with a handkerchief.

Walter said, "And your husband has killed a hundred men, you say?"

"Well, thereabouts, yes. But they were all fair fights."

The kids slipped away into the foyer and silently opened the front door, stepping out onto the large porch. Then they were racing away to tell all their friends that their uncle, Smoke Jensen, the most famous gunfighter in all the world, was coming to Keene for a visit.

Really!

Sally passed around the newspapers she had saved over the months, from both Fontana and Big Rock. The family read them, disbelief in their eyes.

"Monte Carson is your sheriff?" John questioned. "But I have seen legal papers that stated he was a notorious gunfighter."

"He was. But he wasn't an outlaw. And Johnny North is now a farmer/rancher and one of our neighbors and close friends."

They had all heard of Johnny North. He was almost as famous as Smoke Jensen.

"Louis Longmont is a man of great wealth," Jordan muttered, reading a paper. "His holdings are quite vast. Newspaper, hotels, a casino in Europe, and a major stockholder in a railroad."

"He's also a famous gunfighter and gambler," Sally informed them all. "And a highly educated man and quite the gentleman."

Shaking his head, John laid the paper aside. "When is your husband coming out for a visit, Sally?"

"As soon as he finishes with his work."

"His work being with his guns." It was not put as a question.

"That is correct. Why do you ask, Father?"

"I'm just wondering if I should alert the governor so he can call out the militia!"

9

On the morning he set out for Dead River, Smoke dressed in his most outlandish clothing. He even found a long hawk feather and stuck that in his silly cap. He knew he would probably be searched once inside, or maybe outside the outlaw town, and what to do with his short-barreled .44 worried him. He finally decided to roll it up in some dirty longhandles and stick it in his dirty clothes bag, storing it in his pack. He was reasonably sure it would go undetected there. It was the best idea he could come up with.

He adjusted the bonnets on Drifter and his packhorse, with Drifter giving him a look that promised trouble if this crap went on much longer. Smoke swung into the saddle, pointing Drifter's nose north. A few more miles and he would cut west, into the Sangre de Cristo range and into the unknown.

About two hours later, he sensed unfriendly eyes watching him as he rode. He made no effort to search out his watchers, for a foppish gent from back east would not have developed that sixth sense. But White Wolf had told him that there were guards all along the trail, long before one ever reached the road that would take him to Dead River.

Smoke rode on, singing at the top of his lungs, stopping occasionally to admire the beautiful scenery and to make a quick sketch. To ooh and aah at some spectacular wonder of nature. He was just about oohed and aahed out, and Drifter looked like he was about ready to throw Smoke and stomp on him, when he came to a road. He had no idea what to expect, but this startled him with its openness.

A sign with an arrow pointing west, and under the arrow: DEAD RIVER. Under that: IF YOU DON'T HAVE BUSINESS IN DEAD RIVER, STAY OUT!

Smoke dismounted and looked around him. There was no sign of life. Raising his voice, he called, "I say! Yoo, hoo! Oh, yoo hoo! Is anyone there who might possibly assist me?"

Drifter swung his big bonneted head around and looked at Smoke through those cold yellow eyes. Eyes that seemed to say: Have you lost your damn mind!

"Just bear with me, boy," Smoke muttered. "It won't be long now. I promise you."

Drifter tried to step on his foot.

Smoke mounted up and rode on. He had huge mountains on either side of him. To the north, one reared up over fourteen thousand feet. To the south, the towering peaks rammed into the sky more than thirteen thousand feet, snow-capped year-round.

The road he was on twisted and climbed and narrowed dramatically.

The road was just wide enough for a wagon and maybe a horse to meet it, coming from the other direction. Another wagon, and somebody would have to give. But where? Then Smoke began to notice yellow flags every few hundred yards. A signal for wagon masters, he supposed, but whether they meant stop or go, he had no idea.

He had ridden a couple of miles, always west and always climbing, when a voice stopped him.

"Just hold it right there, fancy-pants. And keep your hands where I can see them. You get itchy, and I'll blow your butt out of the saddle."

Smoke reined up. Putting fear into his voice, he called, "I mean you no harm. I am Shirley DeBeers, the artist."

"What you gonna be is dead if you don't shut that goddamn mouth."

Smoke shut up.

The faint sounds of mumbling voices reached him, but

he could not make out the words.

"All right, fancy-britches," the same voice called out. "Git off that horse and stand still."

Smoke dismounted and stood in the roadway. Then he heard the sounds of bootsteps all around him: There was Hart, the backshooter; Gridley, who murdered his best friend and partner, and then raped and killed the man's wife; Nappy, a killer for hire. There were others, but Smoke did not immediately recognize them, except for the fact that they were hardcases.

"Take off that coat," he was ordered, "and toss it to me. Frisk 'im, Nappy."

Smoke was searched and searched professionally; even his boots were removed and inspected. His pack ropes were untied and his belongings dumped in the middle of the road.

"Oh, I say now! Is that necessary, gentlemen?"

"Shut up!"

Smoke shut up.

His belongings were inspected, but his bag of dirty underwear was tossed to one side after only a glance. Luckily the bag landed on a pile of clean clothes and the weight of the .44 did not make a sound.

So far, so good, Smoke thought.

Finally, the search was over and the men stared at him for a moment. One said, "I reckon Cahoon and them others was right. He ain't got nothing but a pocket knife. And it's dull."

"Is my good friend Cahoon in town? Oh, I hope so. He's such a nice man."

"Shut your mouth!"

"What about it, Hart?"

"I reckon some of us can take silly-boy on in."

"I say," Smoke looked around him at the mess in the road. "Are some of you good fellows going to help me gather up and repack my possessions?"

The outlaws thought that was very funny. They told him in very blunt language that they were not. And to make their point better understood, one of them kicked

Smoke in the butt. Smoke yelled and fell to the ground. Drifter swung his head and his yellow eyes were killer-cold. Smoke quickly crawled to the horse and grabbed a stirrup, using that to help pull himself up, all the while murmuring to Drifter, calming him.

Rubbing his butt, Smoke faced the outlaws. "You don't have to be so rough!"

"Oh, my goodness!" Gridley cried, prancing about to the laughter of the others. "We hurt his feelin's, boys. We got to stop bein' so rough!"

And right then and there, Smoke began to wonder if he would be able to last a week.

He calmed himself and waved his hand at his pile of belongings. "I say, as you men can see from your trashing of my possessions, I am low on supplies. Might I be allowed to continue on to Dead River and resupply?" He had left most of his supplies at the head of the Sangre de Cristo creek.

"Cahoon was supposed to have given you a note," a man said. A hardcase Smoke did not know. "Lemmie see the note, sissy-pants."

"I am not a sissy! I am merely a man of great sensibilities."

"Gimme the goddamn note!"

The note was handed over and passed around.

"That's Cahoon's writin' all right. What about it, Hart, it's up to you?"

"Yeah, let him go on in. He can draw us all, and then we'll have some fun with him."

Smoke caught the wink.

"Yeah. That's a good idee. And I know just the person to give him to."

"Who?" Nappy asked.

"Brute!"

That drew quite a laugh and narrowed Smoke's eyes. He had heard of Brute Pitman. A huge man, three hundred pounds or more of savage perversions. He was wanted all over the eastern half of the nation for the most disgusting crimes against humanity. But oddly enough, Smoke had never heard of a warrant against him west of the Mississippi River. Bounty hunters had tried to take him, but Brute was hard to kill.

It was rumored that Brute had preyed on the miners in the gold camps for years, stashing away a fortune. And he had lived in Dead River for a long time, keeping mostly to himself.

But, Smoke thought, if these cruds think Brute is going to have his way with me, I'll start this dance with or without the rest of the band.

Smoke looked from outlaw to outlaw. "This Brute fellow sounds absolutely fascinating!"

The outlaws laughed.

"Oh, he is, sweetie," Hart told him. "You two gonna get along just fine, I'm thinkin'."

Uh-huh, Smoke thought. We'll get along until I stick a .44 down his throat and doctor his innards with lead.

"Oh, I'm so excited!" Smoke cried. "May we proceed onward?"

"Son of a bitch shore talks funny!" Gridley grumbled.

Smoke had killed his first man back on the plains, back when he was fifteen or sixteen; he wasn't quite sure. And he had killed many times since then. But as accustomed as he was to the sights of brutality, he had to struggle to keep his lunch down when they passed by a line of poles and platforms and wooden crosses sunk into the ground. Men and women in various stages of death and dying were nailed to the crosses; some were hung from chains by their ankles and left to rot; some had been horsewhipped until their flesh hung in strips, and they had been left to slowly die under the sun.

Smoke had never seen anything like it in his life. He did not have to force the gasp of horror that escaped from his lips. He turned his face away from the sight.

The outlaws thought it was funny, Hart saying, "That's what happens to people who try to cross the boss, Shirley. Or to people who come in here pretendin' to be something they ain't."

Gridley pointed to a woman, blackened in rotting death, hanging by chains. "She was a slave who tried to escape. Keep that in mind, sissy-boy."

"How hideous!" Smoke found his voice. "What kind of place is this?"

"He really don't know," Nappy said with a laugh. "The silly sod really don't know. Boy, are we gonna have some fun with this dude."

"I don't wish to stay here!" Smoke said, putting fear and panic in his voice. "This place is disgusting!" He tried to turn Drifter.

The outlaws escorting him boxed him in, none of them noticing the firm grip Smoke held on Drifter's reins, steadying the killer horse, preventing him from rearing up and crushing a skull or breaking a back with his steel-shod hooves.

The bonnet had worked in disguising Drifter for what he really was. Worked, so far.

"You just hold on, fancy-pants," Hart told him. "You wanted to come in here, remember?"

"But now I want to leave! I want to leave right this instant!"

"Sorry, sweets. You here to stay."

Jim Wilde looked at the late afternoon sunlight outside his office window. He sighed and returned to his chair. "He ought to be in there by now. God have mercy on his soul; I guess I got to say it."

"Yeah," Sherriff Mike Larsen agreed. "He's got more guts than I got, and I'll stand out in the middle of the damn street and admit that."

Jim sipped his coffee. "You told your boys not a word about this to anybody, right?"

"Damn well bet I did. I told 'em if they even thought hard on it, I'd catch the vibrations and lock 'em up."

And the marshal knew the sheriff would do just that. Mike ran a good solid straight office in a tough town.

"You got the final tally sheet of all that's goin' in, Mike?"

"Yep. The boys is gearin' up now. Quietly. Three sheriffs, including myself. Twenty regular deputies. Twenty volunteers—all of them top riders and good with short gun and rifle—and you and ten marshals."

"The other marshals will be comin' in by train two at a time, starting tomorrow at noon. They're goin' to stay low. I just wish we had some way of findin' out how many hardcases we're gonna be up against."

"I think that's impossible, Jim. But if I had to make a guess on it . . . I'd say two hundred at the low end. We all gonna tie a white handkerchief on our left arm so's the Injuns won't mistake us for outlaws . . . that is still the plan, ain't it?"

"Yeah. Best I can come up with. I've already contracted for horses to be stashed along the way. So when we start ridin', we ain't gonna stop until it's over and done with. One way or the other," he added grimly.

Mike Larsen chose not to elaborate on that last bit. He would tell his wife only at the last moment, just before he stepped into the saddle. It was not a job he looked forward to doing, but he knew it was a job that had to be done. "Where you got the horses?"

"We'll switch to fresh at Spanish Peaks, then again at La Veta Pass. The last stop will be at Red Davis's place. I ain't gonna kill no good horse on that final run. Most of that is gonna be uphill."

Both men knew the fastest way to tire a horse was riding uphill.

"Red is givin' us the best of his line and wanted to go in with us. I thanked him but told him no. Told him he was doin' enough by loanin' us fresh horses."

"He's a tough old man. But you was right in refusin' him. You think he took offense?"

"No. He understands. White Wolf says he'll have at least thirty braves around that town when Jensen opens the dance. And Jensen is goin' to start the music as soon as White Wolf signals him that we've left the trail and entered the pass. White Wolf says the guards along the road will be taken care of. Them Utes ain't got no use for anybody in Dead River. And I told the boys that volunteered that the reward money will be split up amongst 'em."

"That's good, but I don't like Smoke openin' the show by hisself." Larsen frowned. "We're gonna be a good forty-five minutes of hard ridin' away from the town when he starts draggin' iron and lettin' it bang."

"I know it. But he was by hisself when he met them ol' boys up there on the Uncompahgre. And he killed ever' damn one of them."

"Yep," the sherriff agreed. "He damn shore did that, didn't he?"

"Unhand me, you beast!" Smoke shrilled his protest, struggling against the hands that held him in front of the saloon.

"My, my." A man stepped out of the Bloody Bucket and onto the boardwalk. "What manner of creature do we have here, boys?"

"It's that sissy-boy that draws them pitchers, Mr. Davidson. The one that Cahoon told us about."

"Where is my friend, Cahoon?" Smoke asked.

No one from the gathering crowd of thugs and hardcases replied.

"Well, well," Davidson said with a smile, his eyes taking in Smoke's outlandish dress. "So it is. And how do you like our little town, Mr. DeBeers?"

"I think it is appalling and disgusting and most offensive. And I do not like being manhandled by thugs. Tell your henchmen to unhand me this instant!"

Rex Davidson stepped from the boardwalk, faced Smoke and then backhanded him viciously across the face. He slapped him again. Smoke allowed his knees to buckle and he slumped to the ground, whimpering.

"You, silly boy," Rex said, standing over Smoke, "do

not give me orders. Around here, I give the orders, and you obey. I say who lives and dies, and who comes and goes. Do you understand that, Shirley?"

"Yes, sir," Smoke gasped. The blows from Davidson had hurt. The man was no lightweight; he was big and muscled. Smoke decided to remain on the ground, on his hands and knees, until ordered to rise.

"Here, silly-boy," Rex continued, "I am king. You are nothing. However, if I decide you may live—and that is a big if—I might elect to make you my court jester. Would you like that, silly-boy?"

"Yes, sir." Until I shed this costume and put lead in you, you overbearing jackass!

King Rex kicked Smoke in the belly, knocking him flat on the ground. "When you address me, silly-boy, you will address me as Your Majesty. Now, say it, you foppish-looking fool!"

"Yes, Your Majesty." And Smoke knew it was going to take a miracle for him to last out the entire seven days. Maybe two or three miracles.

"That's better, Jester. Some of you men get this fool on his feet and drag him inside the saloon. I wish to talk with him about doing my portrait."

Smoke started to tell him that he didn't do portraits, then decided it would be best if he'd just keep his mouth shut for the moment. He let the hardcases drag him to his feet and shove him up the steps, onto the boardwalk, and through the batwings. And it was all done with a lot of unnecessary roughness and very crude language.

What the hell did you expect, Jensen? Smoke silently questioned. A tea party?

The saloon—and from what Smoke had been able to glean, the only one in town—was a huge affair, capable of seating several hundred people. There was a large stage on one end of the building. The stage had red velvet curtains. Smoke wondered who did the acting and singing.

He was shoved roughly into a chair and then, looking up, got his first good look at Rex Davidson.

The man was a handsome rascal, no doubt about that. And a big man, in his mid-forties, Smoke guessed, solid, with heavily muscled arms and shoulders, thick wrists. Big hands. His eyes were cruel but not tinged with any sign of madness that Smoke could readily detect.

Rex leaned against the polished bar and smiled at Smoke; but the smile did not reach the man's eyes. "Talk to me, Jester."

"About what, Your Majesty?" Smoke promptly responded as instructed.

"Good, good!" Rex shouted to the hardcases gathered in the saloon. "You all see how quickly he learns? I think this one will do just fine. Oh, my, yes. Where are you from, Jester?"

"I am originally from Pennsylvania, Your Majesty."

"What city?"

"I am not from a city, Your Majesty."

"Oh? You certainly don't speak like a hick."

"Thank you, Your Majesty." You royal pain in the ass! "I was born on a small farm. Both my mother and father were highly educated people. They taught us at home." And I'm going to teach you a thing or two, King Jackass! "There were no schools nearby."

"Thank you, Jester. And where did you learn to draw, Jester?"

"I suppose I was born with the talent, Your Majesty." Just like I was born good with a gun, which you shall certainly get the chance to see...briefly. "My brother, Maurice, has the ability to write quite eloquently."

"Ah, yes, Maurice. Did you tell Cahoon that this Maurice person had stopped by here?"

"That is what he wrote and told me. But I have no way of knowing if he did stop or not. Maurice, ah, tends to story a bit."

"I see. In other words, he's nothing more than a goddamned liar?"

"Ah, yes, Your Majesty."

"Where is he now, Jester?"

"I have no idea, Your Majesty."

"I see. Does he look like you, Jester?"

"No, Your Majesty. Maurice was adopted, you see. While my hair is—"

Rex waved him silent as a man carrying a tray of drinks stumbled and went crashing to the floor. The glasses shattered and the smell of raw whiskey and beer filled the huge room.

"Incompetent fool!" Rex yelled at the fallen man.

"I'm sorry, sir. It was an accident."

"Your services will no longer be needed here, idiot."

The man tried to crawl to his feet just as Rex pulled out a .44. "I cannot tolerate clumsiness." He eased back the hammer and shot the man in the chest, knocking him back to the floor. The man began screaming in pain. Rex calmly shot him in the head. The screaming stopped.

Smoke watched it all, then remembered to put a shocked look on his face. Just in time, for Rex had cut his eyes and was watching Smoke carefully.

"Oh, my goodness!" Smoke gasped, putting a hand over his mouth. "That poor fellow."

"Drag him out of here and sprinkle some sawdust over the blood spots," Rex ordered. He punched out the empty brass in the cylinder and replaced the spent cartridges, then cut his eyes to Smoke. "Life is the cheapest commodity on the market around here, Jester. Bear that in mind at all times. Now then, how long were you planning on staying in my town?"

"My original plans were to spend about a week, sketching the scenery, which I was told was lovely. Then I was going to resupply and move on."

"A week, hey?"

"Yes, Your Majesty."

"Give me all your money."

"Sir?"

King Rex slapped Smoke out of the chair. And as he hit the floor, Smoke was really beginning to question his own sanity for getting himself into this snakepit. And wondering if he were going to get out of it alive.

Smoke was jerked up from the floor and slammed into his chair. The side of his face ached and he tasted blood in his mouth. And if Rex, king of Dead River, could just read Smoke's thoughts . . .

"Never, never question me, Jester," Rex told him. "You will obey instantly, or you will die. Very slowly and very painfully. Do you understand me, Jester?"

"Yes, Your Majesty. Just don't hurt me. I can't stand pain. It makes me ill."

"Stop your goddamned babblings, you fool. Give me your money!"

Smoke dug in his trousers and handed the man his slim roll of greenbacks.

Rex counted the money. "Sixty dollars. I charge ten dollars a day to stay here, Jester, unless you work for me, which you don't. What are you going to do at the end of six days, Jester?"

A woman began screaming from one of the rooms upstairs. Then the sounds of a whip striking flesh overrode the screaming. A man's ugly laughter followed the sounds of the lashing.

"A slave being punished, Jester," Rex told him. "We have many slaves in this town. Some live a long, long time. Others last only a few weeks. How long do you think you would last, Jester?"

"I don't know, Your Majesty."

"An honest answer. Now answer my original question, Jester."

"Well, I suppose after my six days are up, I'll just leave, sir." *After I kill you, Davidson.*

From the depths of the crowd, a man laughed, and it was not a very nice laugh. Smoke looked around him; all the hardcases were grinning at him.

"So you think you'll leave, hey, Jester?" Davidson smiled at him.

"Yes, sir. I hope to do that."

"Well, we'll see. If you behave yourself, I'll let

you leave."

Sure you will, Smoke thought. Right. And Drifter is going to suddenly start reciting poetry at any moment.

Davidson shook the greenbacks at Smoke. "This money only allows you to stay in this protected town. You pay for your own food and lodgings. You may leave now, Jester."

Smoke stood up.

"Welcome to Dead River, Mr. DeBeers," Rex said with a smile.

Smoke began walking toward the batwings, half expecting to get a bullet in his back. But it was a pleasant surprise when none came. He pushed open the batwings and stepped out onto the boardwalk. He mounted up, packhorse rope in his hand, and swung Drifter's bonneted head toward the far end of town, away from the sights and sounds and smells of the dead and slowly dying men and woman at the other end of the town. He got the impression that hell must be very much like what he had witnessed coming in.

One thing for sure, he knew he would never forget that sight as long as he lived. He didn't have to sketch it to remember it; it was burned into his brain.

He wondered what had finally happened to that slave woman he had heard being beaten back at the Bloody Bucket. He thought he knew.

How in the name of God could a place like this have existed for so long, without somebody escaping and telling the horrors that were going on?

He had no answers for that question either.

But he knew that this place must be destroyed. And he also knew that when Marshal Jim Wilde and Sheriff Larsen and the posse members saw this chamber of horrors, there would never be any due process of law. No courts with judge and jury would decide the fate of the outlaws of Dead River. It would be decided on the seventh night, with gunsmoke and lead.

If the posse could help it, no outlaw would leave this valley alive.

Smoke pushed those thoughts out of his mind and concentrated on his own predicament: He did not have a cent to his name and had very few supplies left. Maybe enough to last a couple of days, if he was careful.

Smoke Jensen, the most famous and feared gunfighter in all the West, didn't know what in the hell he was going to do.

10

"So that's it." Sally's father's voice was filled with ill-disguised disgust. "What a wretched excuse for a human being."

Abigal's face mirrored her shock and horror.

Sally sat with her mother and father in the book-lined study of the mansion. Her father's room, which few of them had dared enter when they were children. But Sally had never been afraid of doing so. She used to love to sit in her father's chair and look at all the books about law and justice.

The three of them were alone; her brothers and sisters had left for the evening. And the town was fairly buzzing about the news of the famous gunfighter who was soon to be arriving.

"Why didn't you tell us when it happpened, dear?" her mother asked.

"Because he told me he would kill you both. Then, after he left town, after killing that man, I just did my best to put the incident out of my mind, as much as possible. As the years went by, the memory became dimmer and dimmer. But there is no doubt in my mind that Dagget is the same man who tried to molest me years ago."

John rose from his chair to pace the room, his anger very evident. Wife and daughter watched him until he composed himself and returned to his leather chair. "The first thing in the morning, I shall inform the authorities as to this scoundrel's whereabouts. Then we shall begin extradition proceedings to have him returned to New

Hampshire to stand trial."

Sally could not contain the smile that curved her lips. "Father, by the time you do all that legal mumbojumbo, the matter will most probably be taken care of—if it isn't already tended to. However, Smoke did suggest he cut off Dagget's head and bring it back here in a sack."

Abigal turned a bit green around the mouth and began fanning herself. "For heaven's sake!" she finally blurted. "He was joking, of course?"

"Oh, no, Mother. He wasn't joking a bit."

"Just exactly what is your husband doing while you are visiting here, Sally?" John asked.

Sally then explained to her parents what her husband was doing.

"Are you telling us, expecting us to believe," John said, astonishment in his voice, "that your husband . . . ah . . . Smoke, one man, is going to . . . ah . . . attack and destroy an entire town of thugs and hooligans and ne'er-do-wells—all by himself? Now, really, Sally!"

"Oh, he's found some help. And I think you will approve of his methods, Father, or what you think his methods will be—in your New England straight-by-the-book mind."

"You disapprove of law and order, Sally?"

"Of course not, Father. Your way works here; our way works for us in the West. This will not be the first time Smoke has taken on an entire town." Then she told them about the shoot-out at the silver camp and what had happened in Bury, Idaho.

Her parents sat in silence and stared at her.

"And you can believe what I say, the both of you. I was in Bury. I saw it all. When Smoke gets his back up, you better get out of the way. Cause he's going to haul it out, cock it back, and let her bang."

"The finest schools in this country and Europe," John muttered. "And she hauls it out and lets her bang. Incredible."

Sally laughed openly at the expression on her father's face. "It's just a western expression, father."

"It's just that it is terribly difficult for us, here in the long-settled East, to fully understand the ways of the West, Sally," Abigal said. "But we don't doubt for a moment what you've told us. Sally, when Smoke comes out here for a visit, will he be armed?"

"If he's got his pants on."

John looked heavenward, shook his head, and sighed. "Yet another delightful colloquialism."

Sally reached into a pocket of her dress—she was getting too large to wear jeans, but she would have loved to do so, just to see the expression on her parents' faces—and took out a piece of paper. "This wire came this morning, while you both were out. It's from Smoke."

"Shall I contact the governor and have him call out the militia?" John asked his daughter, only half-joking. He wanted to meet his son-in-law, certainly; but he had absolutely no idea what to expect. And just the thought of an armed western gunfighter riding into the town made him slightly nauseous.

Sally laughed at him. "You're both thinking my husband to be some sort of savage. Well," she shrugged her shoulders, "when he has to be, he is, to your way of thinking. Yet, he is a fine artist, well-read, and highly intelligent. He knows the social graces; certainly knows what fork and spoon to use. But we don't go in for much of that where we live. In the West, eating is serious business, and not much chitchat goes on at the table. But I really think you'll like Smoke if you'll give him just half a chance."

Abigal reached over and patted Sally's hand. "I know we will, dear. And of course he'll be welcomed here. Now please tell us what is in the wire. I'm fairly bursting with excitement." She looked at her husband. "This is the most exhilarating thing that's happened in Keene in twenty years, John!"

"Not yet, dear," John said. "Smoke hasn't yet arrived in town, remember."

Sally laughed so hard she had to wipe her eyes with a handkerchief. She read from the wire. "Smoke has been appointed a deputy U.S. Marshal. This is from the marshal's office in Denver. He has entered the outlaw town in disguise. They'll wire me when the operation has been concluded."

"Well!" John said, obviously pleased. "I'm happy to hear that your husband has chosen the legal way, Sally. He'll properly arrest the criminals and bring them to trial the way it's supposed to be, according to the laws of this land."

Sally smiled. "Father, do you believe pigs can fly like birds?"

"What! Of course not."

"Father, the only law Smoke is going to hand out to those outlaws will be coming out of the muzzles of his .44's. And you can believe that."

"But he's an officer of the law!" the man protested. "More than that, he is operating under a federal badge. He must see to due process. That is his sworn duty!"

Sally's smile was grim. "Oh, he'll see that the outlaws get their due, Father. Trust me."

Smoke made his camp at the very edge of town, pitching his tent and unrolling his blankets. He gathered and stacked wood for a fire. Saving his meager supplies, he cut a pole and rigged it for fishing, walking to a little stream not far away. There he caught his supper, all the while letting his eyes stay busy, checking out the terrrain. The stream had to come from somewhere; it didn't just come out of the ground here. For it was full of trout.

He had deliberately made his camp far enough away so he could not hear the terrible cries and the begging of those men and women at the far end of town, being tortured to death. He wished desperately to help, but he knew for the moment, he was powerless to do so.

Huge peaks rose stately and protectively all around the little valley that housed Dead River. Smoke wondered where and how it had gotten its name. At first glance, he could understand why a lot of people would believe the myth of one way in and one way out. But Smoke knew that was crap, and he felt that most of the outlaws knew it as well. But those who would try to seek escape, when the attack came, would be in for a very ugly surprise when they tried those secret trails. White Wolf and his braves would be in hiding, waiting for them.

As Smoke had ridden to his camp, he had seen the compound where some prisoners were being held; but mostly the town itself was a prison, and he had noticed many slaves had free access to the town.

They obviously had been convinced, probably very brutally, that there was no way out except for the road, so why lock them up? But they were probably locked up at night. The compound, then, must be for any newcomers to the town. Or perhaps those were people being punished for some infraction of the rules.

Or waiting to die.

He wondered if the marshal's plant, Hope Ferris, was in the compound.

Or had she been discovered and killed?

He cleaned his fish and cooked his supper, all the while watching the comings and goings of the outlaws. So far, few had paid any attention to him.

Smoke judged the number of outlaws in the town at right around two hundred, and that was not counting the shopkeepers and clerks and whores. Rex Davidson had himself a profitable operation going here, Smoke concluded, and he was sure King Rex got his slice of the pie from every store in town and from every whore who worked.

Not that there were that many stores; Smoke had counted six. But they were all huge stores. By far, the biggest place in town was the livery stable and barns, a half dozen of them, all connected by walkways. And during bad weather, many men, Smoke guessed, would live and sleep in those barns. He knew that this high up the winters would be brutal ones.

And so far, Smoke had not seen the man called Dagget. He felt sure he would recognize him from Sally's description. Already he had seen a dozen or more hardcases he had brushed trails with years back; but his disguise had worked. They had paid him no mind, other than a quick glance and equally quick dismissal as being nothing more than a fop and totally harmless.

He wondered if Lone Eagle had hidden his guns behind the privy yet, then decided he had not. Not enough time had gone by since Smoke had met with the brave at the head of the creek.

Smoke heard a harsh shriek of pain from a shack across the wide road. Then a man's voice begging somebody not to do something again. Wild cursing followed by more shrieks of pain.

The door to the cabin was flung open and Smoke watched as a naked man ran out into the road. He was screaming. Then the obscene bulk of Brute Pitman appeared in the door of the shack. He was shirtless, his galluses hanging down to his knees. Brute held a long-barreled pistol in his hand.

The face of the running man was a mask of terror and pain. His body bore the bruises and markings of the many beatings he had endured until he could no longer take any more of it. And because he was naked, Smoke knew that beatings were not the only thing the man had been forced to endure.

But the man's agony was about to end, Smoke noted, watching as Brute lifted the pistol and jacked the hammer back, shooting the man in the back. The naked man stumbled, screamed, and fell forward, sliding on his face in the dirt and the gravel. The bullet had gone clear through the man, tearing a hole in his chest as it exited. The man kicked once, and then was still.

"How shocking!" Smoke said.

Brute turned, looking at him. "You, come here!" he commanded.

"Not on your life, you obscene tub of lard!"

A dozen outlaws had stopped what they were doing and they were motioning for others to come join them; come listen and watch. For sure, they thought, the fop was about to get mauled.

Brute stepped away from his shack. "What'd you call me, sissy-boy?"

Smoke could see Rex Davidson and another man, dressed all in black from his boots to his hat, walking up the dirt street to join the crowd.

Dagget.

And he wore his guns as Smoke preferred to wear his: the left hand Colt high and butt-forward, using a cross draw.

It was going to be a very interesting match when it came, Smoke thought. For no man wore his guns like that and lived very long, unless he was very, very quick.

Smoke turned his attention back to Brute. The man had moved closer to him. And, Jesus God, was he big and ugly! He was so ugly he could make a buzzard puke.

"I said you were a fat tub of lard, blubber-butt!" Smoke shouted, his voice high-pitched.

"I'll tear your damn head off!" Brute shouted, and began lumbering toward Smoke.

"Only if you can catch me!" Smoke shouted. "Can't catch me, can't catch me!"

He began running around in circles, taunting the huge man.

The outlaws thought it funny, for few among them liked Brute and all could just barely tolerate his aberrant appetites. He lived in Dead River because there he could do as he pleased with slaves, and because he could afford the high rent, paying yearly in gold. He left the place only once a year, for one month to the day. Those who tried to follow him, to find and steal his cache of stolen gold, were never seen again.

Smoke knew that he could never hope to best Brute in any type of rough and tumble fight—not if he stayed within the limits of his foppish charade—for Brute was over three hundred pounds and about six and a half feet tall. But he was out of shape, with a huge pus-gut, and if Smoke could keep the ugly bastard running around after him for several minutes, then he might stand a chance of besting him and staying known as a sissy.

It was either that or getting killed by the huge man, and the odds of Smoke getting killed were strong enough without adding to it.

Smoke stopped and danced around, his fists held in the classic fighter's stance. He knew he looked like a fool in his fancy-colored britches and silk shirt and stupid cap with a feather stuck in it.

"I warn you!" Smoke yelled, his voice shrill. "I am an expert pugilist!"

"I'm gonna pugile you!" Brute panted, trying to grab Smoke.

"First you have to catch me!" Smoke taunted. "Can't catch me!"

The outlaws were all laughing and making bets as to how long Smoke would last when Brute got his hands on him, and some were making suggestions as to how much they would pay to see Brute do his other trick, with Smoke on the receiving end of it.

"No way, hombre!" Smoke muttered, darting around Brute. But this time he got a little too close, and Brute got a piece of Smoke's silk shirt and spun him around.

Jerking him closer, Brute grinned, exposing yellowed and rotted teeth. "Got ya!"

Smoke could smell the stink of Brute's unwashed body and the fetid animal smell of his breath.

Before Brute could better his hold on Smoke, Smoke balled his right hand into a hard fist and, with a wild yell, gave Brute five, right on his big bulbous nose.

Brute hollered and the blood dripped. Smoke tore free and once more began running around and around the man, teasing and taunting him. The crowd roared their approval, but the laughter ceased as Smoke lost his footing, slipping to the ground, and Brute was on him, his massive hands closing around Smoke's throat, clamping off his supply of air.

"I'll not kill you this way," Brute panted, slobber from his lips dripping onto Smoke's face. "I have other plans for you, pretty-boy."

Smoke twisted his head and bit Brute on the arm, bringing blood. With a roaring curse, Brute's hand left his throat and Smoke twisted from beneath him, rolling and coming to his feet. He looked wildly around him, spotting a broken two-by-four and grabbing it. The wood was old and somewhat rotten, but it would still make a dandy club.

Brute was shouting curses and advancing toward him.

Smoke tried the club, right on the side of Brute's head.

The club shattered and the blood flew, but still the big man would not go down.

He shook his head and grinned at Smoke.

"All right, you nasty ne'er-do-well," Smoke trilled at him. "I hate violence, but you asked for this."

Then he hit Brute with everything he had, starting the punch chest-high and connecting with Brute's jaw. This time when Brute hit the ground, he stayed there.

Smoke began shaking his right hand and moaning as if in pain, which he was not.

He heard Davidson say, "Doc, look at DeBeers's hand. See if it's broken. Sheriff Danvers? If DeBeers's hand is broken and he can't draw, shoot Brute."

"Yes, sir," the so-called sheriff said.

An old whiskey-breathed and unshaven man checked Smoke's hand and pronounced it unbroken.

Smoke turned to Rex Davidson. "I am sorry about this incident, sir. I came in peace. I will leave others alone if they do the same for me."

Davidson looked first at the unconscious Brute, then at Smoke. "You start drawing me first thing in the morning. Sheriff Danvers?"

"Yes, sir?"

"When Brute comes out of it, advise him I said to leave Mr. DeBeers alone. Tell him he may practice his sickening perversions on the slaves, but not on paying guests."

"Yes, sir."

He once more looked at Smoke. "Breakfast at my house. Eight o'clock in the morning. Be there."

"Yes, sir," Smoke replied, and did not add the "Majesty" bit.

"Does this place offend your delicate sensibilities, Mr. DeBeers?" Davidson asked.

"Since you inquired, yes, it does."

It was after breakfast, and Davidson was posing for the first of many drawings.

"Why, Mr. DeBeers?" For some reason, Davidson had dropped the "Jester" bit.

"Because of the barbarous way those unfortunate people at the edge of town are treated. That's the main reason."

"I see. Interesting. But in England, Mr. DeBeers, drawing and quartering people in public was only stopped a few years ago. And is not England supposed to be the bastion of civilized law and order . . . more or less?"

"Yes, sir, it is."

"Well, this is still a young country, so it's going to take us a while to catch up."

What an idiotic rationalization, Smoke thought. Louis Longmont would be appalled. "Yes, sir, I suppose you're right."

"Don't pander to me, Mr. DeBeers. You most certainly do not think I am right."

"But when I do speak my mind, I get slapped or struck down."

"Only in public, Mr. DeBeers. When we are alone, you may speak your mind."

"Thank you, sir. In that case, I find this entire community the most appalling nest of human filth I have ever had the misfortune to encounter!"

Davidson threw back his head and laughed. "Of course, you do! But after a time, one becomes accustomed to it. You'll see."

"I don't plan on staying that long, sir." Smoke looked at King Rex, checking for any signs of annoyance. He could see none.

Instead, the man only smiled. "Why would you want to leave here?"

Smoke stopped sketching for a moment, to see if the man was really serious. He was. "To continue on with my journey, sir. To visit and sketch the West."

"Ah! But you have some of the most beautiful scenery in the world right around you. Plus many of the most famous outlaws and gunfighters in the West. You could spend a lifetime here and not sketch it all, could you not?"

"That is true, but two of the people I want to meet and sketch are not here."

"Oh? And who might those be?"

"The mountain man, Preacher, and the gunfighter, Smoke Jensen."

The only sign of emotion from the man was a nervous tic under his right eye. "Then you should wait here, Mr. DeBeers, for I believe Jensen is on his way."

"Oh, really, sir! Then I certainly shall wait. Oh, I'm so excited."

"Control yourself, Shirley."

"Oh, yes, sir. Sorry. Sir?"

"Yes?"

"Getting back to this place . . . The west, from what I have been able to see, is changing almost daily. Settling. Surely this town is known for what it really is?"

Davidson met his eyes. "So?"

"Do you think this will go on forever and ever? As the town becomes known outside of this immediate area, the citizens will eventually grow weary of it and demand that the Army storm the place."

"Ummm. Yes, you're probably right. And I have given that much thought of late. But, young man,"—he smiled and held up a finger, breaking his pose—"this town has been here for twenty years and still going. How do you account for that?"

"Well, when you first came here, I suppose there were no other towns nearby. Now all that has changed. Civilization is all around you and closing in. That, sir, is why I wanted to come west now, before the wild West is finally tamed."

"Ummm. Well, you are a thinking man, Mr. DeBeers, and I like that. There is so little intellectual stimulation to be found around here." He abruptly stood up. "I am weary of posing." He walked around to look at the sketch. "Good. Very good. Excellent, as a matter of fact. I thought it would be. I have arranged for you to take your meals at the Bon Ton Café. I will want at least a hundred of your sketches of me. Some with an outside setting. When that is done, to my satisfaction, then you may leave. Good day, Mr. DeBeers."

Gathering up his pencils and sketch pads, Smoke left the house, which was situated on a flat that sat slightly above the town, allowing Rex a commanding view. As he walked back to his tent, Smoke pondered his situation. Surely, Rex Davidson was insane; but if he was, would that not make all the others in this place mad as well?

And Smoke did not believe that for a moment.

More than likely, Davidson and Dagget and all the others who voluntarily resided in Dead River were not insane. Perhaps they were just the personification of evil, and the place was a human snake pit.

He chose that explanation. Already, people who had committed the most terrible of crimes were saying they were not responsible for their actions because they had been crazy, at the time, before the time, whatever. And courts, mostly back east in the big cities, were accepting that more and more, allowing guilty people to be set free without punishment. Smoke did not doubt for one minute that there were people who were truly insane and could not help their actions.

But he also felt that those types were in the minority of cases; the rest were shamming. If a person were truly crazy, Smoke did not believe that malady could be turned off and on like a valve. If a person were truly insane, they would perform irrational acts on a steady basis, not just whenever the mood struck them.

He knew for an ironclad fact that many criminals were of a high intelligence, and that many were very convincing actors and actresses. Certainly smart enough to fool this new thing he'd heard about called psychiatry. Smoke Jensen was a straight-ahead, right-was-right and wrong-was-wrong man, with damn little gray in between. You didn't lie, you didn't cheat, you didn't steal, and you treated your neighbor like you would want to be treated.

And if you didn't subscribe to that philosophy, you best get clear of men like Smoke Jensen.

As for the scum and filth and perverts in this town of Dead River, Smoke felt he had the cure for what ailed them.

The pills were made of lead.

And the doctor's name was Smoke Jensen.

11

For one hour each day, Smoke sketched Rex Davidson; the rest of the time was his to spend as he pleased. He took his meals at the Bon Ton—the man who owned the place was wanted for murder back in Illinois, having killed several people by poisoning them—and spent the rest of his time wandering the town, sketching this and that and picking up quite a bit of money by drawing the outlaws who came and went. He made friends with none of them, having found no one whom he felt possessed any qualities that he wished to share. Although he felt sure there must be one or two in the town who could be saved from a life of crime with just a little bit of help.

Smoke put that out of his mind and, for the most part, kept it out. He wanted nothing on his conscience when the lead started flying.

He was not physically bothered by any outlaw. But the taunts and insults continued from many of the men and from a lot of the women who chose to live in the town. Smoke would smile and tip his cap at them, but if they could have read his thoughts, they would have grabbed the nearest horse and gotten the hell out of Dead River.

Brute saw Smoke several times a day but refused to speak to him. He would only grin nastily and make the most obscene gestures.

Smoke saw the three who had shoved him around in Trinidad—Jake, Shorty, and Red—but they paid him no mind.

What did worry Smoke was that the town seemed to be

filling up with outlaws. Many more were coming in, and damn few were leaving.

They were not all famous gunfighters and famous outlaws, of course. As a matter of fact, many were no more than two-bit punks who had gotten caught in the act of whatever crimes they were committing and, in a dark moment of fear and fury, had killed when surprised. But that did not make them any less guilty in Smoke's mind. And then as criminals are prone to do, they grabbed a horse or an empty boxcar and ran, eventually joining up with a gang.

It was the gang leaders and lone-wolf hired guns who worried Smoke the most. For here in Dead River were the worst of the lot of bad ones in a three state area.

LaHogue, called the Hog behind his back, and his gang of cutthroats lived in Dead River. Natick and his bunch were in town, as was the Studs Woodenhouse gang and Bill Wilson's bunch of crap. And just that morning, Paul Rycroft and Slim Bothwell and their men had ridden in.

The place was filling up with hardcases.

And to make matters worse, Smoke knew a lot of the men who were coming in. He had never ridden any hoot-owl trails with any of them, but their paths had crossed now and then. The West was a large place but relatively small in population, so people who roamed were apt to meet, now and then.

Cat Ventura and the Hog had both given Smoke some curious glances and not just one look but several, and that made Smoke uneasy. He wanted desperately to check to see if his guns were behind the privy. But he knew it would only bring unnecessary attention to himself, and that was something he could do without. He had stayed alive so far by playing the part of a foolish fop and by maintaining a very high visibility. And with only a few days to go, he did not want to break that routine. He spent the rest of the day sketching various outlaws—picking up about a hundred dollars doing so—and checking out the town of Dead River. But there was not that much more to be learned about the place. Since he was loosely watched every waking moment, Smoke had had very little opportunity to do much exploring.

He was sitting before his small fire that evening, enjoying a final cup of coffee before rolling up in his blankets, for the nights were very cool this high up in the mountains, when he heard spurs jingling, coming toward him. He waited, curious, for up to this point he had been left strictly alone.

"Hello, the fire!" the voice came out of the campfire-lit gloom.

"If you're friendly, come on in," Smoke called. "I will share my coffee with you."

"Nice of you." A young man, fresh-faced with youth, perhaps twenty years old at the most and wearing a grin, walked up and squatted down, pouring a tin cup full of dark, strong cowboy coffee. He glanced over the hat-sized fire at Smoke, his eyes twinkling with good humor.

He's out of place, Smoke accurately pegged the young cowboy. He's not an outlaw. There was just something about the young man; something clean and vital and open. That little intangible that set the innocent apart from the lawless.

"My first time to this place," the young man said. "It's quite a sight to see, ain't it?"

Smoke had noticed that the cowboy wore his six-gun low and tied down, and the gun seemed to be a living extension of the man.

He knows how to use it, Smoke thought. "It is all of that, young man, to be sure."

"Name's York."

"Shirley DeBeers."

York almost spilled his coffee down his shirtfront at that. He lifted his eyes. "You funnin' me?"

Smoke smiled at his expression. "Actually, no. It's a fine old family name. Is York your first or last name?" he inquired, knowing that it was not a question one asked in the West.

York looked at him closely. "You new out here, ain't you?"

"Why, yes, as a matter of fact, I am. How did you know that Mr. York?"

The cowboy's smile was quick. "Just a guess. And it's just York."

"Very well." Smoke noticed that the young man's eyes kept drifting to the pan of bacon and bread he had fixed for his supper. There were a few strips of bacon left, and about half a loaf of bread. "If you're hungry, please help yourself. I have eaten my fill and I hate to throw away good food."

"Thanks," York said quickly and with a grin. "That's right big of you. You don't never have to worry 'bout tossin' out no food when I'm around." He fixed a huge sandwich and then used another piece of bread to sop up the grease from the pan.

Smoke guessed he had not eaten in several days.

When York had finished and not a crumb was left, he settled back and poured another cup of coffee. Smoke tossed him a sack of tobacco and papers.

York caught the sack and rolled and lit. "Thanks. That was good grub. Hit the spot, let me tell you. Anything I can do for you, you just let me know. Most "—he cut his eyes suspiciously—"most of the hombres around here wouldn't give a man the time of day if they had a watch in every pocket. Sorry bastards."

"I agree with you. But you be careful where you say things like that, York."

York nodded his agreement. "Ain't that the truth. Say, you don't neither talk like nor look like a man that's on the dodge, DeBeers."

"On the dodge?" Smoke kept up his act. "Oh! Yes, I see what you mean now. Oh, no. I can assure you, I am not wanted by the authorities."

York studied him across the small fire, confusion on his young face. "Then . . . what in the hell are you doin' in a place like this?"

"Working. Sketching the West and some of its most infamous people. Mr. Davidson was kind enough to give me sanctuary and the run of the place."

"And you believed him?"

Smoke only smiled.

"Yeah. You might look sorta silly—and I don't mean no o-fence by that, it's just that you dress different—but I got a hunch you ain't dumb."

"Thank you." Smoke was not going to fall into any verbal traps, not knowing if York was a plant to sound him out.

The cowboy sipped his coffee and smoked for a moment. "You really come in here without havin' to, huh?"

"That is correct."

"Weird. But," he shrugged, "I reckon you have your reasons. Me, now, I didn't have no choice at all in the matter."

"We all have choices, young man. But sometimes they are disguised and hard to make."

"Whatever that means. Anyways, I'm on the hard dodge, I am."

He tried to sound proud about that statement, but to Smoke, it came across flat and with a definite note of sadness.

"I'm very sorry to hear that, York. Is it too personal to talk about?"

"Naw. I killed a man in Utah."

Smoke studied him. "You don't sound like a man who would cold-bloodedly kill another man."

"Huh? Oh, no. It wasn't nothin' like that. It was a stand-up-and-face-him-down fight. But the law didn't see it thataway. I guess near'bouts all these people in this lousy town would claim they was framed, but I really was." He poured another cup of coffee and settled back against a stump, apparently anxious to talk and have somebody hear him out. "You see, I bought a horse from this feller. It was a good horse for fifty dollars. Too good, as it turned out. I had me a bill of sale and all that. Then these folks come ridin' up to me about a week later and claimed I stole the horse. They had 'em a rope all ready to stretch my neck. I showed 'em my bill of sale and that backed 'em down some. But they was still gonna take the horse and leave me afoot in the Uintah's. Well, I told 'em that they wasn't gonna do no such a thing. I told 'em that if the horse was rightfully theirs, well, I was wrong and they was right. But let me get to a town 'fore they took the horse; don't leave me in the big middle of nowheres on foot."

He sighed and took a swallow of coffee. "They allowed as to how I could just by God walk out of there. I told them they'd better drag iron if that's what they had in mind, 'cause I damn sure wasn't gonna hoof it outta there.

"Well, they dragged iron, but I was quicker. I kilt one and put lead in the other. The third one, he turned yeller and run off.

"I got the hell outta there and drifted. Then I learned that I had a murder charge hangin' over my head. That third man who run off? He told a pack of lies about what really happened.

"Well, bounty hunters come up on me about two/three months later. I buried one of them and toted the other one into a little town to the doc's office. The marshal, he come up all blustered-up and I told him what happened and added that if he didn't like my version of it, he could just clear leather and we'd settle it that way."

He grinned boyishly. "The marshal didn't like it, and I'll admit I had my back up some. But he liked livin' moreun gunfightin'. So I drifted on and things just kept gettin' worser and worser. I couldn't get no job 'cause of them poster out on me. I heard about this place and sort of drifted in. I ain't no outlaw, but I don't know what else to do with all them charges hangin' over my head."

Smoke thought on it. He believed the young man; believed him to be leveling as to the facts of it all. "Might I make a suggestion?"

"You shore could. I'd rather live in hell with rattle-snakes than in heaven with this bunch around here."

Smoke couldn't help it. He laughed at the young man's expression. "York, why don't you just change your name and drift. And by the way, do you still have the horse in question?"

"Naw. I turned him loose and caught me up a wild horse and broke him. He's a good horse."

"Well then, York, drift. Change your name and drift. Chances are that you'll never be caught."

"I thought of that. But damn it, DeBeers, I ain't done nothin' wrong. At least, not yet. And York is my family name. By God, I'm gonna stick with it. I'm doin' some thinkin' 'bout linkin' up with Slim Bothwell's bunch. They asked me to. I guess I ain't got no choice. I don't wanna hurt nobody or steal nothin' from nobody. But, hell, I gotta eat!"

"York, you are not cut out for the outlaw life," Smoke told him.

"Don't I know it! Look, DeBeers, I listened to some of the men talk 'bout all they've done, in here and out there." He jerked his thumb. "Damn near made me puke." He sighed heavily. "I just don't know what to do."

Could this entire thing be a setup? Smoke wondered, and concluded that it certainly could be. But something about the young cowboy was awfully convincing. He decided to take a chance, but to do it without York knowing of it.

"Perhaps something will come up to change your mind, York."

The cowboy looked up across the fire, trust in his eyes. "What?"

"I really have no idea. But hope springs eternal, York. You must always keep that in mind. Where are you staying while you're here?"

"I ain't got no place. Give that Dagget feller my last fifty dollars. He told me that give me five days in here." He shook his head. "After that . . . I don't know."

"You're welcome to stay here. I don't have much, but you're welcome to share with me."

"That's mighty white of you, DeBeers. And I'll take you up on that." He grinned at Smoke. "There is them that say you're goofy. But I don't think so. I think you're just a pretty nice guy in a bad spot."

"Thank you, York. And have you ever thought that

might fit you as well?"

The grin faded. "Yeah, I reckon it might. I ain't never done a dishonest thing in my life. Only difference is, you ain't got no warrants hangin' over your head. You can ride out of this hellhole anytime you take a notion. Me? I'm stuck, lookin' at the wrong side of society!"

The next morning Smoke left the still-sleeping York a full pot of coffee, then took his sketch pad and went walking, as was his custom every morning. As the saloon came into view, Smoke noticed a large crowd gathered out front, in the street. And it was far too early for that many drinkers to have gathered.

"Let's have some fun!" Smoke could hear the excited shout.

"Yeah. Let's skin the son of a bitch!"

"Naw. Let's give him to Brute."

"Brute don't want no dirty Injun."

"Not unless it's a young boy," someone shouted with a hard laugh.

"Hold it down!" a man hollered. "Mr. Davidson's got a plan, and it's a good one."

Smoke stepped up to a man standing in the center of the street. "What on earth has happened here?"

The outlaw glanced at him. "The guards caught them an Injun about dawn. He was tryin' to slip out over the mountains. No one knows what he was doin' in town." The man shut up, appraising Smoke through cool eyes, aware that he might have said too much.

"He must have slipped in on the road," Smoke said quickly, noting the coolness in the man's eyes fading. "It would be impossible to come in through those terribly high mountains around the town."

The outlaw smiled. "Yeah. That's what he done, all right. And there ain't no tellin' how long he's been tryin' to get out, right?"

"Oh, absolutely. I think the savage should be hanged immediately." Smoke forced indignation into his voice.

The outlaw grinned. His teeth were blackened, rotted stubs. "You all right, Shirley. You're beginnin' to fit right in here. Yeah, the Injun's gonna die. But it's gonna be slow."

"Why?" Smoke asked innocently.

"Why, hell's fire, Shirley! So's we can all have some fun, that's why."

"Oh. Of course."

A man ran past Smoke and the outlaw, running in that odd bowlegged manner of one who has spent all his life on a horse.

"What's happenin', Jeff?" the outlaw asked.

"Mr. Davidson tole me to get the kid, York. Says we gotta test him. You know why?"

"Yeah."

Neither man would elaborate.

Smoke felt he knew what the test was going to involve, and he also felt that York would not pass it. There was a sick feeling in the pit of his stomach. Smoke wandered on down to the large crowd gathered in front of the saloon and tried to blend in.

The crowd of hardcases and thugs and guns-for-hire ignored him, but Smoke was very conscious of Rex Davidson's eyes on him. He met the man's steady gaze and smiled at him.

Davidson waved the crowd silent. "I have decided on a better plan," he said as the crowd fell quiet. "Forget York; we know he's a wanted man. There are some of you who claim that our artist friend is not what he professes to be. Well, let's settle that issue right now. Bring that damned Indian out here."

Smoke felt sure it would be Lone Eagle, and it was. He was dragged out of the saloon and onto the boardwalk. He had been badly beaten, his nose and mouth dripping blood. But his face remained impassive and he deliberately did not look at Smoke.

"Drag that damned savage to the shooting post," Davidson ordered. He looked at Smoke and smiled, an evil curving of the lips. "And you, Mr. Artist, you come along, too."

"Do I have to? I hate violence. It makes me ill. I'd be upset for days."

"Yes, damn it, you have to. Now get moving."

Smoke allowed himself to be pushed and shoved along, not putting up any resistance. He wondered if any Indians were watching from the cliffs that surrounded the outlaw town and concluded they probably were.

And he also had a pretty good hunch what the test was going to entail.

The crowd stopped in a large clearing. In the center of the clearing, a bullet-scarred and blood-stained post was set into the ground.

Lone Eagle turned to face the crowd, and when he spoke, his voice was strong. "I do not need to be tied like a coward. I face death with a strong heart, and I shall die well. I will show the white man how to die with honor. Which is something that few of you know anything about."

The crowd of hardcases booed him.

Lone Eagle spat at them in contempt.

He had not as yet looked at Smoke.

Smoke was shoved to the front of the crowd and a pistol placed into his hand.

"What am I supposed to do with this weapon, Mr. Davidson?"

"Kill the Indian," Rex told him.

"Oh, I say now!" Smoke protested shrilly. "I haven't fired a gun in years. I detest guns. I'm afraid of them. I won't be able to hit the savage."

Lone Eagle laughed at Smoke, looking at him. "The white man is a woman!" Lone Eagle shouted. And Smoke knew he was deliberately goading him. Lone Eagle knew he was going to die and preferred his death to be quick rather than slow torture, torture for the amusement of the white men gathered around. He might have chosen the slow way had he been captured by another tribe, for to die slowly and with much pain was an honor—if at the hands of other Indians. But not at the hands of the white men.

"The silly-looking white man is a coward."

"You gonna take that from a damned Injun, Shirley?" a man shouted.

"What am I supposed to do?"

"Hell, sissy-boy. Kill the bastard!"

Smoke lifted the pistol and pretended to have trouble cocking it. He deliberately let it fire, the slug almost hitting an outlaw in the foot. Smoke shrieked as if in fright and the outlaw cussed him.

The others thought it wildly funny.

"Watch it there, Black!" an outlaw yelled. "He lift that muzzle up some you liable to be ridin' side-saddle!"

The man whose foot was just missed by the slug stepped back into the crowd and gave Smoke some dirty looks.

"Shoot the goddamn Indian, DeBeers!" Davidson ordered.

Smoke lifted the pistol and cocked it, taking careful aim and pulling the trigger. The slug missed Lone Eagle by several yards, digging up dirt. The outlaws hooted and laughed and began making bets as to how many rounds it would take for Smoke to hit his target.

"Try again, Shirley," Davidson told him, disgust in his voice.

"What a silly, silly man you are!" Lone Eagle shouted. "If you had two pistols and a rifle and shotgun beside you, you still would not be able to hit me. It is good they are out of your sight. You might hurt yourself, foolish man."

Lone Eagle was telling Smoke that his weapons had been hidden as planned.

"Shoot the damned Injun, Shirley!" Dagget hollered in Smoke's ear.

"All right! All right!" Smoke put a hurt expression on his face. "You don't have to be so ugly about it!"

Smoke fired again. The slug missed Lone Eagle by a good two feet.

"Jesus Christ, DeBeers!" Dagget said, scorn thick in his voice.

"The pistol was fully loaded, Shirley," Davidson told him. "You have four rounds left."

Lone Eagle turned his back to Smoke and hiked up his loincloth, exposing his bare buttocks; the height of insult to a man.

Facing the crowd, Lone Eagle shouted, "There are little girls in my village who are better shots than the white man. Your shots are nothing more than farts in the wind."

"If you don't kill him," Davidson warned, "you shall be the one to gouge out his eyes. And if you refuse, I'll personally kill you. After I let Brute have his way with you."

Smoke cocked the pistol.

Lone Eagle began chanting, and Smoke knew he was singing his death song.

He fired again. This time, the slug came much closer. Lone Eagle's words changed slightly. Smoke listened while he fumbled with the gun. Lone Eagle was telling him to miss him again, and then he would charge and make the outlaws kill him; it was too much to ask a friend to do so. He told him that his death could not be avoided, that it was necessary for the plan to work. That for years it would be sung around the campfires about how well Lone Eagle had died, charging the many white men with only his bare hands for a weapon.

And it was a good way to die. The Gods had allowed a beautiful day, warm and pleasant.

Smoke cocked the pistol and lifted it, taking aim.

Lone Eagle sang of his own death, then abruptly he screamed and charged the line of outlaws and gunslingers. Using the scream as a ruse to miss him, Smoke emptied the pistol and fell to the ground just as Lone Eagle, with a final scream, jumped at the line and a dozen guns barked and roared, stopping him in midair, flinging him to the ground, bloody and dead.

Rex helped Smoke up. "You'll never change, Shirley," he said disgustedly. "Do us all a favor and don't ever carry a gun. You'd be too dangerous. Hell, you might accidentally hit something!"

Smoke fanned himself. "I feel faint!"

"If you pass out, DeBeers," Dagget told him, contempt

in his eyes and his voice, "you'll damn well lie where you fall."

"I can probably make it back to the camp before I collapse," Smoke trilled.

"Stand aside, boys!" an outlaw said with a laugh. "Shirley's got the vapors!"

"Come on, boys! The drinks are on me."

As they passed by him, several hardcases jokingly complimented Smoke on his fine shooting.

Smoke looked first at Davidson and Dagget, standing by his side, and then at the bullet-riddled and bloody body of Lone Eagle. "Isn't anyone going to bury the savage?"

Dagget laughed, cutting his eyes to Davidson. "I think that'd be a fine job for Shirley, don't you, Rex?"

"Yes." That was said with a laugh. "I do. There is a shovel right over there. DeBeers." He pointed. "Now get to it."

It took Smoke more than a hour to dig out a hole in the rocky soil, even though he dug it shallow, knowing the chief would take the body from the ground and give it a proper Indian burial.

When he got back to his camp, York was laying on his blankets, looking up at him, disgust in his eyes.

Smoke flopped down on his own blankets. "What a horrible experience."

"They wasn't no call to kill that Injun. He wasn't even armed and probably was lookin' for food. You was missin' him deliberate, wasn't you?"

Smoke made up his mind and took the chance. "Yes, York, I was."

"I figured as much. Can't nobody shoot that bad. 'Specially a man who was raised up on a farm the way you claim to be. You puttin' on some sort of act, DeBeers. But you best be damn careful around here. This is a hellhole, and they ain't nothin' but scum livin' here."

"I know. Davidson at first said if I didn't kill the Indian, he was going to give me to Brute Pitman and then have me gouge out the Indian's eyes." Smoke let the mention of his putting on an act fade away into nothing, hoping York would not bring it up again.

York lay on the ground and gazed at him. "I heard of Brute; seen him around a couple of times. He's a bad one. If they'd a tried that, I'd have been forced to deal myself in and help you out."

"You'd have gotten yourself killed."

"You befriended me. Man don't stand by his friends when they in trouble ain't much of a man or a friend. That's just the way I am."

And Smoke felt the young cowboy was sincere when he said it. "I agree with you. You know, at first, they were going to make you kill the Indian."

"I'd a not done it," he said flatly. "My ma was part Nez Percé. And I'm damn proud of that blood in my veins. And I don't make no effort to hide that fact, neither."

And judging by the scars on his flat-knuckled hands, York had been battling over that very fact most of his life, Smoke noted.

York followed Smoke's eyes. "Yeah. I'm just as quick with my fists as I am with my guns." His eyes dropped to Smoke's big hands. "And you ain't no pilgrim, neither, Mr. Shirley DeBeers. Or whatever the hell your name might be."

"Let's just leave it DeBeers for the time being, shall we?"

"'Kay." York took off his battered hat and ran fingers through his tousled hair. "DeBeers?"

"Yes, York?"

"Let's you and me get the hell gone from this damn place!"

12

There was no doubt in Smoke's mind that York was serious and was no part of Davidson's scheme of things in or around Dead River. The young cowboy was no outlaw and had made up his mind never to become one. But Smoke had three days to go before the deadline was up and the posse would strike. He had a hunch that would be the longest three days of his life. He looked at York for a moment before replying.

"I'm just about through sketching Davidson. He has indicated that he would allow me to leave after that."

"Like I said before—and you believed him?"

"I have no choice in the matter."

"I guess not. But I still think you're draggin' your boots for some reason. But I'll stick around just to see what you're up to. Don't worry, DeBeers. I'll keep my suspicions to myself."

Again, Smoke had nothing to say on that subject. "What are you going to do on the outside, York?"

York shook his head. "I don't know. Drift, I reckon. I just ain't cut out for this kind of life. I think I knowed that all along. But I think I owe it to you for pointin' it out."

"Stay out of sight, York." Smoke picked up his sketch pad. "I have to go sketch Davidson. Even though I certainly don't feel up to it."

"What if Davidson won't let you leave here like he says he will?"

"I don't know. Let's cross that bridge when we come to it."

"Bridges don't worry me," York said glumly. "It's that damn guarded pass that's got me concerned."

The next two days passed without incident. York stayed at Smoke's camp—and stayed close. Smoke continued his sketching of Rex Davidson, and his opinion that the man was a conceited and arrogant tyrant was confirmed. The man remained friendly enough—as friendly as he had ever been to Smoke—but Smoke could detect a change in him. He appreared tense and sometimes nervous. And there was distance between them now, a distance that had not been there before. Smoke knew that Davidson had never really intended to let him leave. He did not think that Rex suspected he was anything except the part he was playing, what he claimed to be. It was, Smoke felt, that Rex had been playing a game with him all along; a cat with a cornered mouse. A little torture before the death bite.

"I'm becoming a bit weary of all this," Davidson suddenly announced, breaking his pose. The afternoon of the sixth day.

"Of what, sir?" Smoke lifted his eyes, meeting the hard gaze of the man.

"Of posing, fool!" Davidson said sharply. "I have enough pictures. But as for you, I don't know what to do about you."

"Whatever in the world are you talking about, Mr. Davidson?"

Rex stared at him for a long moment. Then, rising from the stool where he'd been sitting, posing, he walked to a window and looked out, staring down at his outlaw town. He turned and said, "I first thought it was you; that you were the front man, the spy sent in here. Then I realized that no one except a professional actor could play the part of a fool as convincingly as you've done . . . and no actor has that much courage. Not to come in here and lay his life on the line. So you are what you claim to be. A silly fop. But I still don't know what to do with you. I do know that you are beginning to bore me. It was the Indian. Had to be.

The marshals hired the Indian to come in here and check on us."

"Sir, I have no idea what you're talking about." But Smoke knew. Somewhere in the ranks of the marshals or the sheriffs or the deputies, there was a turncoat. Now he had to find out just how much Rex Davidson knew about the plan just twenty-four hours away from bloody reality.

And stay alive long enough to do something about it, if he could.

"That damn woman almost had me fooled," Davidson said, more to himself than to Smoke. He had turned his back again, not paying any attention to Smoke. "It was good fun torturing her, DeBeers; I wish you had been here to see it. Yes, indeed. I outdid myself with inventiveness. I kept her alive for a long time. I finally broke her, of course. But by the time I did, she was no more than a broken, babbling idiot. The only thing we learned was that the marshals were planning on coming in here at some time or the other. She didn't know when."

"Sir, I—"

Davidson whirled around, his face hard with anger. "Shut your goddamn mouth, DeBeers!" he shouted. "And never interrupt me when I'm speaking."

"Yes, sir."

"Of course, she was raped—among other things. The men enjoyed taking their perversions upon her." He was pacing the room. "Repeatedly. I enjoyed listening to her beg for mercy. Dagget can be quite inventive, too. But finally I wearied of it, just as I am rapidly wearying of you, DeBeers. You're really a Milquetoast, Shirley. I think I'll put you in a dress and parade you around. Yes. That is a thought."

Smoke kept his mouth shut.

Davidson turned back to the window, gazing out over his town of scum and filth and perversion. "I have not left this place in years. I stay aware of what is going on outside, of course. But I have not left this valley in years. It's mine, and no one is going to take it from me. I will not permit it. I know an attack is coming. But I don't know when."

Smoke knew then why the sudden influx of outlaws. Somehow, probably through outriders, Davidson had gotten the word out to them: If you want to save your refuge, you'd better be prepared to fight for it.

Or something like that.

With King Rex, however, it had probably been put in a much more flowery way.

"Ah, sir, Your Majesty?" Smoke verbally groveled, something he was getting weary of.

"What do you want, Shirley?"

"May I take my leave now, Your Majesty?"

"Yes, you silly twit!" Davidson did not turn from the window. "And stay out of my sight, goofy. I haven't made up my mind exactly what I'm going to do with you. Get out, fool!"

I've made up my mind what to do with you, King Rex, Smoke thought, on his way out. And about this time tomorrow, you're going to be in for a very large surprise. One that I'm going to enjoy handing you.

He gently closed the door behind him. He was smiling as he walked down the hill from the King's house. He had to work to get the smile off his lips before he entered the long main street of Dead River.

In twenty-four hours, he would finally and forever shed his foppish costume and strap on his guns.

And then Dr. Jensen would begin administering to a very sick town.

With gunsmoke and lead.

Smoke was conscious of York staring at him. He had been sliding furtive glances his way for several hours now, and Smoke knew the reason for the looks. He could feel the change coming over him. He would have to be very careful the remainder of this day, for he was in no mood to continue much longer with his Shirley DeBeers act.

York had just returned from town and had been unusually quiet since getting back. He finally broke his silence.

"DeBeers?"

"Yes, York?"

"I gotta tell you. The word is out that come the morning, you're gonna be tossed to the wolves. Davidson is gonna declare you fair game for anybody. And you know what that means."

Mid-afternoon of the seventh day.

"Brute Pitman."

"Among other things," York said.

"What size boots do you wear, York?"

"Huh! Man, didn't you hear me? We got to get the hell gone from this place. And I mean we got to plan on how to do it right now!"

"I heard you, York. Just relax. What size boots do you wear?"

The cowboy sighed. "Ten."

"That's my size. How about that?" Smoke grinned at him.

"Wonderful!" The comment was dryly given. "You lookin' at gettin' kilt, and you all het up about us wearin' the same size boots. You weird, DeBeers."

With a laugh, Smoke handed York some money. "Go to the store and buy me a good pair of boots. Black. Get me some spurs. Small stars, not the big California rowels. Don't say a word about who you're buying them for. We'll let that come as a surprise for them. Think you can do that for me, York?"

"Why, hell, yes, I can! What do you think I am, some sort of dummy? Boots? 'Kay. But I best get you some walkin' heels."

"Riding heels, York," Smoke corrected, enjoying the look of bewilderment on his new friend's face. "And how many boxes of shells do you have?"

"One and what's in my belt. Now why in the hell are you askin' that?"

"Buy at least three more boxes. When you get back, I'll explain. Now then, what else have you heard about me, York?"

"You ain't gonna like it."

"Oh, I don't know. It might give me more incentive to

better do the job that faces me."

York shook his head. "Weird, DeBeers. That's you. Well, that Jake feller? He's been makin' his brags about how he's gonna make you hunker down in the street and eat a pile of horse-droppin's."

"Oh, is he now?"

"Yeah. He likes to be-little folks. That Jake, he's cruel mean, DeBeers. That one and them that run with him is just plain no-good. He makes ever' slave that comes in here do that. I've had half a dozen or more men tell me that. All the men here, they think it's funny watchin' Jake force folks to eat that mess."

"I wonder how Jake would like to eat a poke of it himself?"

York grinned. "Now that'd be a sight to see!"

"Don't give up hope, York. Would you please go get my stuff for me?"

"Sure." He turned, then stopped and whirled around to face Smoke. "I can't figure you, DeBeers. You've changed. I noticed that this morning."

"We'll talk when you get back, York. Be careful down in town. I think things are getting a bit tense."

"That ain't exactly the way I'd put it, but whatever you say." He walked off toward town, mumbling to himself and shaking his head. Smoke smiled at the young man and then set about preparing himself mentally for what the night held in store.

And he knew only too well what lay before him when the dusk settled into darkness in the outlaw town.

There was no fear in Smoke; no sweaty palms or pounding heart. He was deathly calm, inside and out. And he did not know if that was an asset or liability. He knew caution, for no man lived by the gun without knowing what was about him at all times. But Smoke, since age sixteen, had seldom if ever at all experienced anything even remotely akin to fear.

He sat down on his ground sheet and blankets and calmly set about making a pot of coffee. He looked up at the sound of boots striking the gravel. Brute Pitman stopped a few yards away, grinning at him.

"Go away, Brute. The smell of you would stop a buzzard in flight."

Brute cussed him.

Smoke smiled at him.

"I'm gonna enjoy hearin' you holler, pretty-boy," Brute told him, slobber leaking past his fat lips. "With you, I'm gonna make it las' a long, long time."

Smoke made no reply, just sat on the ground and stared at the hulking mass of perversion. He allowed his eyes to do the talking, and they silently spoke volumes to the big slob.

Brute met the gaze and Smoke's smile was wider still as something shifted in the hulk's eyes. Was it fear touching Brute's dark eyes? Smoke felt sure that it was, and that thought amused him. Brute Pitman was like so many men his size, a bully from boyhood. He had bulled and heavy-shouldered his way through life, knowing his sheer size would keep most from fighting back. But like most bullies, Brute was a coward at heart.

"Something the matter, Brute?"

That took him by surprise. "Huh! Naw, they ain't nothin' the matter with me, sissy-boy. Nothin'," he added, "that come night won't clear."

"You best watch the night, Brute," Smoke cautioned. "Night is a time when death lays close to a man."

"Huh! Whatda you talkin' 'bout now, pretty-boy. I don't think you even know. I think you so scared you peein' your drawers."

Smoke laughed at him. Now he didn't care. It was too close to the deadline to matter. By now, the men from the posse would be approaching the ranch and would be changing horses for the last time before entering the mountain pass. Already, the Utes would be slipping into place, waiting for the guards to change.

Everything was in motion; it could not be stopped now.

"Get out of my sight, Brute. You sicken me."

Brute hesitated, then mumbled something obscene under his breath and walked down the small hill. Twice he stopped and looked back at Smoke. Smoke gave him the finger, jabbing the air with his middle finger.

"Crazy!" Brute said. "The bassard's crazy! Done took leave of his senses."

Smoke heard the comment and smiled.

Brute met Cat Ventura on his way down. The men did not speak to each other. Cat stood over Smoke, staring down at him.

"I would wish you a good afternoon," Smoke told him, "but with you here, it is anything but that."

Cat stared at him, ignoring the remark; Smoke was not sure the man even knew what he meant by it. "I seen you somewheres before, artist," the gunfighter, outlaw, and murderer said. "And you wasn't drawin' no pitchers on paper, neither."

"Perhaps if you dwell on it long enough, it will come to you in time, Mister-whatever-your-name is. Not that I particularly care at this juncture."

"Huh! Boy, you got a damn smart mouth on you, ain't you? I'm Cat Ventura."

"Not a pleasure, I'm sure. Very well, Mr. Meow. If you came up here to ask me to sketch you, my studio is closed for the time being. Perhaps some other time; like in the next century."

"You piss-headed smart ass! When the time comes, I think I'll jist stomp your guts out; see what color they is. How 'bout that, sissy-pants?"

"Oh, I don't think so, Mr. Purr. I really have my doubts about you doin' that."

Before he turned away to walk back down the hill, Cat said, "I know you from somewheres. It'll come to me. I'll be back."

"I'll certainly be here."

Smoke lay on his ground sheet and watched a passing parade of outlaws visit him during the next few minutes. Some walked up and stared at him. A few made open threats on his life.

He would have liked to ask why the sudden shift in their attitude toward him, but he really wasn't all that interested in the why of it.

Smoke checked the mountain sky. About three hours until dusk. He rose from the ground and got his fishing pole, checking the line and hook. Jake and Shorty and Red had been watching him, hunkered down at the base of the hill. Out of the corner of his eyes, Smoke saw them all relax and reach for the makings, rolling and lighting cigarettes. He stepped back into the timber behind his camp, as if heading for the little creek to fish and catch his supper. Smoke assumed his line of credit at the Bon Ton Café had been cut off. The food hadn't been all that good anyway.

Out of sight of the trio of outlaws, Smoke dropped his pole and walked toward the center of town, staying inside the thin timber line until he was opposite the privy and the pile of lumber behind the saloon. He quickly stepped to the lumber, moved a couple of boards, and spotted the rolled-up packet.

The back door to the saloon opened, a man stepping out. "What you doin', boy? Sneakin' around here. You tryin' to slip out, pretty-pants?"

Smoke looked up as the man closed the door behind him and walked toward him. His hand closed around a sturdy two-by-four, about three feet long and solid. "Just borrowing a few boards, sir. I thought I might build a board floor for my tent. Is that all right with you?"

The outlaw stepped closer, Smoke recognizing him as a wanted murderer. "No, it ain't all right with me. You jist git your butt on out of here."

Smoke could smell the odor of rotting human flesh from those unfortunates hanging from the meat hooks at the edge of town. Those few still alive were moaning and crying out in pain.

Smoke looked around him. They were alone. He smiled at the outlaw. "Playtime is all over, you bastard."

"What'd you say to me, fancy-pants?" The man stepped closer, almost within swinging distance. Just a few feet more and Smoke would turn out the man's lights. Forever.

"I said you stink like sheep-shit and look like the ass end

of a donkey."

Cursing, growling deep in his throat, the outlaw charged Smoke. Smoke jerked up the two-by-four and laid the lumber up against the man's head. The outlaw stopped, as if he had run into a stone wall. His skull popped under the impact. He dropped to the earth, dying, blood leaking from his ears and nose and mouth.

Smoke dropped the two-by-four and quickly dragged the man behind the privy, stretching him out full length behind the two-holer. He could only be seen from the timber.

Smoke took the man's two .44's and punched out the shells from the loops of his belt. He grabbed up his own guns and walked back into the timber, heading for his campsite.

He was smiling, humming softly.

They had said their good-byes to their wives and kids and girlfriends and swung into the saddle, pointing the nose of their horses north, toward the outlaw town.

One deputy from an adjoining county had been caught trying to make it alone to Dead River. He had been brought back to face Jim Wilde. It turned out his brother was one of the outlaws living in Dead River. The deputy was now locked down hard in his own jail, under heavy guard.

The members of the posse were, to a man, hard-faced and grim. All knew that some of them would not live through the night that lay before them. And while none of them wanted to die, they knew that what lay ahead of them was something that had to be done, should have been done a long time back. The outlaw town had been a blight on society for years, and the time had come to destroy it and all who chose to reside within its confines.

The riders each carried at least two pistols belted around their waists. Most had two more six-guns, either tucked behind their belts or carried in holsters, tied to their saddles. All carried a rifle in the boot; some had added a shotgun, the express guns loaded with buckshot. The men had stuffed their pockets full of .44's, .45's, and shotgun shells.

The posse rode at a steady, distance-covering gait; already they had changed horses and were now approaching Red Davis's place. While the hands switched saddles, the men of the posse grabbed and wolfed down a sandwich and coffee, then refilled canteens. All checked their guns, wiping them free of dust and checking the action.

"Wish I was goin' with you," Davis said. "I'd give a thousand dollars to see that damn town burned slap to the ground."

Wilde nodded his head. "Red, there'll be doctors and the like comin' out here and settin' up shop 'bout dark. Some of us are gonna be hard-hit and the slaves in that town are gonna be in bad shape. You got your wagons ready to meet us at the mouth of the pass?"

"All hitched up." He spat on the ground. "And me and my boys will take care of any stragglers that happen to wander out when the shootin' starts."

Jim Wilde smiled grimly. Between the Utes and Red Davis's hard-bitten hands, any outlaws who happened to escape were going to be in for a very rough time of it. Red's ranch had been the first in the area, and the old man was as tough as leather—and so were his hands.

Red clasped Jim on the shoulder. "Luck to you, boy. And I wanna meet this Smoke Jensen. That there is my kind of man."

Jim nodded and turned, facing the sixty-odd men of the posse. The U.S. Marshal wore twin .44's, tied down. He carried another .44 in a shoulder holster and a rifle and a shotgun in the boots, on his horse. "All right, boys. This is the last jumpin'-off place. From here on in, they's no turnin' back. You gotta go to the outhouse, get it done now. When we get back into the saddle, we ain't stoppin' until we're inside Dead River." He glanced at the sinking sun. "Smoke's gonna open up the dance in about an hour—if he's still alive," he added grimly. "And knowin' him, he is. Anybody wanna back out of this?"

No one did.

"Let's ride!"

The guards along the pass road had just changed, the new guards settling in for a long and boring watch. Nothing ever happened; a lot of the time many of them dozed off. They would all sleep this dusky evening. Forever.

One guard listened for a few seconds. Was that a noise behind him? He thought it was. He turned, brought his rifle up, and came face to face with a war-painted Indian. He froze, opening his mouth to yell a warning. The shout was forever locked in his throat as an axe split his skull. The Ute caught the bloody body before it could fall to the ground and lowered it to the earth. The body would never be found; time and wind and rain and the elements and animals would dispose of the flesh and scatter the bones. A hundred years later, small boys playing would discover the gold coins the outlaw had had in his pockets and would wonder how the money came to be in this lonely spot.

His job done, for the moment, the brave slipped back into the timber and waited.

Up and down the heavily guarded narrow road, the guards were meeting an end just as violent as the life they had chosen to live. And they had chosen it; no one had forced them into it. One outlaw guard, who enjoyed torturing Indians, especially children, and raping squaws, was taken deep into the timber, gagged, stripped, and staked out. Then he was skinned—alive.

Their first job done, the Indians quietly slipped back and took their positions around the outlaw town of Dead River. With the patience bred into them, they waited and watched, expressionless.

York looked up and blinked, at first not recognizing the tall muscular man who was walking toward him, out of the timber. Then he recognized him.

"Damn, DeBeers. I didn't know you at first. How come you shaved off your beard?"

"It was time. And my name is not DeBeers."

"Yeah. I kinda figured it was a phony. And I didn't believe that Shirley bit, neither."

"That's right. You get my boots and spurs?"

York pointed to a bag on the ground. He had never seen such a change in any man. The man standing in front of him looked . . . awesome!

Smoke was dressed all in black, from his boots to his shirt. His belt was black with inlaid silver that caught the last glows of the setting sun. He wore a red bandana around his neck. He had buckled on twin .44's, the left handgun worn butt-forward, cross-draw style. He had shoved two more .44's behind his belt.

"Ah . . . man, you best be careful with them guns," York cautioned. "You packin' enough for an army. Are you fixin' to start a war around here?"

"That is my hope, York."

"Yeah?" Somehow, that did not come as any surprise to York. There was something about this tall man that was just . . . well, unsettling. He poured a cup of coffee and sipped it, hot, strong, and black. He looked at the tall man. Naw, he thought, it couldn't be. But he sure looked like all the descriptions York had ever heard about the gunfighter. "Who are you, man?"

Smoke pulled a badge from his pocket and pinned it to his shirt. "I'm a United States Deputy Marshal. And as far as I'm concerned, York, all those warrants against you are not valid. And when we get out of here, I'll see that they are recalled. How does that sound to you?"

York took a sip of coffee. Oddly, to Smoke, he had shown no surprise. "Sounds good to me, Marshal." He stood up and pulled a gold badge out of his pocket and pinned it on his shirt. "Buddy York is the name. Arizona Rangers. I was wonderin' if you plan on corralin' this town all by your lonesome."

"That's a good cover story of yours, Ranger," Smoke complimented him.

"Well, took us six months to set it up. The dodgers that are out are real. Had to be that way."

"I gather you have warrants for some people in here?"

"A whole passel of them, including some on Dagget."

"There is a large posse on the way in. They'll be here just at dusk. The Utes have taken care of the guards along the road."

York looked up at the sky. "That's a good hour and a half away, Marshal." He was grinning broadly.

"That's the way I got it figured, Ranger. Of course, you do know that you have no jurisdiction in this area?"

"I'll worry about that later."

"Consider yourself deputized with full goverment authority."

"I do thank you, Marshal."

"You ready to open this dance, Ranger?" Smoke sat down on a log and buckled on his spurs. He looked up as York opened another bag and tossed him a black hat, low crowned and flat brimmed. "Thanks. I am ever so glad to be rid of that damned silly cap." He tried the hat. A perfect fit.

"You did look a tad goofy. But I got to hand it to you. You're one hell of a fine actor."

Both men stuffed their pockets full of shells.

Rifle in hand, York said, "What is your handle, anyways?"

"Smoke Jensen," the tall, heavily muscled man said with a smile.

York's knees seemed to buckle and he sat down heavily on a log. When he found his voice, he said, "Holy jumpin' Jesus Christ!"

"I'm new to the marshaling business, Ranger. I just took this on a temporary basis." Then he explained what had happened at his ranch, to his wife.

"Takes a low-life SOB to attack a lone woman. I gather you want Davidson and Dagget and them others all to yourself, right?"

"I would appreciate it, Ranger."

"They're all yours."

Smoke checked his guns, slipping them both in and out of leather a few times. He filled both cylinders and every loop on his gunbelt, then checked the short-barreled pistol he carried in his shoulder holster. Breaking open the sawed-off shotgun, he filled both barrels with buckshot loads. Smoke looked on with approval as the ranger pulled two spare .44's out of his warbag and loaded them full. He tucked them behind his belt and picked up a Henry repeating rifle, loading it full and levering in a round, then replacing that round in the magazine.

"I'll tell you how I see this thing, Ranger. You don't have to play this way, but I'm going to."

"I'm listenin', Smoke."

"I'm not taking any prisoners."

"I hadn't planned on it myself."

The men smiled at each other, knowing then exactly where the other stood.

Their pockets bulging with extra cartridges, York carrying a Henry and Smoke carrying the sawed-off express gun, they looked at each other.

"You ready to strike up the band, Ranger?"

"Damn right!" York said with a grin.

"Let's do it!"

13

Marshal Jim Wilde's posse had an hour to go before reaching Dead River when Smoke and York stepped into the back of the saloon. Inside, the piano player was banging out and singing a bawdy song.

"How do we do this?" York asked.

"We walk in together," Smoke whispered.

The men slipped the thongs off their six-guns and eased them out of leather a time or two, making certain the oiled interiors of the holsters were free.

York eased back the hammer on his Henry and Smoke jacked back the hammers on the express gun.

They stepped inside the noisy and beer-stinking saloon. The piano player noticed them first. He stopped playing and singing and stared at them, his face chalk-white. Then he scrambled under the lip of the piano.

"Well, well!" an outlaw said, laughing. "Would you boys just take a look at Shirley. He's done shaven offen his beard and taken to packin' iron. Boy, you bes' git shut of them guns, 'fore you hurt yourself."

Gridley stood up from a table where he'd been drinking and playing poker—and losing. "Or I decide to take 'em off you and shove 'em up your butt, lead and all, pretty-boy. Matter of fact, I think I'll jist do that, right now."

Smoke and York had surveyed the scene as they had stepped in. The barroom was not nearly filled to capacity . . . but it was full enough.

"The name isn't pretty-boy, Gridley," Smoke informed him.

"Oh, yeah? Well, mayhaps you right. I'll jist call you shit! How about that?"

"Why don't you call him by his real name?" York said, a smile on his lips.

"And what might that be, punk?" Gridley sneered the question. "Alice?"

"First off," York said, "I'll tell you I'm an Arizona Ranger. Note the badges we're wearing? And his name, you blow-holes, is Smoke Jensen!"

The name was dropped like a bomb. The outlaws in the room sat stunned, their eyes finally observing the gold badges on the chests of the men.

Smoke and York both knew one thing for an ironclad fact: The men in the room might all be scoundrels and thieves and murderers, and some might be bullies and cowards, but when it came down to it, they were going to fight.

"Then draw, you son of a bitch!" Gridley hollered, his hands dropping to his guns.

Smoke pulled the trigger on the express gun. From a distance of no more than twenty feet, the buckshot almost tore the outlaw in two.

York leveled the Henry and dusted an outlaw from side to side. Dropping to one knee, he levered the empty out and a fresh round in and shot a fat punk in the belly.

Shifting the sawed-off shotgun, Smoke blew the head off another outlaw. The force of the buckshot lifted the headless outlaw out of one boot and flung him to the sawdust-covered floor.

York and his Henry had put half a dozen outlaws on the floor, dead, dying, or badly hurt.

The huge saloon was filled with gunsmoke, the crying and moaning of the wounded, and the stink or relaxed bladders from the dead. Dark gray smoke from the black powder cartridges stung the eyes and obscured the vision of all in the room.

The outlaws had recovered from their initial shock and had overturned tables, crouching behind them, returning the deadly hail of fire from Smoke and Arizona

Ranger York.

Smoke had slipped to the end of the bar closest to the batwing doors, and York had worked his way to the side of the big stage, crouching behind a second piano in the small orchestra pit. Between the two of them, Smoke and York were laying down a deadly field of fire. Both men had grabbed up the guns of the dead and dying men as they slipped to their new positions and they now had a pile of .44's, .45's, and several shotguns and rifles in front of them.

A half-dozen outlaws tried to rush the batwings in a frantic attempt to escape and were met by a half-dozen other outlaws attempting to enter the saloon from the outside. It created a massive pileup at the batwings, a pileup that was too good for Smoke to resist.

Slipping to the very end of the long bar, Smoke emptied a pair of .45's taken from a dead man into the panicked knot of outlaws. Screaming from the men as the hot slugs tore into their flesh added to the earsplitting cacophony of confusion in the saloon.

Smoke grabbed up an armload of weapons and ran to the end of the bar closest to the rear of the saloon. He caught York's attention and motioned to the storeroom where they had entered. York nodded and left his position at a run. The men ran through the darkened storeroom to the back door.

Just as they reached the back door it opened and two outlaws stepped inside, guns drawn. Smoke and York fired simultaneously, their guns booming and crashing in the darkness, lancing smoke and fire, splitting the heavy gloom of the storeroom. The outlaws were flung backward, outside. They lay on the ground, on their backs, dying from wounds to the chest and belly.

"York, you take the north end of town," Smoke said. "I'll take the south end." He was speaking as he was stripping the weapons from the dead men.

York nodded his agreement and tossed Smoke one of two cloth sacks he'd picked up in the storeroom. The men began dumping in the many guns they'd picked up along the way.

"Find and destroy the heathens!" a man's strong voice cut the night. "The Philistines are upon us!"

"Who in the hell is that?" York whispered.

"That's Tustin, the preacher. Has to be."

"A preacher? Here?" The ranger's voice was filled with disbelief.

The gunfire had almost ceased, as the outlaws in the saloon could not find Smoke or York.

"Oh, Lord!" Tustin's voice filled the night. "Take these poor unfortunate bastards into the gates of Heaven and give us the strength and the wherewithal to find and shoot the piss outta them that's attackin' us!"

"I ain't believein' this," York muttered.

Smoke smiled, his strong white teeth flashing in the night. "Good luck, York."

"Same to you, partner."

Carrying their heavy sacks of weapons and cartridge-filled belts, the men parted, one heading north, the other heading south.

York and Smoke both held to the edge of the timber as they made their way north and south. The town's inhabitants had adopted a panicked siege mentality, with outlaws filling the streets, running in every direction. No one among them knew how many men were attacking the town. Both York and Smoke had heard the shouts that hundreds of lawmen were attacking.

Just before Smoke slipped past the point where he could look up and see the fine home of Davidson, he saw the lamps in the house being turned off, the home on the hill growing dark.

And Smoke would have made a bet that Davidson and Dagget had a rabbit hole out of Dead River, and that both of them, and probably a dozen or more of their most trusted henchmen, were busy packing up and getting out.

Just for a moment, Smoke studied the darkened outline of the home on the hill. And then it came to him. A cave. He would bet a hundred dollars that King Rex had built his home in front of a cave, a cave that wound through the mountain and exited out in the timbered range behind

Dead River. And he would also bet that White Wolf and his braves knew nothing of it. It might exit out into a little valley where horses and gear could be stored.

Cursing in disgust for not thinking of that sooner, Smoke slipped on into the night, seeking a good spot to set up a defensive position.

He paused for a moment, until York had opened fire, showing Smoke where the ranger had chosen to make his stand. And it was a good one, high up on the right side of the ridge overlooking the town, as Smoke stood looking north. With a smile, Smoke chose his position on the opposite side of the street, above the first store one encountered upon entering the outlaw town.

Below him, the outlaws had settled down, taking up positions around the town. Smoke could see several bodies sprawled in the street, evidence of York's marksmanship with his Henry.

A handful of outlaws tried to rush the ranger's position. Hard gunfire broke out on either side and above York's position. White Wolf's Utes were making their presence known, in a very lethal manner. For years, the outlaws had made life miserable for the Utes, and now it was payback time. With a vengeance.

A horseman came galloping up the street, toward the curve that exited the town. The man was riding low in the saddle, the reins in his teeth and both hands full of six-guns. Smoke took careful aim with a rifle he'd picked up in the saloon and knocked the man out of the saddle. The rider hit the ground hard and rolled, coming up on his feet. A dozen rifles spat lead. The man was hit a dozen times, shot to bloody rags. He dropped to the roadway, his blood leaking into the dirt.

The horse, reins trailing, trotted off into an alley.

Smoke hit the ground, behind a series of boulders, as his position was found and rifles began barking and spitting in the night, the lead ricocheting and whining off the huge rocks, spinning into the night.

A Ute came rolling down the hill crashing against the boulder behind which Smoke was hiding. Smoke rolled the brave over and checked his wound—a nasty wound in the brave's side. Smoke plugged it with moss and stretched the Indian out, safe from fire. The Ute's dark eyes had never left Smoke's face, and he endured the pain without a sound.

Smoke made the sign for brother and the Indian, flat on his back returned the gesture. Gunfighter and Indian smiled at each other in the gunfire-filled night above the outlaw town.

Smoke picked up his rifle as the Indian, who had never let go of his rifle, crawled to a position on the other end of the line of boulders. Smoke tossed him a bag of cartridges and the men began lacing the town with .44 rifle fire. The .44's, which could punch through a good three inches of pine, began bringing shouts and yells of panic from the outlaws in the town below.

Several tried to run; they were knocked down in the street. One outlaw, his leg twisted grotesquely, tried to crawl to safety. A slug to the head stopped his strugglings.

Smoke spoke to the Ute in his own language. "If they ever discover how few we are up here, we're in trouble, brother."

The Ute laughed in the night and said, "My people have always fought outnumbered, gunfighter. It is nothing new to us."

Smoke returned the laugh and began working the lever on his Henry, laying a line of lead into a building below their position. The sudden hard fire brought several screams of pain from inside the building. One man fell through a shattered window to hang there, half in and half out of the building.

The Ute shouted a warning as a dozen outlaws charged their position, the men slipping from tree to tree, rock to rock, working closer.

Smoke quickly reloaded the Henry and laid two .44's on the ground beside him, one by each leg. There was no doubt in his mind that the outlaws would certainly breach their position, and then the fighting would be hand to hand.

Smoke heard the ugly sound of a bullet striking flesh and bone, and turning his head, he saw the Ute fall backward, a blue-tinged hole in the center of his forehead. With his right hand, Smoke made the Indian sign for peaceful journey and then returned to the fight.

He took out one outlaw who made the mistake of exposing too much of his body, knocking the man spinning from behind a tree; a second slug from Smoke's rifle forever stilled the man.

Then there was no time for anything except survival, as the outlaws charged Smoke's position.

Smoke fought savagely, his guns sending several outlaws into that long darkness. Then his position was overrun. Something slammed into the side of his head, and Smoke was dropped into darkness.

14

He was out for no more than a few seconds, never really losing full consciousness. He felt blood dripping down the side of his face. He was still holding onto his guns, and he remembered they were full. Lifting them, as a dozen shapes began materializing around him in the night, Smoke began cocking and pulling the triggers.

Hoarse screams filled the air around him as the slugs from his pistols struck their mark at point-blank range. Unwashed bodies thudded to the ground all around him, the dead and dying flesh unwittingly building a fort around his position, protecting him from the returning fire of the outlaws.

Then, half-naked shapes filtered silently and swiftly out of the timber, firing rifles and pistols. By now, the remaining outlaws were too confused and frightened to understand how a man whom they believed to be dead from a head wound had managed to inflict so hideous a toll on them.

And then the Utes came out of the timber, and in a matter of seconds, what had been twenty outlaws were no more than dying cooling flesh in the still-warm mountain air slightly above Dead River.

The Utes vanished back into the timber, as swiftly and as silently as they had come.

Smoke reloaded his guns, pistols, and rifles, and slung the rifles across his shoulders. He wrapped his bandana around his head and tied it, after inspecting his head-wound with his fingers and finding it not serious; he knew that a head wound can bleed hard and fast for a few moments, and then, in many cases, stop.

He loaded his pistols, then loaded the sawed-off shotgun. Then he began making his way down the hill, back into the town of Dead River. He was going to take the fight to the outlaws.

He stopped once to tie a white handkerchief around his arm, so not only the Indians would know who he was but so the posse members would not mistakenly shoot him.

He slipped down to the building where the outlaw was still hanging half out of the window and quietly checked out the interior. The building was void of life. Looking up the street, he could see where he, York, and the Utes had taken a terrible toll on the population of the outlaw town. The street, the alleys, and the boardwalks were littered with bodies. Most were not moving.

He did not know how much time had transpired since he and Ranger had opened the dance. But he was sure it was a good half hour or forty-five minutes.

He slipped to the south a few yards and found a good defensible position behind a stone wall that somebody had built around a small garden. Smoke pulled a ripe tomato off the vine, brushed the dust off it, and ate it while his eyes surveyed the street, picking out likely targets.

He unslung the rifles, laid his sack of guns and cartridges by one side, the express guns by his other side, and then picked up and checked out a Henry.

He had found a man stationed on top of a building. Sighting him in, Smoke let the other outlaws know he was still in the game by knocking the man off the roof with one well-placed shot to his belly. The sniper fell screaming to the street below. His howling stopped as he impacted with earth.

Putting his hand to the ground, Smoke thought he could detect a trembling. Bending over, being careful not to expose his butt to the guns of the outlaws, he pressed his ear to the ground and picked up the sound of faint rumblings. The posse was no more than a mile away.

"York!" he yelled.

"Yo, Smoke!" came the call.

"Here they come, Ranger! Shovel the coals to it!"

Smoke began levering and pulling the trigger, laying down a blistering line of fire into the buildings of the town. From his position at the other end, York did the same. The Utes opened up from both sides of the town, and the night rocked with gunfire.

"For the love of God!" Sheriff Larsen cried out, reining up by the lines of tortured men and women on the outskirts of town. His eyes were utterly disbelieving as they touched each tortured man and woman.

"Help us!" came the anguished cry of one of the few still alive. "Have mercy on us, please. We were taken against our will and brought here."

The posse of hardened western men, accustomed to savage sights, had never seen anything like this. All had seen Indian torture; but that was to be expected from ignorant savages. But fellow white men had done this.

Several of the posse leaned out of their saddles and puked on the ground.

"Three or four men stay here and cut these poor wretches down," Jim Wilde ordered, his voice strong over the sound of gunfire. "Do what you can for them."

"Jim!" Smoke called. "It's Jensen. Hold your fire, I'm coming over."

Smoke zigzagged over to the posse, catching the reins of a horse as the man dismounted. "Your horses look in good shape."

"We rested them about a mile back. Let them blow good and gave them half a hatful of water. How's your head?"

"My Sally has hit me harder," Smoke grinned, swinging into the saddle. He patted the roan's neck and rubbed his head, letting the animal know he was friendly.

"You comin' in with us?" the marshal asked.

"I got personal business to tend to. There's an Arizona Ranger named York up yonder." He pointed. "I forgot to tell him to tie something about his arm. He's a damn good man. Good luck to you boys."

Smoke swung the horse's head, and with a screaming yell from the throats of sixty men, the posse hit the main street hard. The reins in their teeth, the posse members had their hands full of .44's and .45's, and they were filling anybody they saw with lead.

Smoke rode behind the buildings of the town and dismounted, ground-reining the horse. He eased the hammers back on the express gun and began walking, deliberately letting his spurs jingle.

"Jensen!" a voice shouted from the forward darkness. "Smoke Jensen!"

Stepping behind a corner of a building, Smoke said, "Yeah, that's me."

"Cat Ventura here. You played hell, Jensen."

"That's what I came here to do, Ventura."

"Step out and face me, Jensen?"

Step out and face an ambush, you mean, Smoke thought. "No, thanks, Ventura. I don't trust you."

As soon as he said it, Smoke dropped to the ground. A half-dozen guns roared and sparked, the lead punching holes in the corner of the building where he'd been standing.

Smoke came up on one knee and let the hammers fall on both barrels of the sawed-off shotgun. He almost lost the weapon as both barrels fired, the gun recoiling in his strong hands.

The screaming of the wounded men was horrible in the night. Smoke thought of those poor people at the end of town and could not dredge up one ounce of sympathy for the outlaws he'd just blasted.

He reloaded the shotgun just as Cat called out. "Goddamn you, Jensen."

Smoke fired at the sound of the voice. A gurbling sound reached his ears. Then silence, except for the heavy pounding of gunfire in the street.

He slipped out of the alley and looked down at what was left of Cat Ventura. The full load of buckshot had taken him in the chest and throat. It was not pretty, but then,

Cat hadn't been very pretty when he was alive.

Smoke stepped over the gore and continued his walking up the back alley. The posse had dismounted and were taking the town building by building. But the outlaws remaining were showing no inclination to give up the fight. The firing was not as intense as a few moments past, but it was steady.

Smoke caught a glimpse of several men slipping up the alley toward him. He eased back the hammers of the express gun and stepped deeper into the shadows, a privy to his left.

Smoke recognized the lead man as an outlaw called Brawley, a man who had been in trouble with the law and society in general since practically the moment of birth. There were so many wanted posters out on Brawley that the man had been forced to drop out of sight a couple of years back. Now Smoke knew where he'd been hiding.

Smoke stepped out of the shadows and pulled both triggers. The sawed-off shotgun spewed its cargo of ball bearings, nails, and assorted bits of metal. Brawley took one load directly in the chest, lifting the murderer off his feet and sending him sprawling. The man to Brawley's right caught part of a load in the face. Smoke recalled that the man had thought himself to be handsome.

That was no longer the case.

The third man had escaped most of the charge and had thrown himself to the ground. He pulled himself up to his knees, his hands full of .44's. Holding the shotgun in his left hand, Smoke palmed his .44 and saved the public the expense of a trial.

"The goddamn Injuns got Cahoon!" a hoarse yell sprang out of the night.

Smoke turned, reloading the sawed-off, trying to determine how close the man was.

"Hell with Cahoon!" another yelled. Very close to Smoke. "It's ever' man for hisself now."

Smoke pulled the triggers and fire shot out of the twin barrels, seeming to push the lethal loads of metal. Horrible screaming was heard for a moment, and then the sounds of bootheels drumming the ground in death.

Smoke reloaded and walked on.

At a gap between buildings, Smoke could see York, still in position, still spitting out lead from his Henry. The bodies in the street paid mute testimony to the ranger's dead aim.

A man wearing a white armband ducked into the gap and spotted Smoke.

"Easy," Smoke called. "Jensen here."

Smoke could see the badge on his chest, marking him as a U.S. Marshal.

"Windin' down," the man said. "Thought I'd take me a breather. You and that Arizona Ranger played hell, Smoke."

"That was our intention. You got the makin's? I lost my sack."

The man tossed Smoke a bag of tobacco and papers. Squatting down, out of the line of fire, Smoke and the marshal rolled, licked, and lit.

Smoke could see the lawman had been hit a couple of times, neither of the wounds serious enough to take him out of the fight.

"I figure the big boys got loose free," Smoke spoke over a sudden hard burst of gunfire. He jerked his head. "That's Davidson's big house up yonder on the ridge. . . ."

Jim Wilde almost got himself plugged as he darted into the alley and slid to a halt, catching his breath.

"I dearly wish you would announce your intentions, ol' hoss," the marshal said to him. "You nearbouts got drilled."

"Gimmie the makin's, Glen. I lost my pouch." Jim holstered his guns.

While Jim rolled a cigarette, Smoke elaborated on his theory of the kingpins escaping.

"Well, lets us rest for a minute and then we'll take us a hike up yonder to the house. Check it out." He puffed for a moment. "I've arranged for a judge to be here at first light," he said. "The hands from Red Davis's place is gonna act as jury. Red'll be jury foreman. Soon as we clean out the general store, I got some boys ready to start workin' on ropes."

"Hezekiah Jones the judge?" Glen asked.

"Yep."

"Gonna be some short trials."

"Yep."

"And they's gonna be a bunch of newspaper folks and photographers here, too."

"Yep."

An outlaw tried to make a break for it, whipping his horse up the street toward the edge of town. A dozen guns barked, slamming the outlaw out of the saddle. He rolled on the street and was still.

Glen looked at the body of the outlaw. "I'm thinkin' there might not be all that many to be tried."

Jim Wilde ground out the butt of his smoke under his heel and stood up. "Yep," he said.

Jim was known to be a spare man with words.

15

The battle for the outlaw town of Dead River was winding down sharply as Smoke and the marshals made their way up the hill to Rex Davidson's fine home. They passed a half-dozen bodies on the curving path, all outlaws. All three men were conscious of eyes on them as they walked up the stone path. . . . Utes, waiting in the darkness, watching.

Somewhere back in the timber, a man screamed in agony.

"Cahoon," Smoke told the men.

Glen replied, "Whatever he gets, he earned."

That pretty well summed up the feelings of all three men. Jim pulled out his watch and checked the time. Smoke was surprised to learn it was nearly ten o'clock. He stopped and listened for a moment. Something was wrong.

Then it came to him: The gunfire had ceased.

"Yeah," Jim remarked. "I noticed it too. Eerie, ain't it?"

The men walked on, stepping onto the porch of the house. Motioning the lawmen away from the front door in case it was booby-trapped, Smoke stepped to one side and eased it open. The door opened silently on well-oiled hinges.

Smoke was the first in, the express gun ready. Jim and Glen came in behind him, their hands full of pistols. But the caution had been unnecessary; the room was void of human life.

The men split up, each taking a room. They found

nothing. The big house was empty. But everywhere there were signs of hurried packing. The door to the big safe was open, the safe empty of cash. Jim began going through the ledgers and other papers, handing a pile to Glen while Smoke prowled the house. At the rear of the house he found the rabbit hole, and he had been correct in his thinking. The home had been built in front of a cave opening. He called for Jim and Glen.

"You was right," Jim acknowledged. "We'll inspect it in the morning. I'll post guards here tonight." He held out the papers taken from the safe. "Interestin' readin' in here, Smoke. All kinds of wanted posters and other information on the men who lived here. What we've done—it was mostly you and York—is clean out a nest of snakes. We've made this part of the country a hell of a lot safer."

On the way back to the town, Smoke spotted the Ute chief, White Wolf. The men stopped, Jim saying, "We're goin' to try them that's still alive, White Wolf. Do that in the mornin'. We should be out of the town by late tomorrow afternoon. When we pull out, the town and everything in it is yours."

"I thank you," the chief said gravely. "My people will not be cold or hungry this winter." He turned to Smoke and smiled. "My brother, Preacher, would be proud of you. I will see that he hears of this fight, young warrior."

"Thank you, Chief. Give him my best."

White Wolf nodded, shook hands with the men, and then was gone.

Cahoon was still screaming.

It was a sullen lot that were rounded up and herded into the compound for safekeeping. A head count showed fifty hardcases had elected to surrender or were taken by force, usually the latter.

But, as Smoke had feared, many of the worst ones had slipped out. Shorty, Red, and Jake were gone. Bill Wilson's body had been found, but Studs Woodenhouse, Tie Medley, Paul Rycroft, and Slim Bothwell were gone.

Hart and Ayers were dead, riddled with bullets. But Natick, Nappy, LaHogue, and Brute Pitman had managed to escape. Tustin could not be found among the dead, so all had to assume the so-called minister had made it out alive. Sheriff Danvers had been taken prisoner, and Sheriff Larsen had told him he was going to personally tie the noose for him. Dagget, Glen Moore, Lapeer and, of course, Rex Davidson were gone.

Smoke knew he would have them to deal with—sooner or later, and probably sooner.

Smoke bathed in the creek behind his campsite, and he and York caught a few hours sleep before the judge and his jury showed up. They were to be in Dead River at dawn.

As had been predicted, there were several newspaper men with the judge, as well as several photographers. The bodies of the outlaws still lay in the street at dawn, when the judge, jury, reporters, and photographers showed up. Two of the half-dozen reporters were from New York City and Boston, on a tour of the wild West, and they were appalled at the sight that greeted them.

Old Red Davis, obviously enjoying putting the needle to the Easterners, showed them around the town, pointing out any sight they might have missed.

"See that fellow over yonder?" he pointed. The reporters and a photographer looked. "The man with a gold badge on his chest? That's the most famous gunfighter in all the West. He's kilt two/three hundred men. Not countin' Injuns. That's Smoke Jensen, boys!"

The Easterners gaped, one finally saying, "But why is the man wearing a badge? He's an outlaw!"

"He ain't no such thing," Red corrected. "He's just fast with a gun, that's all. The fastest man alive. Been all sorts of books writ about Smoke. Want to meet him?"

Foolish question.

Luckily for Smoke, Jim Wilde intercepted the group and took them aside. "You boys from back east walk light around the men in this town. This ain't Boston or New

York. And while Smoke is a right nice fellow, with a fine ranch up north of here, he can be a mite touchy at times." Then the marshal brought the men up to date on what Smoke had done in Dead River.

The photographer set up his awkward equipment and began taking pictures of Smoke and the Arizona Ranger, York. Both men endured it, Smoke saying to York, "You got any warrants on any of them that cut and run?"

"Shore do. What you got in mind?"

The camera popped and puffed smoke into the air.

"I think Sally told me she was going to give birth about October. I plan on bein' there when she does. That gives us a few months to prowl. Tell your bosses back in Arizona not to worry any about the expenses; it's on me."

The camera snapped and clicked, and smoke went into the air as the chemical dust was ignited.

And Marshal Jim Wilde, unintentionally, gave the newspaper reporters the fuel that would, in time, ignite the biggest gunfight, western-style, in Keene, New Hampshire history.

"Smoke's wife is back in New Hampshire. He'll be going back there when she gives birth to their child. Now come on, I'll introduce you gentlemen to Smoke Jensen."

Judge Hezekiah Jones had set up his bench, so to speak, outside the saloon, with the jury seated to his left, on the boardwalk. Already, a gallows had been knocked together and ropes noosed and knotted. They could hang three at a time.

The trial of the first three took two and a half minutes. A minute and a half later, they were swinging.

"Absolutely the most barbaric proceedings I have ever witnessed," the Boston man sniffed, scribbling in his journal.

"Frontier justice certainly does leave a great deal to be desired," the New York City man agreed.

"I think I'm going to be ill," the photographer said, a tad green around the mouth.

"Hang 'em!" Judge Jones hit the table with his gavel, and three more were led off to meet their maker.

Sheriff Danvers stood before the bench, his hands tied behind his back. "I have a statement to make, Your Honor," he said.

Hezekiah glared at him. "Oh, all right. Make your goddamn statement and then plead guilty, you heathen!"

"I ain't guilty!" Danvers shouted.

The judge turned to face the men of the jury. "How do you find?"

"Guilty!" Red called.

"Hang the son of a bitch!" Hezekiah ordered.

And so it went.

The hurdy-gurdy ladies and shopkeepers were hauled off in wagons. Smoke didn't ask where they were being taken because he really didn't care. The bodies of the outlaws were tossed into a huge pit and dirt and gravel shoveled over them. "I'd like to keep my federal commission, Jim," Smoke said. "I got a hunch this mess isn't over."

"Keep it as long as you like. You're makin' thirty a month and expenses." He grinned and shook Smoke's hand, then shook the hand of the ranger. "I'll ride any trail with you boys any time."

He wheeled his horse and was gone.

The wind sighed lonely over the deserted town as Smoke and York sat their horses on the hill overlooking the town. White Wolf and his people were moving into the town. The judge had ordered whatever money was left in the town to remain there. Let the Indians have it for their help in bringing justice to the godforsaken place, he had said.

Smoke waved at White Wolf and the chief returned the gesture. Smoke and York turned their horses and put their backs to Dead River.

"What is this?" York asked. "July, August . . . what? I done flat lost all track of the months."

"I think it's September. I think Sally told me the first

month she felt she was with child was March. So if she's going to have the baby the last part of October . . ."

York counted on his fingers, then stopped and looked at Smoke. "Do you count March as one?"

"Damned if I know!"

"We'll say you do." He once more began counting. "Yep. But that'd be eight months. So this must be August."

Smoke looked at him. "York . . . what in the hell are you talking about?"

York confessed that what he knew about the process of babies growing before the birth was rather limited.

"I think I better wire Sally and ask her," Smoke suggested.

"I think that'd be the wise thing to do."

Jim Wilde had told Smoke he would send a wire to Sally, telling her the operation was over and Smoke was all right. And he would do the same for York, advising the Arizona Ranger headquarters that York was in pursuit of those who had escaped.

Smoke and York cut across the Sangre de Cristo range, in search of the cave Davidson and his men had used to escape.

Sally got the wire one day before the Boston and New York newspapers ran the front-page story of the incident, calling it: JUSTICE AT DEAD RIVER. The pictures would follow in later editions.

John read the stories, now carried in nearly all papers in the East, and shook his head in disbelief, saying to his daughter, "Almost fifty men were hanged in one morning. Their trials took an average of three minutes per man. For God's sake, Sally, surely you don't agree with these kangaroo proceedings?"

"Father," the daughter said, knowing that the man would never understand, "it's a hard land. We don't have time for all the niceties you people take for granted back here."

"It doesn't bother you that your husband, Smoke, is credited—if that's the right choice of words—with killing some thirty or forty men?"

Sally shook her head. "No. I don't see why it should. You see, Father, you've taken a defense attorney's position already. And you immediately condemned Smoke and the other lawmen and posse members, without ever saying a word about those poor people who were kidnapped, enslaved, and then hung up on hooks to die by slow torture. You haven't said a word about the people those outlaws abused, robbed, murdered, raped, tortured, and then ran back to Dead River to hide and spend their ill-gotten gain. Even those papers there," she pointed, "admit that every man who was hanged was a confessed murderer, many of them multiple killers. They got what they deserved, Father. No more, and no less."

The father sighed and looked at his wife. "The West has changed you, Sally. I don't know you anymore."

"Yes, I've changed, Father," she admitted. "For the better." She smiled. "It's going to be very interesting when you and Smoke meet."

"Yes," John agreed. "Quite."

It took Smoke and York three days after crossing the high range to find the cave opening and the little valley beneath it.

"Slick," York said. "If they hadn't a knocked down the bushes growin' in front of the mouth of that cave, we'd have had the devil's own hard time findin' it."

The men entered the cave opening, which was barely large enough to accommodate a standing man. And they knew from the smell that greeted them what they would find.

They looked down at the bloated and maggot-covered bodies on the cave floor.

"You know them?" Smoke asked.

"I seen 'em in town. But I never knowed their names. And I don't feel like goin' through their pockets to find out who they was, do you?"

Smoke shook his head. Both men stepped back outside, grateful to once more be out in the cool, fresh air. They breathed deeply, clearing their nostrils of the foul odor of death.

"Let's see if we can pick up a trail," Smoke suggested.

Old Preacher had schooled Smoke well. The man could track a snake across a flat rock. Smoke circled a couple of times, then called for York to join him.

"North." He pointed. "I didn't think they'd risk getting out into the sand dunes. They'll probably follow the timber line until they get close to the San Luis, then they'll ride the river, trying to hide their tracks. I'll make a bet they'll cut through Poncha Pass, then head east to the railroad town. They might stop at the hot springs first. You game?"

"Let's do it,"

They picked up and lost the tracks a dozen times, but it soon became apparent that Smoke had pegged their direction accurately. At a village called Poncha Springs, past the San Luis Valley, Smoke and York stopped and resupplied and bathed in the hot waters.

Yes, about a dozen hard-looking men had been through. Oh, five or six days back. They left here ridin' toward Salida. They weren't real friendly folks, neither. Looked like hardcases.

Smoke and York pulled out the next morning.

At Salida, they learned that Davidson and his men had stopped, bought supplies and ammunition, and left the same day they'd come.

But one man didn't ride out with the others.

"He still in town?" Smoke asked.

"Shore is. Made his camp up by the Arkansas. 'Bout three miles out of town. But he's over to the saloon now."

Salida was new and raw, a railroad town built by the Denver and Rio Grande railroad. Salida was the division point of the main line and the narrow-gauge lines over what is called Marshall Pass.

"What's this ol' boy look like?" York asked.

The man described him.

"Nappy," Smoke said. "You got papers on him?"

"'Deed I do," York said, slipping the hammer thong off his .44.

"I'll back you up. Let's go."

"You look familiar, partner," the citizen said to Smoke. "What might be your name?"

"Smoke Jensen."

As soon as the lawmen had left, the man hauled his ashes up and down the muddy streets, telling everyone he could find that Smoke was in town.

"I know Nappy is wanted for rape and murder," Smoke said. "What else did he do?"

"Killed my older brother down between the Mogollon Plateau and the Little Colorado. Jimmy was a lawman, workin' out of Tucson. Nappy had killed an old couple just outside of town and Jimmy had tracked him north." York talked as they walked. "Nappy ambushed him. Gut-shot my brother and left him to die. But Jimmy wasn't about to die 'fore he told who done him in. He crawled for miles until some punchers found him and he could tell them what happened, then he died. I was fifteen at the time. I joined the Rangers when I was eighteen. That was six years ago."

"I figured you for some younger than that."

"It's all the clean livin' I done," York said with a straight face.

Then they stepped into the saloon.

And Nappy wasn't alone.

The short, barrel-chested, and extremely ugly outlaw stood at the far end of the bar, his hands at his sides. Across the room were two more hardcases, also standing, each wearing two guns tied down low. To Smoke's extreme right, almost in the shadows, was another man, also standing.

"Napoleon Whitman?" York spoke to the stocky outlaw.

"That's me, punk."

"I'm an Arizona Ranger. It is my duty to inform you that you are under arrest for the murder of Tucson deputy sheriff Jimmy York."

"Do tell? Well, Ranger, this is Colorado. You ain't jack-shit up here."

"I have also been appointed a deputy U.S. Marshal, Nappy. Now how is it gonna be?"

"Well," Nappy drawled, as the men at the tables drifted back, out of the line of fire. And since Nappy had men posted all around the room, that meant getting clear outside, which is what most did. "I think I'm gonna finish my drink, Ranger. That's what I think I'm gonna do. And since both you squirts is about to die, why don't y'all order yourselves a shot?"

Then he arrogantly turned his left side to the man and faced the bar. But both Smoke and York knew he was watching them in the mirror.

"He's all yours," Smoke murmured, just loud enough for York to hear. "Don't worry about the others."

York nodded. "I don't drink with scum," he told the ugly outlaw.

Nappy had lifted the shot glass to his mouth with his left hand. With that slur, he set the glass down on the bar and turned, facing the younger man. "What'd you say to me, punk?" The outlaw was not accustomed to be talked to in such a manner. After all, he was a famous and feared gunfighter, and punk kids respected him. They sure didn't talk smart to him.

"I said you're scum, Nappy. You're what's found at the bottom of an outhouse pit."

All were conscious of many faces peering inside the dark barroom; many men pressed up against the glass from the boardwalk.

"You cain't talk to me lak 'at!" Nappy almost screamed the words, and he could not understand the strange sensation that suddenly filled him.

It was fear.

Fear! The word clutched at Nappy's innards. Fear! Afraid of this snot-nosed pup with a tin star? He tried to shrug it off but found he could not.

"I just did, Nappy," York said. He smiled at the man; he could practically smell the fear-stink of the outlaw.

Nappy stepped away from the bar to stand wide-legged, facing York. "Then fill your hand, you son of a bitch!"

16

Smoke had been standing, half turned away from York, about three feet between them, his arms folded across his lower chest. When Nappy grabbed for iron, Smoke went into a low crouch and cross-drew, cocking and firing with one blindingly fast motion. First he shot the man in the shadows with his right hand .44, then took out the closest of the two men to Nappy's immediate left.

Nappy had beaten York to the draw, but as so often happens, his first slug tore up the floor in front of York's boots. York had not missed a shot, but the stocky outlaw was soaking up the lead as fast as York could pump it into him and was still standing on his feet, tossing lead in return. He was holding onto the bar with his left hand and firing at York.

Smoke rolled across the floor and came up on his knees, both .44's hammering lead into the one man he faced who was still standing. The .44 slugs drew the life from the man and Smoke turned on one knee, splinters from the rough wood floor digging into his knee with the move. The man in the shadows was leaning against a wall, blood all over his shirt front, trying to level his .45. Smoke shot him in the face, and the man slid down the wall to rest on his butt, dead.

As the roaring left his ears and Smoke could once more see, Nappy was still standing, even though York had emptied his .44 into the man's chest and belly.

But Smoke could see he was not going to be standing much longer. The man's eyes were glazing over, and blood was pouring out of his mouth. His guns were laying on the floor beside his scuffed and dirty boots.

Nappy cut his eyes to Smoke. "That you, Jensen?" he managed to say.

"It's me, Nappy." Smoke stood up and walked toward the dying outlaw.

"Come closer, Jensen. I cain't see you. Dark in here, ain't it?"

Death's hand was slowly closing in on Nappy.

"What do you want, Nappy?"

"They'll get you, Jensen. They're gonna have their way with your uppity wife in front of your eyes, then they're gonna kill you slow. You ain't gonna find them, Jensen. They're dug in deep. But they'll find you. And that's a promise, Jensen. That's . . ."

His knees buckled and his eyes rolled back into his head until only the whites were showing. Nappy crashed to the barroom floor and died.

Both lawmen punched out empties and reloaded. York said, "I'll send a wire to the Tucson office and tell them to recall the dodgers on Nappy. You hit anywhere?"

"'Bout a dozen splinters in my knee is all."

"I'll be back, and then we'll have us a drink."

"Sounds good. I'll have one while I'm waiting. Hurry up, I hate to drink alone."

Smoke lost the trail. It wasn't the first time it had happened in his life, but it irked him even more this time. Smoke and York had trailed the outlaws to just outside of Crested Butte, and there they seemed to just drop off the face of the earth.

The lawmen backtracked and circled, but it was no use; the trail was lost.

After five more days of fruitless and frustrating looking, they decided to give it up.

They were camped near the banks of Roaring Fork, cooking some fish they'd caught for supper, both their mouths salivating at the good smells, when Drifter's head and ears came up.

"We got company," Smoke said softly.

"So I noticed. Injuns, you reckon?"

"I don't think so. Drifter acts different when it's Indians."

"Hallo, the fire!" a voice called.

"If you're friendly," Smoke returned the shout, "come on in. We caught plenty of fish and the coffee's hot."

"Music to my ears, boys." A man stepped into camp, leading his horses, a saddle mount and a packhorse. "Name's McGraw, but I'm called Chaw."

"That's Buddy York and I'm Smoke Jensen."

Chaw McGraw damn near swallered his chaw when he heard the name Smoke Jensen. He coughed and spat a couple of times, and then dug in his kit for a battered tin cup. He poured a cup of coffee and sat down, looking at Smoke.

"Damned if it ain't you! I figured you for some older. But there you sit, bigger 'en life. I just read about you in a paper a travelin' drummer gimmie. Lemmie git it for you; it ain't but a week old. Outta Denver."

The paper told the story of the big shoot-out and the hangings and the final destruction of the outlaw town of Dead River. It told all about Smoke and York and then, with a sinking feeling in the pit of his stomach, Smoke read about Sally being back in Keene, New Hampshire, awaiting the birth of their first child.

"What's wrong, partner?" York asked, looking at the strange expression on Smoke's face.

Not wanting to take any chances on what he said being repeated by Chaw, Smoke minutely shook his head and handed the paper to York. "Nothing."

York read the long article and lifted his eyes to Smoke. The men exchanged knowing glances across the fire and the broiling fish.

"Help yourself, Chaw," Smoke offered. "We have plenty."

"I wanna wash my hands 'for I partake," Chaw said. "Be right back. Damn, boys, but that do smell good!"

Chaw out of earshot, Smoke said, "You ever been east of the Big Muddy, York?"

"Never had no desire to go." Then he added, "Until now, that is."

"Davidson is crazy, but like a fox. We destroyed his little kingdom, brought his evil down on his head. And now he hates you as much as he does me. And I would just imagine this story is all over the West." He tapped the newspaper. "It would be like King Rex to gather up as many hardcases as he could buy—and he's got the money to buy a trainload of them—and head east. What do you think?"

"I think you've pegged it. Remember what Nappy said back in the bar, just before he died?"

"Yes. But I'm betting he wants the child to be born before he does anything. It would be like him. What do you think?"

"That you're right, all the way down the line. Dagget was one of the men who shot your wife, right?"

"Yes."

"But she wasn't showin' with child then, right?"

"Yes."

"Well, Rex can count. He'll time it so's the baby will be born, I'm thinkin'."

"I think you're right. And I'm thinking none of them would want to get back east too soon. Dagget is wanted back there, remember? You with me, York?"

"All the way, Smoke."

"We'll pull out in the morning. Here comes Chaw. We'd better fix some more fish. He looks like he could eat a skunk, and probably has."

They said their good-byes to Chaw and headed east, taking their time, heading for Leadville, once called Magic City and Cloud City, for it lies just below timberline, almost two miles above sea level. Some have described the climate as ten months winter and two months damn late in the fall. Smoke and York followed old Indian trails, trails that took Smoke back in time, when he and Preacher roamed wild and free across the land, with Preacher teaching first the boy and then the man called Smoke. It brought back memories to Smoke, memories that unashamedly wet his eyes. If York noticed—and Smoke was sure he did—the ranger said nothing about it.

Located in the valley of the Arkansas, Leadville was once the state's second largest city. It was first a roaring gold town, then a fabulous silver boom town, and then once more a gold-rush town. When Smoke and York rode into Leadville late one afternoon, the town was still roaring.

Smoke and York had experienced no trouble on their way into the boom town, unlike so many other not-so-lucky travelers. Roving gangs of thugs and outlaws had erected toll booths on several of the most important roads leading into the town, and those who refused to pay were robbed at gunpoint; many were killed. Robberies, rapes, assaults, and wild shoot-outs were almost an hourly occurrence within the town's limits.

When Smoke and York rode into the busy city, Leadville's population was hovering between fifty thousand and sixty thousand—no one ever really knew for sure. It was the wildest place in the state, for a time. The town's only hospital was guarded by a hundred men, day and night, to keep it from being torn down by thugs. Churches were forced to hire armed guards to work around the clock. The handful of police officers were virtually powerless to keep any semblance of order, so that fell to various vigilante groups. It was a town where you took your life in your hands just by getting out of bed in the morning.

"I ain't too thrilled about no hotel, Smoke," York commented on the way in.

"There wouldn't be a room anyway. We'll stable the horses, pick up some supplies, and hit the saloons. We might be able to hear something. Let's take off these badges."

The only "hotel" in town that might have had empty beds was the Mammoth Palace, a huge shed with double bunks that could easily sleep five hundred. A guest paid a dollar for a eight-hour sleeping turn.

And in the midst of it all, churches were flourishing. If not spiritually, then financially. One member suggested that he buy a chandelier for the church. Another member asked, "Why? None of us knows how to play it!"

Smoke and York turned their horses onto State Street, where several famous New York chefs operated fancy eating places. Oxtail soup cost five cents a bowl at Smoothey's, and it was famous from the Coast to the Rockies.

Smoke waved at a ragged newsboy and bought a local newspaper, *The Chronicle*. They rode on and found a stable that had stalls to spare.

"We'll sleep with our horses," Smoke told the livery man.

"That'll be a dollar extra, boys. Apiece."

York started to protest, then noted the look on Smoke's face and held his peace.

"Give them a bait of corn and all the hay they can handle," Smoke told the man. "And do it now. If you go into Drifter's stall after I'm gone, he'll kill you."

"Son of a bitch tries to stomp on me," the liveryman blustered, "I'll take a rifle to him."

"Then I'll kill you," Smoke said softly, but with steel in his voice.

The man looked into those cold, hard eyes. He swallowed hard. "I was jokin', mister."

"I wasn't."

The liveryman gulped, his Adam's apple bobbing up and down. "Yes, sir. I'll take the best of care of your horses. Whatever you say, mister . . . ah? . . ."

Smoke smiled and thought, To hell with trying to disguise who we are. "Smoke Jensen."

The liveryman backed up against a stall. "Yes, sir, Mr. Jensen. I mean, whatever you say, sir."

Smoke patted the man on the shoulder. "We'll get along fine, I'm sure."

"Yes, sir. You can bet I'll do my damndest!"

Smoke and York stepped out into the hustle and confusion of the boom town. Both knew that within the hour, every resident of the town would know that Smoke Jensen had arrived.

They stepped into a general store, checked the prices of goods, and decided they'd resupply further on.

"Legal stealin'," York said, looking at the price of a pair of jeans. He put the jeans back on the table.

They walked back outside.

"We can cover more ground if we split up," the Arizona Ranger suggested. "I'll take the other side of the street. What say we meet back at the stable in a couple of hours?"

"Sounds good to me. Watch your back, York."

"I hear you." York checked the busy street, found his chance, and darted across. As it was, he almost got run over by a freighter. The freighter cursed him, and rumbled and rattled on.

Smoke walked on. There was something about the tall man with the two guns, in cross-draw style, that made most men hurry to step out of his way. If someone had told Smoke that he looked menacing, he would not have believed it. He could never see the savage look that was locked into his eyes.

Smoke turned a corner and found himself on Harrison Avenue, a busy business thoroughfare. He strolled the avenue, left it, and turned several corners, cutting down to hit State and Main.

Then he saw Natick, stepping out of a brothel. Smoke stopped and half turned, blending in better with the crowd. He backed against a building and began reading the paper he'd bought, still keeping a good eye on Natick. He hoped the outlaw might lead him to Davidson and Dagget.

But Natick stepped out into the street and walked toward a saloon. Smoke turned away and walked in the opposite direction, not wanting to stare too long at the man, knowing how that can attract someone's attention.

Smoke lounged around a bit, buying a cup of coffee and a sandwich at prices that would make a Scotsman squall in outrage. The coffee was weak and the sandwich uneatable. Smoke gave both to a ragged man who seemed down on his luck, and then he waited.

Soon he saw York walking up the street and turning into the saloon. Smoke hurriedly crossed the street and stepped into the crowded saloon, elbowing and shouldering his way through the crowd. Several turned to protest, looked into the unforgiving eyes of the tall stranger with the two six-guns, and closed their mouths much faster than they opened them.

York was facing Natick and two other hard-looking men that Smoke did not know and did not remember seeing in Dead River.

And the crowd was rapidly moving back and away, out of the line of fire.

It was almost a repeat performance of Nappy and his crew. Except that this time a photographer was there and had his equipment set up, and he was ready to start popping whenever the action began.

The town marshal, a notorious bully and killer, was leaning up against the bar watching it all, a faint smile on his face. He was not going to interfere on behalf of either side.

"Mort!" Smoke called.

The marshal turned and faced Smoke, and his face went a shade paler.

"Jensen," he whispered.

"Either choose a side or get out," Smoke warned him, clear menace in his voice.

It was a warning and a challenge that rankled the town marshal, but not one he wanted to pick up. Quick with his guns and his fists, boasting that he had killed seven men, Mort's reputation was merely a dark smudge on the ground when compared to Smoke's giant shadow.

The marshal nodded and walked outside, turning and going swiftly up the street.

"All right, boys," York said. "You all know Smoke Jensen. Make your play."

The three outlaws drew together. One did not even clear leather before Smoke's guns belched fire and smoke, the slug striking the outlaw in the center of the chest. The second outlaw that Smoke faced managed to get the muzzle free of leather before twin death-blows of lead hammered at his belly and chest.

York's guns had roared and bucked and slammed Natick against a rear wall of the saloon, down but not quite dead.

Smoke walked to him. "Natick?"

"What do you want, Jensen?" the outlaw gasped.

"I know why you broke with Davidson and the others."

"Yeah? Why?"

"Because you may be a lot of bad things, but you're no baby killer."

Natick nodded his bloody head. "Yeah. I couldn't go along with that. I'm glad it was you boys who done me in. Pull my boots off for me, Jensen?"

Smoke tugged off the man's boots. One big toe was sticking through a hole in his sock.

"Ain't that pitiful?" Natick observed. "I've stole thousands and thousands of dollars and cain't even afford to buy a pair of socks." He cut his eyes to Smoke. "Rex and Dagget's got some bad ones with them, Jensen. Lapeer, Moore, The Hog, Tustin. Shorty, Red, and Jake. Studs Woodenhouse, Tie Medley, Paul Rycroft, Slim Bothwell, and Brute Pitman. I don't know where they're hidin', Jensen, and that's the truth. But Davidson plans on rapin' your woman and then killin' your kid."

Natick was whispering low, so only Smoke and York could hear his dying words. The photographer was taking pictures as fast as he could jerk plates and load his dust.

Smoke bent his head to hear Natick's words, but the outlaw would speak no more. He was dead.

Smoke dug in his own pocket and handed some money to a man standing close by. "You'll see that he gets a proper burial?"

"I shore will, Mr. Jensen. And it was a plumb honor to

see you in action."

The photographer fired again.

The batwings snapped open and a dirty man charged into the bar, holding twin leather bags. "She's pure, boys. Assayed out high as a cat's back. The drinks is on me! Git them damn stiffs outta the way!"

17

John and his sons and daughters and their families looked at the pictures John had sent in from New York, looked at them in horror.

Bodies were sprawling in the street, on the boardwalks, hanging half in and half out of broken windows. One was facedown in a horse trough, another was sprawled in stiffened death beside the watering trough.

And John's son-in-law, Smoke Jensen, handsome devil that he was, was standing on the boardwalk, calmly rolling a cigarette.

"That's my Smoke!" Sally said, pointing.

Smoke was wearing his guns cross-draw, and he had another one tucked behind his gunbelt. In another picture, the long-bladed Bowie knife he carried behind one gun could be clearly seen. In still another picture, Smoke was sitting on the edge of the boardwalk, eating an apple. In the left side of the picture, bodies could be seen hanging from the gallows.

John's stomach felt queasy. He laid the pictures aside and stifled a burp when Sally grabbed them up and began glancing at them.

"There's a bandage on Smoke's head," she noted. "But I can't see that he was shot anywhere else."

"Who is that handsome man standing beside him?" Walter's sister-in-law asked. "He's so . . . rugged-looking!"

"Lord, Martha!" her sister exclaimed. "He's savage-looking!"

"He's some sort of law enforcement officer," Walter explained, examining the picture. But his badge is somewhat different from . . . ah . . . Smoke's. Excuse my hesitation, Sister, but I never heard of a man being called Smoke."

"Get used to it, Walt," Sally said, a testy note to her statement. After being in the West, with its mostly honest and open and non-pompous people, the East was beginning to grate on her more and more.

Her father picked up on her testiness. "Sally, dearest, it'll soon be 1882. No one carries a gun around here except the law officers, and many times they don't even carry a gun, only a club. There hasn't been an Indian attack in this area in anyone's memory! We are a quiet community, with plans underway to have a college here; a branch of the state university. We are a community of laws, darling. We don't have gunfights in the streets. Keene was settled almost a hundred and fifty years ago. . . ."

"Yes, Father," Sally said impatiently. "I know. 1736, as a matter of fact. It's a nice, quiet, stable, pleasant little community. But I've grown away from it. Father, Mother, all of you . . . have you ever stood on the Great Divide? Have you ever ridden up in the High Lonesome, where you knew you could look for a hundred miles and there would be no other human being? Have any of you ever watched eagles soar and play in the skies, and knew yours were the only eyes on them? No, no you haven't. None of you. You don't even have a loaded gun in this house. None of you women would know what to do if you were attacked. You haven't any idea how to fire a gun. All you ladies know how to do is sit around looking pretty and attend your goddamn teas!"

John wore a pained expression on his face. Abigail started fanning herself furiously. Sally's brothers wore frowns on their faces. Her sisters and sisters-in-law looked shocked.

Martha laughed out loud. "I have my teacher's certificate, Sally. Do you suppose there might be a position for me out where you live?"

"Martha!" her older sister hissed. "You can't be serious. There are . . . savages out there!"

"Oh . . . piddly-poo!" Martha said. She would have liked to have the nerve to say something stronger, like Sally, but didn't want to be marked as a scarlet woman in this circle.

"We're looking for a schoolteacher right this moment, Martha," Sally told her. "And I think you'd be perfect. When Smoke gets here, we'll ask him. If he says you're the choice, then you can start packing."

Martha began clapping her hands in excitement.

"Smoke is a one-man committee on the hiring of teachers?" Jordan sniffed disdainfully.

"Would you want to buck him on anything, Brother?"

Jordan stroked his beard and remained silent. Unusually so for a lawyer.

Smoke and York left Leadville the next morning, riding out just at dawn. They rode north, past Fremont Pass, then cut east toward Breckenridge. No sign of Davidson or Dagget or any of the others with him. They rode on, with Bald Mountain to the south of them, following old trails. They kept Mount Evans to their north and gradually began the winding down toward the town of Denver.

"We gonna spend some time in Denver City?" York asked.

"Few days. Maybe a week. We both need to get groomed and curried and bathed, and our clothes are kind of shabby-looking."

"My jeans is so thin my drawers is showin'," York agreed. "If we goin' east, I reckon we're gonna have to get all duded up like dandies, huh?"

"No way," Smoke's reply was grim. "I'm tired of pretending to be something I'm not. We'll just dress like what we are. Westerners."

York sighed. "That's a relief. I just cain't see myself in one of them goofy caps like you wore back in Dead River."

Smoke laughed at just the thought. "And while we're

here, I've got to send some wires. Find out how Sally is doing and find out what's happened up on the Sugarloaf."

"Pretty place you got, Smoke?"

"Beautiful. And there's room for more. Lots of room. You ever think about getting out of law work, York?"

"More and more lately. I'd like to have me a little place. Nothin' fancy; nothin' so big me and a couple more people couldn't handle it. I just might drift up that way once this is all over."

"You got a girl?"

"Naw. I ain't had the time. Captain's been sendin' me all over the territory ever since I started with the Rangers. I reckon it's time for me to start thinking about settlin' down."

"You might meet you an eastern gal, York." Smoke was grinning.

"Huh! What would I do with her? Them eastern gals is a different breed of cat. I read about them. All them teas and the like. I got to have me a woman that'll work right alongside me. You know what ranchin' is like. Hard damn work."

"It is that. But my Sally was born back east. Educated all over the world. She's been to Paris!"

"Texas?"

"France."

"No kiddin'! I went to Dallas once. Biggest damn place I ever seen. Too damn many people to suit me. I felt all hemmed in."

"It isn't like that up in the High Lonesome. I think you'd like it up there, York. We need good stable people like you. Give it some thought. I'll help you get started; me and Sally."

"Right neighborly of y'all. Little tradin' post up ahead. Let's stop. I'm out of the makin's."

While York was buying tobacco, Smoke sat outside, reading a fairly recent edition of a Denver paper. The city was growing by leaps and bounds. The population was now figured at more than sixty thousand.

"Imagine that," Smoke muttered. "Just too damn many

folks for me."

He read on. A new theatre had been built, the Tabor Grand Opera House. He read on, suddenly smiling. He checked the date of the paper. It was only four days old.

"You grinnin' like a cat lickin' cream, Smoke," York said, stepping out and rolling a cigarette. "What got your funny bone all quiverin'?"

"An old friend of mine is in town, York. And I just bet you he'd like to ride east with us."

"Yeah? Lawman?"

"Businessman, scholar, gambler, gunfighter."

"Yeah? Who might that be?"

"Louis Longmont."

"By the Lord Harry!" Louis exclaimed, standing up from his table in the swanky restaurant and waving at Smoke. "Waiter! Two more places here, s'il vous plait."

"What the hell did he say?" York whispered.

"Don't ask me," Smoke returned the whisper.

The men all shook hands, Smoke introducing York to Louis. Smoke had not seen Louis since the big shoot-out at Fontana more than a year ago. The man had not changed. Handsome and very sure of himself. The gray just touching his hair at the temples.

Smoke also noted the carefully tailored suit, cut to accommodate a shoulder holster.

Same ol' Louis.

After the men had ordered dinner—Louis had to do it, the menu being in French—drinks were brought around and Longmont toasted them both.

"I've been reading about the exploits of you men," Louis remarked after sipping his Scotch. York noticed that all their liquor glasses had funny-looking square bits of ice in them, which did make the drink a bit easier on the tongue.

"We've been busy," Smoke agreed.

"Still pursuing the thugs?"

"You know we are, Louis. You would not have allowed

your name to appear in the paper if you hadn't wanted us to find you in Denver."

York sat silent, a bit uncomfortable with the sparkling white tablecloth and all the heavy silverware—he couldn't figure out what he was supposed to do; after all, he couldn't eat but with one fork and one knife, no how. And he had never seen so many duded-up men and gussied-up women in all his life. Even with new clothes on, it made a common fella feel shabby.

"Let's just say," Louis said, "I'm a bit bored with it all."

"You've been traveling about?"

"Just returned from Paris a month ago. I'd like to get back out in the country. Eat some beans and beef and see the stars above me when I close my eyes."

"Want to throw in with us, Louis?"

Louis lifted his glass. "I thought you were never going to ask."

Smoke and York loafed around Denver for a few days, while Louis wrapped up his business and Smoke sent and received several wires. Sally was fine; the baby was due in two months—approximately.

"What does she mean by that?" York asked, reading over Smoke's shoulder.

"It means, young man," Louis said, "that babies do not always cooperate with a timetable. The child might be born within several weeks of that date, before it or after it."

Louis was dressed in boots, dark pants, gray shirt, and black leather vest. He wore two guns, both tied down and both well-used and well-taken care of, the wooden butts worn smooth with use.

York knew that Louis Longmont, self-made millionaire and world-famous gambler, was a deadly gunslinger. And a damn good man to have walkin' with you when trouble stuck its head up, especially when that trouble had a six-gun in each hand.

"Do tell," York muttered.

"What's the plan, Smoke?" Louis asked.

"You about ready to pull out?"

"Is tomorrow morning agreeable with you?"

"Fine. The sooner the better. I thought we'd take our time, ride across Kansas; maybe as far as St. Louis if time permits. We can catch a train anywhere along the way. And by riding, we just might pick up some information about Davidson and his crew."

"Sounds good. Damn a man who would even entertain the thought of harming a child!"

"We pull out at dawn."

Sally had not shown her family all the wires she'd received from Smoke. She did not wish to alarm any of them, and above all, she did not wish to alert the local police as to her husband's suspicions about Davidson and his gang traveling east after her and the baby. Her father would have things done the legal way—ponderous and, unknowing to him, very dangerous for all concerned. John had absolutely no idea of what kind of man this Rex Davidson was.

But Sally did. And Smoke could handle it, his way. And she was glad Louis and York were with him.

York just might be the ticket for Martha out of the East and into the still wild and wide-open West. He was a good-looking young man.

The servant answered the door and Martha entered the sitting room. Sally waved her to a chair with imported antimacassars on the arms and back. The day was warm, and both women fanned themselves to cool a bit.

"I was serious about going west, Sally."

"I thought as much. And now," she guessed accurately, "you want to know all about it."

"That's right."

Where to start? Sally thought. And how to really explain about the vastness and the emptiness and the magnificence of it all?

Before she could start, the door opened again, and this time the room was filled with small children: Sally's nieces and nephews and a few of their friends.

"Aunt Sally," a redheaded, freckle-faced boy said. "Will you tell us about Uncle Smoke?"

"I certainly will." She winked at Martha. "I'll tell you all about the High Lonesome and the strong men who live there."

They pulled out at first light. Three men who wore their guns as a part of their being. Three men who had faced death and beaten it so many times none of them could remember all the battles.

Louis had chosen a big buckskin-colored horse with a mean look to his eyes. The horse looked just about as mean as Smoke knew Drifter really was.

Before leaving Denver, Smoke had wired Jim Wilde and asked for both York and Louis to be formally deputized as U.S. Marshals. The request had been honored within the day.

So they were three men who now wore official badges on their chests. One, a millionaire adventurer. One, a successful rancher. One, a young man who was only weeks away from meeting the love of his life.

They rode east, veering slightly south, these three hard-eyed and heavily armed men. They would continue a southerly line until reaching a trading post on the banks of the Big Sandy; a few more years and the trading post would become the town of Limon.

At the trading post, they would cut due east and hold to that all the way across Kansas. They would stay south of Hell Creek, but on their ride across Colorado, they would ford Sand Creek, an offshoot of the Republican River. They would ride across Spring Creek, Landsman, East Spring, and cross yet another Sand Creek before entering into Kansas.

Kansas was still woolly but nothing like it had been a few years back when the great cattle herds were being driven up from Texas, and outlaws and gunfighters were just about anywhere one wished to look.

But the three men rode with caution. The decade had rolled into the eighties, but there were still bands of Indians who left the reservation from time to time; still bands of outlaws that killed and robbed. And they were riding into an area of the country where men still killed other men over the bitterness of that recent unpleasantness called by some the Civil War and by others the War Between the States.

The days were warm and pleasant or hot and unpleasant as the men rode steadily eastward across the plains. But the plains were now being dotted and marred and scarred with wire. Wire put up by farmers to keep ranchers' cattle out. Wire put up by ranchers to keep nesters out of water holes, creeks, and rivers. Ranchers who wished to breed better cattle put up wire to keep inferior breeds from mixing in and to keep prize bulls at home.

But none of the men really liked wire, even though all could see the reasons—most of the time—behind the erecting of barbed wire fences.

They did not seek out others as they rode toward the east and faraway New Hampshire. Every third or fourth day, late in the afternoon, if a town was handy, they would check into a hotel and seek out a shave and a bath. If not, they would bathe in a handy stream and go unshaven until a town dotted the vast prairie.

"Ever been to this New Hamp-shire, Louis?" York asked the gambler.

"Never have, my friend. But it is an old and very settled state. One of the original thirteen to ratify the Constitution. The first settlement—I can't recall the name—was back in 1623. But I can assure you both, if we ride in like this, armed to the teeth and looking like buccaneers on horseback, we are," he smiled, "going to raise some eyebrows."

"How's that?" York asked. "We don't look no different than anybody else?"

Louis laughed pleasantly and knowingly. "Ah, but my young friend, we are much different from the folks you are about to meet in a few weeks. Their streets are well-lighted with gas lamps. A few might have telephones—marvelous devices. The towns you will see will be old and settled towns. No one carries a gun of any type; many villages and towns have long banned their public display except for officers of the law. And thank you, Smoke, for commissioning us; this way we can carry firearms openly.

"No, York, the world you are only days away from viewing is one that you have never seen before. Smoke, my suggestion would be that we ride the trains well into Massachusetts and then head north on horseback from our jumping-off place. I would suggest Springfield. And get ready for some very strange looks, gentlemen."

"I'm beginnin' not to like these folks and I ain't even met none of 'em yet," York groused. "Don't tote no gun! What do they do if somebody tries to mess with 'em?"

"They are civilized people," Louis said, with more than a touch of sarcasm in his statement. "They let the law take care of it."

"Do tell," York said. "In other words, they ain't got the sand to fight their own fights?"

"That is one way of putting it, York," the gambler said with a smile. "My, but this is going to be a stimulating and informative journey."

Louis cantered on ahead.

"Smoke?" York asked.

"Huh?"

"What's a telephone?"

18

"They're in Salina," Sally read from the wire. "Smoke, York and Louis Longmont."

"The millionaire?" John sat straighter in his chair. "Mr. Longmont is coming east by horseback!"

Sally put eyes on her father. She loved him dearly, but sometimes he could be a pompous ass. "Father, Louis is an adventurer. He is also one of the most famous gunfighters in all the West. He's killed a dozen men on the Continent, in duels. With sword and pistol. He's killed—oh, I don't know, twenty or thirty or maybe fifty men out west, with guns. He's such a gentleman, so refined. I'll be glad to see him again."

John wiped his face with a handkerchief. In one breath, his daughter spoke of Louis killing fifty men. In the next breath, she spoke of him being so refined.

Not normally a profane man, John thought: What kind of goddamned people are going to be staying in my house!

Louis lay on his blankets and watched Smoke unroll a warbag from the pack animal. He laughed aloud when he saw what his friend was unpacking: a buckskin jacket, one that had been bleached a gray-white and trimmed ornately by a squaw.

"You have a touch of the theatrical in you, my friend," Louis observed.

"I got to thinking we might as well give the folks a show. I had it stored in Denver."

"Going to be interesting," Louis smiled, pouring another cup of coffee and turning the venison steaks.

York returned from his bath in the creek, his trousers on but shirtless. For the first time, Smoke and Louis noticed the old bullet scars that pocked the young man's hide.

"You've picked up a few here and there," Louis noted.

"Yeah." York slipped into his shirt. "Me and another ranger, name of McCoy, got all tangled up with some bad ones down in the Dos Cabezas mountains; I hadn't been with the Rangers long when it happened. McCoy got hit so bad he had to retire from the business. Started him up a little general store up near Prescott. But we buried them ol' boys where they fell. I was laid up for nearbouts a month. 'Nother time I was trackin' a bank robber up near Carson Mesa. He ambushed me; got lead in me. But I managed to stay in the saddle and rode on up into Utah after him. I nailed him up near Vermillion Cliffs. Picked up a few other scratches here and there."

And Louis knew then what Smoke had already learned: York was a man to ride the river with. There was no backup in the Arizona Ranger.

York looked up from the cooking steaks. "Where you plannin' on us pickin' up the steam cars, Smoke?"

"I'll wire Sally from Kansas City and see how she's doing. If she's doin' all right and doesn't feel like the baby's due any day, we'll ride on to St. Louis and catch the train there."

The three waited in Kansas City for two days. Sally felt fine and the baby was not due for a month. She urged him to take his time.

Smoke, York, and Louis rode out of Kansas City the next morning, riding into Missouri. It would be days later, when the trio rode into St. Louis and Smoke wired Keene, that he would learn Sally had been taken to the hospital the day after his wire from Kansas City. Sally and babies were doing fine.

"Babies!" Smoke shouted, almost scaring the telegraph operator out of his seat.

"Babies?" Louis exclaimed.

"More 'un one?" York asked.

"Boys," the stationmaster urged, "don't shoot no holes in the ceiling. We just got 'er fixed last month."

They arranged bookings for their horses and themselves, and chugged out of St. Louis the next morning. It was the first time Smoke or York had ever seen a sleeping car, and both were amazed at the luxury of the dining cars and at the quality of the food that was served.

When the finger bowl was brought around, Louis had to leave his seat to keep from laughing when York rolled up his sleeves and washed his elbows in it.

"Ain't you got no soap to go with this thing?" York asked the colored man.

The Negro rolled his eyes and looked heavenward, maintaining his composure despite the situation.

The train stopped in Ohio and the three got off to change trains. It was an overnighter, so they could exercise their horses, get their ground-legs back, and take a genuine bath in a proper tub. All were getting just a little bit gamey. The three big men, broad-shouldered and lean-hipped, with their boots and spurs and western hats, twin six-shooters tied down low, drew many an anxious look from a lot of men and more than curious looks from a lot of ladies.

"Shore are a lot of fine-lookin' gals around these parts," York observed. "But kinda pale, don't y'all think?"

Smoke and York stood on the shores of Lake Erie and marveled at the sight of it.

"Never seen so damn much water in all my life!" York said, undisguised awe in his voice. "And would you just look at them big boats!"

"Ships," Louis corrected. He pointed to one flying an odd-looking flag. "That one just came down the St. Lawrence. That's a German flag."

"How'd it git here?" York asked.

"Across the Atlantic Ocean."

"Lord have mercy!"

When they stomped and jingled back into the fancy hotel, a platoon of cops were waiting for them.

A captain of the police approached them, caution in his eyes and his step. "Lads, I can see that you're U.S. Marshals, but are ye after someone in our city?"

The cop was Irish through and through. "No," Smoke said. "But neither have we bothered anyone here." He looked at the mass of cops and smiled. "Kinda reminds me of that time I took on 'bout twenty-five guns at that silver camp."

"You fought twenty-five desperadoes all by yourself?" the captain asked.

"Yep."

"How did it turn out?"

"I killed them all."

"You . . . killed them all!"

"Yep."

Several news reporters and one photographer had gathered around, for real cowboys and western gunslingers were rare in Cleveland.

"Might I ask your name, sir?" the captain inquired.

"Smoke Jensen."

Pandemonium set in.

Smoke, Louis, and York were given the keys to the city. All three answered an almost endless barrage of questions and endured dozens of cameras popping and clicking at them. A hasty parade was called, and the men rode up and down the city's streets in an open carriage.

"Goddamnedest thing I ever heard of," York muttered. "What the hell have we done to deserve something this grand?"

"You're an Arizona Ranger, York," Louis leaned over and told him. "And a gunfighter, just like Smoke and myself."

"If you say so," York told him. "Seems like a whole bunch to do about nothin' if you ask me."

"Shakespeare felt the same way," the gambler told him, smiling.

"No kiddin'? Seems to me I heard of him. Ain't he from down around El Paso?"

They chugged east the next morning, Smoke and York glad to be out of the hustle and bustle of it all. Louis waved good-bye to a dark-haired young woman who smiled and blushed as the train moved out of the station.

Louis settled back in his seat. "Ah, boys, the freshness and vitality of youth never ceases to amaze me."

Smoke grinned. "I noticed you left the party very early last night, Louis. She certainly is lovely."

But Louis would only smile in reply to questions.

They rolled on through the day and night, across Pennsylvania and into New York. In New York's massive and confusing station, they were met by a large contingent of New York's finest and personally escorted to the train heading to Springfield, with numerous stops along the way.

"It ain't that we don't respect fellow officers, boys," the commander of the police unit said. "It's just that your reputations precede you." He looked at Smoke. "Especially yours, son."

"Yes," a fresh-faced cop said. "Were it up to me, I would insist you remove those guns."

Smoke stopped, halting the parade. He turned to face the helmeted copy. "And if refused? . . ."

The young cop was not in the least intimidated. "Then I would surely have to use force, laddy."

Louis and York joined Smoke in a knowing smile. Smoke said, "You have a pencil in your pocket, officer. I can see it. Would you jerk it out as quickly as you can?"

The older and more wiser of the cops—and that was just about all of them—backed up, with many of them holding their hands out from their sides, smiles on their faces. A half-dozen reporters had gathered around and were scribbling furiously. Photographers were taking pictures.

"So we're going to play games, eh, gunfighter?" the young cop asked.

"No. I'm going to show you how easy it is for a loudmouth to get killed where I come from."

The young officer flushed, and placed his thumb and forefinger on the end of the pencil, and jerked it out.

Smoke swept back his beaded buckskin jacket, exposing his guns. He slipped the hammer-thong off his right hand .44. "Want to try it again?"

The young officer got exactly half of the pencil out of his pocket before he was looking down the muzzle of Smoke's .44.

"Do you get my point, officer?" Smoke asked.

"Ah . . . 'deed, I do, sir! As one fellow officer to another, might I say, sir, that you are awfully quick with that weapon."

Smoke holstered. It was unlike him to play games with weapons, but he felt he just might have saved the young man's life with an object lesson. He held out his hand, and the cop smiled and shook it.

The rest of the walk to their car was an easy one, with chatter among men who found they all had something in common after all.

It was growing late when they finally detrained in Springfield. They stabled their horses and found a small hotel for the night.

The weeks on the road had honed away any city fat that might have built up on Louis and had burned his already dark complexion to that of a gypsy. They were big men, all over six feet, with a natural heavy musculature; they were the kind of men that bring out the hostility in a certain type of man, usually the bully.

And with the knowledge that Sally and the babies—

twins, Smoke had discovered when he wired during a train refueling stop—were now in danger, none of the men were in any mood for taking any lip from some loudmouth.

They elected to have their supper in the hotel's dining room to further avoid any trouble. As had been their custom, they wore their guns, and to hell with local laws. None of them knew when they might run into Davidson or Dagget or their ilk.

Louis had bought York a couple of suits in St. Louis, and Smoke had brought a suit with him. Longmont was never without a proper change of clothes; if he didn't have one handy, he would buy one.

When the men entered the dining room, conversation ceased and all eyes were on them as they walked to their table, led by a very nervous waiter. With their spurs jingling and their guns tied down low, all three managed to look as out of place as a saddle on a tiger.

The three of them ignored several comments from some so-called "gentlemen"—comments that might have led to a fight anywhere west of the Mississippi—and were seated without incident.

Louis frowned at the rather skimpy selections on the menu, sighed, and decided to order a steak. The others did the same.

"Sorry we don't have no buffalo here for you range-riders," a man blurted from the table next to them. His friend laughed, and the women with them, hennaed and painted up and half drunk, also thought fat boy's comments to be hysterically amusing.

Louis ignored the man, as did Smoke and York. "A drink before ordering, gentlemen?" a waiter magically appeared.

"I'm sure they'll want rye, George," fat boy blurted. "That's what I read that all cowboys drink. Before they take their semi-yearly bath, that is."

His table erupted in laughter.

"I could move you to another table, gentlemen," the waiter suggested. "That"—he cut his eyes to the man seated with fat boy and the women—"is Bull Everton."

"Is that supposed to mean something to us?" Smoke asked.

"He's quite the bully," the waiter whispered, leaning close. "He's never been whipped."

"That he's admitted," Louis commented dryly. "If he can't fight any better than he can choose women, he must have never fought a man."

Smoke and York both laughed at that.

"We'll have Scotch," Louis ordered.

"Yes, sir." The waiter was glad to get away from the scene of what he presumed would soon be disaster for the western men.

"You take them damn guns off," the voice rumbled to the men, "and I'll show you what a real man can do."

Smoke lifted his eyes to the source of the voice. Bull Everton. He surveyed the man. Even sitting, Smoke could see that the man was massive, with heavy shoulders and huge wrists and hands. But that old wildness sprang up within Smoke. Smoke had never liked a bully. He smiled at the scowling hulk.

"I'll take them off anytime you're ready, donkey-face," he threw down the challenge and insult.

Bull stood up, and he was big. "How about right now, cowboy? Outside."

"Suits me, tub-butt." Smoke stood up and unbuckled and untied, handing his guns to a waiter.

The waiter looked as though he'd just been handed a pair of rattlesnakes.

"Where is this brief contest to take place?" Louis asked Bull.

"Brief, is right," Bull laughed. "Out back of the hotel will do."

"After you," Smoke told him.

When the back door closed and the Bull turned around, Smoke hit him flush in the mouth with a hard right and followed that with a vicious left to the wind. Before the Bull could gather his senses, Smoke had hit him two more times, once to the nose and another hook to the body.

With blood dripping from his lips and nose, the Bull hollered and charged. Smoke tripped him and hit him once on the way down, then kicked him in the stomach while he was down.

Smoke was only dimly aware of the small crowd that had gathered, several of the spectators dressed in the blue uniform of police officers. He did not hear one of the cops say to Louis, "I've been waiting to see Everton get his due for a long time, boys. Don't worry. There will be no interference from us."

Smoke backed up and allowed the Bull to crawl to his feet. There was a light of fury and panic in the man's eyes.

Bull lifted his hands in the classic boxer's stance: left fist held almost straight out, right fist close to his jaw.

Smoke whirled and kicked the bully on his knee. Bull screamed in pain and Smoke hit him a combination of blows, to the belly, the face, the kidneys. Smoke trip-hammered his fists, brutalizing the bigger man, knocking him down, hauling him back up, and knocking him down again.

Bull grabbed Smoke's knees and brought him down to the dirt of the alley. Pulling one leg free, Smoke savagely kicked the bully in the face. Teeth flew, glistening in the night.

Smoke pulled Bull to his feet and leaned him up against the rear wall, then went to work on the man's belly and sides. Only after he had felt and heard several ribs break did he let the man fall unconscious to the ground.

"Drag the Bull to the paddy wagon, boys," the cop in charge ordered. "We'll take him to the hospital. I can tell by looking that his jaw is broken, and I'll wager half a dozen ribs are broken as well." He looked at Smoke. "You don't even look angry, young man."

"I'm not," Smoke told him.

"Lord suffer us all!" the officer said. "What would you have done had you been angry?"

"Killed him."

"I'd not like to get on the wrong side of the road with you, young man. But I would like to know your name."

"Smoke Jensen."

The crowd gasped and the cop smiled grimly. "Are you as good with your guns as you are with your dukes, me boy?"

"Better."

Louis handed Smoke a towel and held his coat while his friend wiped his face and hands. York had stood to one side, his coat brushed back, freeing the butts of his .44's.

And the cops had noticed that, too.

The cop looked at all three of the men. "You boys are here for a reason. I'm not asking why, for you're officers of the law, and federal officers at that. But I'd not like to see any trouble in this town."

"There won't be," Smoke said, raising up from a rain barrel where he had washed his face and hands. "We'll be leaving at first light."

"You wouldn't mind if I stopped by the stable to see you off, would you now?"

"Not a bit," Smoke said, smiling.

The waiter stuck his head out the back door. "Gentlemen," he said, "I've freshened your drinks. The management has instructed me to tell you that your dinners are on the house this evening."

"That won't be necessary," Smoke told him. "I assure you, we have ample funds."

The waiter smiled. "Gentlmen, Bull Everton will not be returning to this establishment for quite some time, thanks to you. And," he grinned hugely, "if it isn't worth a free meal to get rid of a big pain in the ass, nothing is!"

19

The men were in the saddle and moving out before first light; they would take their breakfast at the first inn they came to once outside of Springfield. It was cold in the darkness before dawn, with more than a hint of fall in the air, and it was going to be a beautiful day for traveling.

The road followed the Connecticut River. The men stayed on the east side of the river, knowing they would have to veer off toward the northeast once inside New Hampshire.

All were taken in by the beauty of the state. Although the leaves were turning as fall approached, the lushness of nature was a beautiful thing to see. As they traveled, the road was bordered by red spruce, red oak, white pine, sugar maple, yellow birch, and white birch.

"It's shore purty," York observed, his eyes taking in the stone fences that surrounded the neat fields and farms. "I can't rightly describe the way I feel about this place. It's, well—" He paused and shook his head.

"Civilized," Louis finished it.

"I reckon that's it, Louis. The only gun I've seen all day is the ones we're totin'. Gives me sort of a funny feelin'."

"Bear in mind," Louis sobered them all, "that all that will change with the arrival of Davidson and his thugs."

By mid-afternoon, the schools out for the day, boys and girls began to appear by the fences and the roadways, staring in mute fascination as the cowboys rode slowly by. Smoke and Louis and York all smiled and waved at the young people, and just to give the kids something to talk about and remember, they swept back their jackets, exposing the butts of their guns for the kids' wide eyes.

And the children loved it.

They could have easily made the distance to Keene by nightfall but decided to break it off at an inn on the New Hampshire/Massachusetts line. The innkeeper was a bit startled as the three jingled into his establishment.

"Innkeeper," Louis said, "rooms for three, if you please. And we'll stable our own horses."

"Yes . . . sir," the man said. "Right around back. You'll see the corn bin."

"And warn people to stay away from our horses," Smoke told him. "Anybody gets into Drifter's stall, he'll kill them."

"Sir!"

"That's what he did to the last man who owned him."

"Yes, sir! I will so advise any locals."

The man and his wife and the girls who worked in the tavern and dining room were having a hard time keeping their eyes off the twin-guns belted around each man's lean waist.

"We'll freshen up a bit and then come down for a drink at the bar," Louis told the man and woman.

Louis, York, and Smoke waited.

The man and woman and hired help continued to stare at the three tall men. No one seemed able to move.

Louis rapped gently on the desk. "The keys, please?"

The man came alive. "Oh! Yes! Here you are, gentlemen."

Smoke smiled at the lady behind the desk. "We don't bite, ma'am. I promise you we don't."

His smile broke the barriers between old, settled, and established codes and those who came from the free-wheeling western part of the nation. She returned his smile and glanced down at the register.

"Enjoy your stay, Mr. Jensen. Jensen! Smoke Jensen?"

And once more, pandemonium reigned.

*　　　*　　　*

The trio crossed into New Hampshire at first light, having paid their bill and slipped out quietly before dawn.

York was dressed in jeans, a red and white checkered shirt, and a leather waist-length jacket. Louis dressed in a dark suit, a white shirt with black string tie, highly polished black boots, and a white duster over his clothing to keep away the dust. Smoke was dressed in dark jeans, a black shirt, a red bandana, and his beaded buckskin jacket. All wore western hats. Only York and Smoke's big bowie knives could be seen; Louis' duster covered his own knife.

About ten miles inside New Hampshire, they picked up the Ashuelot River and followed that toward Keene. Some fifteen miles later, the outskirts of town came into view.

The men reined up, dismounted, and knocked the dust from their clothing. Louis, loving every minute of it, removed his linen duster and tied it behind his saddle. A farmer came rattling along in a wagon, stopped, and sat his seat, staring at the heavily armed trio.

"The Reynolds house," Smoke said, walking to the man. "How do we find it?"

The man sat his wagon seat and stared, openmouthed.

"Sir?" Smoke asked. "Are you all right?"

"It's really you," the farmer said, awe in his voice. "I been readin' 'bout you for years. Knew you by your picture."

"Thank you. I'm glad to meet you, too. Could you direct us to the Reynolds house?"

"Oh . . . sure! That's easy. Cross the bridge and go three blocks. Turn right. Two blocks down they's a big white two-story house on the corner. You can't miss it. Wait'll I tell my wife I seen Smoke Jensen!" He clucked to his team and rattled on.

"What day is this?" York asked. "I'm havin' the damndest time keepin' track of things."

"Saturday," Louis told them. "Smoke, do we inform the local authorities as to why we are here?"

"I think not. If we did that, they'd want to handle it the legal way. With trials and lawyers and the such. We'd be tied up here for months. So let's keep it close to the vest and wait until Davidson makes his play. Then we'll handle it our way."

"Sounds good to me," York said. He swung into the saddle.

Smoke and Louis mounted up.

They cantered across the wooden bridge, three big men riding big western horses. They slowed to a walk on the other side of the street. People began coming out of houses to stand and stare at the men as they rode slowly by. Little children stood openmouthed; for all, it was the first time they had ever seen a real western cowboy, much less three real gunslingers like they'd been reading about in the penny dreadfuls and the tabloids.

Louis tipped his hat to a group of ladies, and they simpered and giggled and twirled their parasols and batted their eyes.

A little boy spotted them as they turned the street corner, and he took off like the hounds of hell were nipping at his feet.

"Aunt Sally! Aunt Sally!" he hollered. "They're here, Aunt Sally!"

He ran up the steps of the huge house and darted inside.

The front porch filled with people, all staring at the three horsemen walking their mounts slowly up the street.

"Your relatives, Smoke," Louis said. "Looks like quite a gathering."

"I am not looking forward to this, Louis," Smoke admitted. "I just want to get this over with, see Davidson and his bunch dead in the streets, and take Sally and the babies and get the hell back to the Sugarloaf."

"You'll survive it," the gambler said. "I assure you, my friend. But I feel it will be somewhat trying for the lot of us."

And then Sally stepped out onto the porch to join her family. Smoke felt he had never seen anything so beautiful in all his life. She stood by an older man that Smoke guessed was her father.

The entire neighborhood had left their houses and were standing in their front yards, gawking at the gunslingers.

"Smoke Jensen!" a teenager said, the words reaching Smoke. "He's killed a thousand men with those guns. Bet he took that coat off an Indian after he killed him."

Smoke grimaced and cut his eyes at Louis. The gambler said, "I feel awed to be in the presence of someone so famous." Then he smiled. "A thousand men, eh? My how your reputation has grown in such a short time."

Smoke shook his head and could not help but smile.

John Reynolds said, "That horse he's riding looks like it came straight out of the pits of hell!"

"That's Drifter," Sally told him. "He's a killer horse. Killed the last man who tried to own him."

John looked at his daughter. "Are you serious?"

"Oh, yes. But he's really quite gentle once he gets to know you. I was baking pies one afternoon and he stuck his head into the kitchen and ate a whole pie before I realized it. I picked up a broom and spanked him."

"You . . . spanked him," John managed to say. He muttered under his breath and Sally laughed at his expression.

The riders turned and reined up, dismounting at the hitchrail. Sally stepped off the porch and walked toward the picket fence, a smile on her lips.

Smoke stood by the gate and stared at her, not trusting his voice to speak.

"You've lost weight," Sally said.

"I've been missing your cooking."

He opened the gate.

Her eyes sparkled with mischief. "Is that all you've been missing?" She spoke low, so her words reached only his ears.

Smoke stepped through the open gate, his spurs jingling. He stopped a few feet from her. "Well, let's see. I reckon I might have missed you just a tad."

And then she was in his arms, loving the strong feel of him. Her tears wet his face as she lifted her lips to his.

York lifted his hat and let out a war whoop.

Walter Reynolds swallowed his snuff.

20

"Should you be out of bed this soon?" Smoke asked his wife.

"Oh, the doctors tried to get me to stay in bed much longer, but since I didn't have the time to get to the city to have the babies, and they came so easily, I left the bed much earlier than most, I imagine."

"I keep forgetting how tough you are." Smoke smiled across the twin cradles at her.

"Have you thought about names, Smoke?"

"Uh . . . no, I really haven't. I figured you'd have them named by now."

"I have thought of a couple."

"Oh?"

"How about Louis Arthur and Denise Nicole?"

Louis for Louis Longmont. Arthur for Old Preacher. And Nicole for Smoke's first wife, who was murdered by outlaws, and their baby son, Arthur, who was also killed. Denise was an old family name on the Reynolds side.

"You don't object to naming the girl after Nicole?"

"No," Sally said with a smile. "You know I don't."

"Louis will be pleased."

"I thought so."

Smoke looked at the sleeping babies. "Are they ever going to wake up?"

She laughed softly. "Don't worry. You'll know when they wake. Come on. Let's go back and join the rest of the family."

Smoke looked around for Louis and York. John caught his eye. "I tried to get them to stay. I insisted, told them we had plenty of room. But Mr. Longmont said he felt it would be best if they stayed at the local hotel. Did we offend them, Son?"

Smoke shook his head as the family gathered around. "No. We're here on some business as well as to get Sally. It would be best if we split up. I'll explain."

John looked relieved. "I was so afraid we had somehow inadvertently offended Mr. Longmont."

John Reynolds stared at Smoke as his son-in-law laughed out loud. "Hell, John. Louis just wanted to find a good poker game, that's all!"

It was after lunch, and the family was sitting on the front porch. Smoke had not removed his guns and had no intention of doing so.

And it was not just the young people who stared at him with a sort of morbid fascination.

"Tell me about Dead River," Sally spoke. She glanced at her nieces and nephews. "You, scoot! There'll be lot of times to talk to your Uncle Smoke."

The kids reluctantly left the porch.

Smoke shaped and rolled and licked and lit. He leaned back in his chair and propped his boots up on the porch railing. "Got kind of antsy there for the last day or two before we opened the dance."

"You went to a dance?" Betsy asked.

Smoke cut his eyes. "Opening the dance means I started the lead flying, Betsy."

"Oh!" Her eyes were wide.

"You mean as soon as you told the hooligans to surrender, they opened fire?" Jordan inquired.

Smoke cut his eyes to him. "No," he drawled. "It means that me and York come in the back way of the saloon, hauled iron, and put about a half a dozen of them on the floor before the others knew what was happening." It wasn't really accurate, but big deal.

"We don't operate that way in the East," Walter said, a note of disdain in his voice.

"I reckon not. But the only thing Dead River was east of was Hell. And anybody who thinks they can put out the fires of Hell with kindness and conversation is a damn fool. And fools don't last long in the wilderness."

John verbally stepped in before his son found himself slapped on his butt out in the front yard. "A young lady named Martha will be along presently. She had some foolish notion of traveling back west with you and Sally. She wants to teach school out there."

"Fine with me." He looked at Sally. "Has she got the sand and the grit to make it out there?"

"Yes. I believe she does."

"Tell her to start packing."

"But don't you first have to get the permission of the school board?" Jordan asked.

"Ain't got none," Smoke slipped back into the loose speech of the western man. "Don't know what that is, anyways."

Sally laughed, knowing he was deliberately using bad grammar.

And cutting her eyes to her mother, she knew that Abigal did, too.

But her father appeared lost as a goose.

And so did her brothers.

"Well, sir," Jordan began to explain. "A school board is a body of officials who—"

"—sit around and cackle like a bunch of layin' hens and don't accomplish a damn thing that's for the good of the kids," Smoke finished it.

Abigal smiled and minutely nodded her head in agreement.

With a sigh, Jordan shut his mouth.

Smoke looked at him. "Are you a lawyer?"

"Why, yes, I am."

"Thought so."

"Do I detect a note of disapproval in your voice, Son?" John asked.

"Might be some in there. I never found much use for lawyers. The ones I knowed, for the most part, just wasn't real nice people."

"Would you care to elaborate on that?" Walter stuck out his chin. What there was of it to stick out.

Smoke took a sip of coffee from the freshly made pot. Made by Sally and drinkable only by Smoke. Jordan said it was so strong it made his stomach hurt. Walter poured half a pitcher of cream in his, and John took one look at the dark brew and refused altogether.

"I reckon I might," Smoke replied. But first he rolled another cigarette. "Man chooses a life of crime, he does that deliberate. It's his choice. Hell with him. You ladies pardon my language. On the other side of the coin, a man breaks into another house and starts stealing things, the homeowner shoots him dead, and they'll be those in your profession who'll want to put the property-owner in jail. It don't make any sense. And now, so I read and hear, you folks are beginning to say that some criminals was drove to it, and the courts ought to take into consideration about how poor they was. Poor!" he laughed. "I was a man grown at thirteen; doing a man's work and going to school and looking after my sick mother, all at once. My daddy was off fighting in the war—for the gray," he added proudly. "Not that he believed in slaves, because he didn't. War wasn't fought over slaves nohow.

"We didn't have any money. Tied the soles of our shoes on with rawhide. Ate rabbit stew with wild onions for flavor. Shot them when we had the ammunition; trapped them and chunked rocks at them when we didn't.

"Or didn't eat at all," he added grimly. "But I never stole a thing in my life. Some of our neighbors had more than they needed; but I didn't envy them for it, and if I caught myself covetin' what they had, I felt ashamed.

"Y'all got a big fine house here, and I 'spect you all got lots of money. But how many times have you turned a begger-man away from your back door without givin' him a bite to eat? That don't happen often out where me and Sally live. If that man is able, we hand him an axe and tell him to chop some wood, then we'll feed him. If he ain't able, we'll feed him and see to his needs. There ain't no need to talk on it a whole lot more. Y'all know what I'm talkin' about. But if I find somebody tryin' to steal from me, I'm gonna shoot him dead."

Smoke stood up. "I'm gonna take me a ride around your pretty town." He looked down at John. "We'll talk after supper."

He stepped off the porch and around the stables, his spurs jingling.

John smiled, then he laughed. "I like your man Smoke, Sally. I didn't think I would, but I do. Even though, or perhaps because, he is a man of conviction."

"And is more than willing, just anytime at all, to back up those convictions, Father."

"Yes," John's words were dryly given. "I just bet he is."

"That's the way it shapes up, John Reynolds," Smoke finished telling his father-in-law.

The men were in the study, the door closed. Sally was the only woman present. Her brothers had not been included in the discussion. It was after dinner, and the men had smoked their cigars and had their brandy.

John looked at York; the young Arizona Ranger met his gaze without flinching. He looked at Louis Longmont; the man was handling a rare book from John's library, obviously enjoying and appreciating the feel of the fine leather. There was no doubt in John's mind that the gambler had read it.

He cut his eyes to his son-in-law. "Of course you are going to inform our local police department of these?"

"No."

"But you must!"

"No, I must not. I don't want these men tried in some damn eastern court of law and have them serve five to ten years and then walk scot-free. And you know far better than I that is exactly what would happen, John."

"Then what do you propose to do, Son?"

"I propose to notify your local police when we see them ride into town. Louis has alerted people along the way, people who work both sides of the law. Davidson is not going to ride all the way here from Colorado. Neither is Bothwell or Rycroft or Brute or any of the others. They'll be coming in on trains, one by one, and pick up horses as close to here as possible. I got a hunch they're going to try to tree this town."

"Tree?"

"Hold it hostage. You can't do that to a western town; folks there would shoot you so full of holes your mother wouldn't recognize you. But an eastern town is different. You don't have a loaded gun in this house and damn few others do, either. But I am about to correct that little problem."

"How?" John asked, seemingly stunned by the news.

"I gave York some money this afternoon. He rode over to Brattleboro and picked up some weapons."

"You are going to arm the boys and me?"

"No." Smoke dashed that. "I'm going to arm Sally." Her father looked crestfallen.

"John," Louis asked, "have you ever killed a man?"

"What? Why . . . no."

"Any of your sons ever used a gun in anger?"

"Ah . . . no."

"That's why we're not arming you, John," Smoke told him. "It isn't that we don't believe you're a one hundred percent man. It's just that you'd be out of your element. You, and ninety percent of the people in this town. Oh, a lot of men in this town fought in the War Between the States and were heroes, I'm sure. But that was war, John. I'd be very surprised if one of them could ambush a man and shoot him in cold blood."

"Yes," the lawyer agreed. "So would I."

"There you have it, Mr. Reynolds," York said. "You'd be thinkin' about them bein' human bein's and all that. Well, these people ain't worth a cup of puke."

"How quaintly put," John muttered. "And you have other officers coming in to assist you, right?"

206

"What for?" Smoke asked.

"Well, how many outlaws will there be?"

"Oh . . . probably twenty or so. We'll handle it."

John jumped up. "Are you serious?" he shouted.

"Hell, Mr. Reynolds," York said, "that ain't but six or seven apiece. I recall the time down near the Painted Rock me and two other guys fought off a hundred or more 'paches. Kilt about forty of 'em."

He turned his head and winked at Louis.

"But those were savages!" John protested, not sure he believed the ranger's story or not.

Louis said, "Believe you me, John, Davidson and his bunch are as just as savage as any Apache that ever lived."

Then Smoke told the man about some of the methods of torture Rex and Dagget enjoyed at Dead River.

The lawyer left the room. A few seconds later, they could hear him retching in the water closet.

"I believe you finally convinced him," Sally said.

John returned to the study, his face pale. "Son," he said to Smoke, "I'll start cleaning my shotguns and my rifle."

21

The nights were cool and the days were pleasantly warm as autumn slipped into the northeast. Smoke, for the most part, stayed close to the Reynolds house; York and Louis spent their days riding around the countryside, ranging from the Vermont line to the west, up to Claremont to the north, over to Manchester to the east, and down to the state line to the south.

There was no sign of Davidson or any of his men, and Smoke began to wonder if he had figured wrong. But there was still that nagging suspicion in his guts that the outlaws were on their way and that they would make their move before the first snow. And the first possible snow, John had said, would probably come around the middle of November.

The twins were growing fast. They were fat and healthy babies, who laughed and gurgled and hollered and bawled and messed their diapers.

It was fascinating to John to watch the gunslinger with the big rough hands handle the babies with such gentleness. And the twins responded to the firm gentleness, apparently loving the touch of the big, rough-looking man who, or so it seemed to John Reynolds, never took off his guns.

The sheriff of the county and the chief of police of the town came to see Smoke, demanding to know what was going on: Why had the three come to town? What were they still doing in town?

Smoke answered that he had come to town to see his

wife's family, and that he was still in town waiting for the babies to get big enough to travel.

Neither the sheriff nor the chief believed Smoke's explanation. But neither the sheriff nor the chief wanted to be the one to call him a liar.

For exercise, Smoke took a wagon out into the timber and spent the better part of several days chopping wood. He chopped enough wood to last the Reynolds family most of the winter, and he stacked it neatly.

On one cool and crisp afternoon in November, Louis rode over and chatted with Smoke, who was currying Drifter. York lounged nearby, the thongs off the hammers of his .44's. Only Smoke and Sally noticed that.

"Four of them left St. Louis a week ago," Louis said, leaning up against a stall wall. "My man was certain that one of them was Davidson. They bought tickets for Boston. Six hard-looking western men pulled out of New York City day before yesterday, after buying some fine horseflesh. Some others pulled into Pittsburgh on the river more than a month ago, bought supplies and horses, and left within a week. Still another group rode the cars from Nebraska to St. Louis, bought horses, and left weeks ago. It's taken my people some time to put all this together."

Louis's people, Smoke had learned, included not only foot-padders and whores, but paid members of the Pinkertons.

"So we can look for them by the end of the week," Smoke said, continuing to curry Drifter. "But Davidson is too smart to come riding into town in a gang, shooting the place up. From what you're said, I gather we'll be looking at twenty to twenty-five men."

"At least," the gambler agreed. "I'd guess close to thirty." Smoke was silent for a moment, trying to recall a news article he'd read several weeks back. Then it came to him.

"There was an Army depot robbed down in Maryland several weeks back. Did either of you read that article?"

Louis snapped his fingers. "Yes! I did. Uniforms and

military equipment taken. Smoke, do you think—?"

"Yes. Yes, I do. That would probably be the group who left St. Louis weeks ago." He was thoughtful. "Let's play it that way. I sure wish we had Jim Wilde and a few of the boys up here with us."

"Yes. That would be nice," Louis concurred. "But it's too late to get them here. Do we still play it close to the vest?"

Smoke sighed. "Louis, I've been thinking about that. I can't put these peoples' lives in danger. They've got a right to know what and who is about to enter this area. As bad as I hate to do it, when the so-called Army patrol is sighted, I'm going to level with the sheriff and the chief of police."

"And Mr. Reynolds?" York asked.

"I'll do that as soon as he comes in from the office."

John Reynolds listened, his face impassive. When Smoke concluded, he leaned back in his chair and sighed. "I'm glad you decided to confide in me, Son. I felt that you would, after further thought, take the lives of the people of this community under deeper consideration."

"John, listen to me," Smoke urged. "Where is the nearest military unit based?"

"Why . . . New York State, I'm sure. But we have a fine militia here in New Hampshire. I'll get right on it the first thing in the morning. I'll wire the governor and he'll see to it immediately."

John did not see the look that passed between the three gunfighters.

"How long is this going to take, sir?" York was the one who asked.

"Oh, several days, I'm sure. The governor has to sign the orders mobilizing the unit, then the men have to be notified and moved into place . . ." He fell silent with a curt wave of Smoke's hand. "What is it, Son?"

"We don't have time, John. Not for all that. Can you contact the governor tonight and have him notify the Army?"

"I'm . . . why, certainly. And tell the Army what?"

"Of our suspicions."

"I'll get a wire off immediately." He shrugged into his coat and called for his buggy. He looked at Smoke. "I'll handle this part of it, Son. Be back in half an hour."

When he returned, his face was long. "The governor is taking an early Thanksgiving vacation." He grimaced. "A very early Thanksgiving vacation. I sent a wire to the commanding officer of the Army post over in New York State. He's in Washington, D.C. for some sort of hearings. Son, we appear to be hitting a stone wall every way we turn in this matter."

"I got a bad feelin' about this thing," York said. "I got a feelin' it's all gonna break loose on us tomorrow."

"And those are my sentiments, as well," Louis agreed. "What is your opinion of the sheriff and the chief of police, John?"

"Oh, they're good men. But with only a small force between them."

Smoke and Louis and York had already checked on the cops in the town and county. A very small force. Five men, to be exact. But they all agreed the cops and deputies checked out to be good, stable men. But not gunfighters.

The hall clock chimed. It was growing late. "We see them first thing in the morning," Smoke said.

"I've packed my things," Louis said. "I'll stay here, with your permission, John."

"Of course, of course. I insist that the both of you stay." He glanced at York, received a nod, then looked at Smoke. "We'll see the sheriff and the chief first thing in the morning."

The sheriff was very indignant. "I don't see why you couldn't have leveled with us first thing, Marshal," he said to Smoke.

"Because by doing that, you would have alerted the militia and the Army and deputized every man in the county. And that would have scared them off."

"So? That would have been a bad thing?"

"In a way, yes. They would have just laid back and hit you when you stood the men down and sent them home. How many men can you muster? Good men, Sheriff."

"Jensen, we don't have gunfighters in this town. We have shopkeepers and schoolteachers and farmers and small businessmen. And a nice fat bank," he added grimly.

"How fat?" Louis inquired.

The sheriff hesitated. But Louis Longmont was known worldwide, not only for his talents with a gun and with cards, but also as a very rich man. "Very fat, Mr. Longmont. And need I remind you all that today is the last day of the month?"

Payday for most working people. The bank would have pulled in more money to meet the demand.

"They planned it well," Smoke said, as much to himself as to the others. "How well do the people listen to you, Sheriff?"

The question caught the lawman off guard. "Why . . . I don't know what you mean. They elected me."

"What I mean is, if you told them to stay off the streets today, would they heed your words?"

"I feel certain they would."

The door to the office burst open and a flustered-looking stationmaster stepped in.

"What's the matter, Bob?" Chief of Police Harrison asked.

"I can't get a wire out in any direction, Harrison. My unit is dead as a hammer."

Louis snapped his fingers. "They're planning on using the train to get away. Remember all the horses I was told they'd bought, Smoke? They've stashed them along the railway, and they'll ride the train north to their horses."

"Huh? Huh?" the stationmaster asked, his eyes darting from man to man.

"And the uniforms they stole were not meant to be used here," Smoke added. "They'll be used as a getaway after they've ridden the train north. And it will be north. When they get close to the Canadian line, they'll peel out of those

213

uniforms and ride across as civilians, after splitting up."

The mayor of Keene had stepped in while Louis was talking. "What's all this?" George Mahaffery asked. "I'm trying to get a wire out to my sister in Hanover, Bob. Old Sully tells me the wires are down. What's going on here?"

Nobody paid any attention to Hizzonor.

Sheriff Poley pointed at his lone deputy on duty that day. "Peter, get the women and the kids off the streets. Arm the men."

"Oh, crap!" York muttered.

"I demand to know what is going on around here?" the mayor hollered.

Nobody paid any attention to him.

Smoke stopped the deputy. "Just hold on, partner." To Sheriff Poley: "You're gonna get a bunch of good men hurt or killed, Sheriff."

Poley stuck out his chest. "What the hell do you mean by that, Marshal?"

"This is New Hampshire, Sheriff, not Northfield, Minnesota. Parts of Minnesota is still wild and woolly. When is the last time any man in this town fired a gun in anger?"

That brought the sheriff up short.

"Goddamnit!" Mayor Mahaffery hollered. "Will somebody tell me what the hell is going on around here?"

"Shut up," York said to him.

Hizzonor's mouth dropped open in shock. Nobody ever talked to him in such a manner.

"And keep it shut," York added.

"I'd guess the Civil War, Marshal," Poley finally answered Smoke's question.

"That's what I mean, Sheriff. Ten men, Sheriff. That's all I want. Ten good solid men. Outdoorsmen if possible."

The deputy named a few and the sheriff added a few more. The stationmaster named several.

"That'll do," Smoke halted the countdown. "Get them, and tell them to arm themselves as heavily as possible and be down here in one hour." He glanced at the clock. Eight-thirty. "When's the next train come in?"

"Two passengers today, Marshal," Bob told him. "Northbound's due in at eleven o'clock."

"They'll hit the bank about ten-forty-five then," Louis ventured a guess.

"That's the way I see it," Smoke's words were soft. "But when will they hit the Reynolds house? Before, or after?"

Farmer Jennings Miller and his wife had left the day before to visit their oldest daughter over in Milford. That move saved their lives, for the Miller farm was the one that had been chosen by Dagget for a hideout until it was time to strike.

The outlaws had moved in during the last two nights, riding in by ones and twos, stabling their horses in the Millers' huge barn.

The outlaws had been hitting banks on their way west and had amassed a goodly sum of money. This was to be their last bank job before moving into Canada to lay low for as long as need be.

And Davidson was paying them all extra for this job, and paying them well. The bank was only secondary; the primary target was Sally Jensen and the babies.

Studs Woodenhouse had three men with him. Tie Medley had four from his original gang left. Paul Rycroft had brought two men with him. Slim Bothwell had three. Shorty, Jake, and Red. Brute Pitman. Tustin. LaHogue. Glen Moore. Lapeer. Dagget. Rex Davidson.

Twenty-six men in all. Over one hundred thousand dollars in reward money lay on their heads.

All were wanted for multiple murders, at least. The outlaws had nothing at all to lose.

"Let's start gettin' the saddles on the horses," Davidson ordered. He laughed. "One damn mile from the center of town, and nobody ever thought to look here. It was a good plan, Dagget."

"All I want is a shot at that damned John Reynolds," Dagget growled. "I want to gut-shoot that fancy-talkin' lawyer so's it'll take him a long time to die."

"They any kids in the Reynolds house?" Brute asked. "Say ten or eleven years old?"

No one answered the man. He was along solely because of his ability to use a gun and his nerves of steel. Other than that, no one had any use at all for Brute Pitman.

Not even his horse liked him.

The outlaws began a final check of their guns. They were going in heavily armed, and Rex Davidson had said he wanted the streets to run red with Yankee bluenose blood: Men, women, and kids; didn't make a damn to him.

And it didn't make a damn to the outlaws. Just as long as Davidson paid in cash or gold.

They had gotten a third of the money. The other two thirds they'd receive in Canada.

Two men eased out of the cold house and slipped to the barn to curry and then saddle their mounts.

"I sure will be glad to have me a hot cup of coffee," Tie bitched.

"You want to take a chance on smoke being seen from the chimney?" Dagget asked him.

"I ain't complainin'," Tie replied. "I just wish I had a cup of coffee, that's all."

"Coffee on the train," Rex told them all. "And probably some pretty women."

"Yeah!" several of the outlaws perked up.

"And maybe some children," Brute grinned.

The outlaw seated next to Brute got up and moved away, shaking his head.

22

Good men, Smoke thought, after looking at the ten that had been chosen. Not gunfighters, but good, solid, dependable men. Their weapons were not what Smoke would have chosen for his own use, but they seemed right in the hands of local citizens. Their pistols were worn high, in flap holsters; but they wouldn't be called upon to do any fast-draw work.

Smoke looked outside. The streets of the town were empty. The storeowners had locked their doors but left the shades up, to give the impression that all was well.

"You men are going to protect the bank and other buildings along Main Street," Smoke told the locals. "When you get the bastards in gunsights, pull the damn trigger! We don't have time to be nice about it. You're all veterans of the Army. You've all seen combat. This is war, and the outlaws are the enemy. The sheriff has deputized you, and I've give you federal commissions. You're protected both ways. Now get into the positions the sheriff has assigned you and stay put. Good luck."

The men filed out and began taking up positions. Some were hidden behind barrels and packing crates in alley openings. Others were on the second floor of buildings on both sides of the street.

The sheriff and his deputy, the chief of police and his one man on duty, armed themselves and took their positions.

Smoke, Louis, and York swung in their saddles and

began a slow sweep of the town.

At the Reynolds home, the twins had been taken down into the basement, where a warm fire had been built, and they were being looked after by Abigal and her daughter-in-law.

"I say, Father," Walter asked, his hair disheveled and his face flushed with excitement, "whatever can Jordan and I do?"

"Stand aside and don't get in the way," the father ordered, picking up a double-barreled shotgun and breaking it down, loading it with buckshot. He did the same to two more shotguns and then loaded a lever-action rifle. He checked the loads in the pistols Smoke had given him and poured another cup of coffee. Cowboy coffee. John was beginning to like the stuff. Really pepped a man up!

He shoved two six-shooters in his belt, one on each side. Then he took up another notch in his belt to keep his pants from falling down.

"Who is that man running across the street?" Walter asked, peering out the window.

John looked. "That isn't a man, Son. That's Martha, in men's jeans."

"Good Lord, Father!" Jordan blurted. "That's indecent!"

John looked at the shapely figure bounding up onto the front porch. He smiled. "That's . . . not exactly the way I'd describe the lass, boy." He opened the door and let her in.

Martha carried a Smith & Wesson pocket .32 in her right hand. She grinned at John. "You know me, Mr. Reynolds. I've always been somewhat of a tomboy."

"Sally is guarding the back door, Martha. She is . . . ah . . . also in men's britches."

"Yes." Martha grinned. "We bought them at the same time." She walked back to the rear of the house.

Sally was sitting by the rear window, a rifle in her hand.

She had a shotgun leaning up against the wall and wore a six-gun belted around her waist.

"Can you really shoot all those guns?" Martha asked.

"Can and have, many times. And if you're moving west, you'd better learn how."

"I think today is going to be a good day for that."

"The Indians have a saying, Martha: It's a good day to die."

"I say, Father," Jordan asked, "wherever do you want us to be posted?"

John looked at his two sons. He loved them both but knew that they were rather on the namby-pamby side. Excellent attorneys, both of them. But in a situation like the one about to face them all, about as useless as balls on a bedpost.

John laughed at his own vulgarity. "I think it would please your mother very much, boys, if you would consent to guard them in the basement."

They consented and moved out. Smartly.

Sally came in and checked on her father. She grinned at him and patted him on the shoulder. "You look tough as a gunslinger, Father."

"I feel like an idiot!" He grinned at her. "But I do think I am capable of defending this house and all in it against thugs and hooligans."

"There isn't a doubt in my mind about that, Father. Don't leave your post. I'll handle the back."

Probably with much more proficiency and deadliness than I will handle the front, he thought.

He leaned down and kissed her cheek and winked at her.

"Don't let them get on the porch, Father," she cautioned the man. "When you get them in gunsights, let 'er bang."

He laughed. "I shall surely endeavor to do that, darling!"

Smoke rode alone to the edge of town, and the huge barn to the southeast caught his eyes. There was no smoke coming from the chimney of the house, and the day was

219

cool enough for a fire. He wondered about that, then put it out of his mind. He turned Drifter's head and rode slowly back to town.

The town appeared deserted.

But he knew that behind the closed doors and shuttered windows of the homes, men and women and kids were waiting and watching. And the people of the town were taking the news of the outlaws' arrival calmly, obeying the sheriff's orders without question.

Smoke, York, and Louis, all in the saddle, met in the center of town.

"What's the time, Louis?" Smoke asked.

The gambler checked his gold watch. "Ten-fifteen, and not a creature is stirring," he said with a small smile.

"Unless they're hidin' awful close," York said, rolling a tight cigarette, "they're gonna have to make their first move damn quick."

Smoke looked around him at the quiet town. "They're close. Maybe no more than a mile or two outside of town. I've been thinking, boys. Jim Wilde told me that those ledger books of Davidson's showed him to be a very rich man; money in all sorts of banks . . . in different banks, under different names, Jim guessed. The assumed names weren't shown. So why would he be interested in knocking off a bank? It doesn't make any sense to me."

"You think the primary target is Sally and the babies?" Louis asked.

"Yes. And something else. John Reynolds told me that Dagget has hated the Reynolds family for years, even before he got into trouble and had to leave."

"So John and Abigal might also be targets."

"Yes."

"This Dagget, he have any family still livin' in town?" York asked.

Smoke shook his head. "I don't know. But I'd bet he does."

"But Dagget would still know the town," Louis mused aloud.

"Yes. And he would know where the best hiding places were."

"And he just might have supporters still livin' here," York interjected.

"There is that, too."

The men sat their horses for a moment, quiet, just listening to the near silence.

"Me and Louis been talkin'. Smoke, we'll take the main street. You best head on over toward the Reynolds place."

Smoke nodded and tightened the reins. "See you boys." He rode slowly toward the Reynolds house.

York and Louis turned the other way, heading for the main street of town.

Smoke put Drifter in the stable behind the house but left the saddle on him. Pulling his rifle from the boot, he walked around the big house on the corner. The house directly across the street, on the adjacent corner, was empty. The home facing the front porch was occupied. John had said the family had taken to the basement. To the rear and the left of the Reynolds house, looking from the street, the lots were owned by John; in the summers, neat patches of flowers were grown by Abigal.

Smoke stood on the front porch, the leather hammer thongs off his .44's, the Henry repeating rifle, loaded full with one in the chamber, held in his left hand. Without turning around, he called, "What's the time, John?"

"Ten-thirty, Son," John called through the closed front door.

"They'll hit us in about ten minutes. Relax, John. Have another cup of coffee. If you don't mind, pour me one while you're at it. I'll keep an eye on the front."

The man is utterly, totally calm, John thought, walking through the house to the kitchen. Not a nerve in his entire body. He looked at his daughter. Sally was sitting in a straight-back chair by a kitchen window, her rifle lying across her lap. She looked as though she just might decide to take a nap.

"Coffee, girls?"

"Thanks, Father. Yes, if you don't mind."

Calm, John thought. But then, he suddenly realized, so am I!

Amazing.

"Why hasn't the Army been notified?" Mayor Mahaffery demanded an answer from the sheriff.

Sheriff Poley puffed on his pipe before replying. "Wire is down, George. 'Sides Mr. Reynolds tried to get in touch with the governor last night. He's on a vacation. Tried to get in touch with the commander of that Army base over in New York State. He's in Washington, D.C. Relax, George, we'll handle it."

George pulled a Dragoon out of his belt, the barrel about as long as his arm.

Sheriff Poley looked at the weapon dubiously. "Is that thing loaded, George?"

"Certainly, it's loaded!" Hizzoner replied indignantly. "I carried it in the war!"

"What war?" Poley asked. "The French and Indian? Git away from me before you try to fire that thing, George. That thing blow up it'd tear down half the building."

Muttering under his breath, George moved to another spot in the office.

"Look at those guys," Deputy Peter Newburg said, awe in his voice.

"What guys?" Poley asked.

"Mr. Longmont and that Arizona Ranger, York. They're just standing out on the sidewalks, big as brass. Got their coats pulled back so's they can get at their guns. That York is just calm as can be rolling a cigarette."

"Hell, the gambler is reading a damn newspaper!" George spoke up. "They behave as though they're just waiting for a train!"

"In a way," Poley said, "they are."

"What time is it?" George asked.

Sheriff Poley looked at him. "About a minute later than the last time you asked."

Before George could tell the sheriff what he could do with his smart remarks, the deputy said, "The gambler just jerked up his head and tossed the paper to the street. He's lookin' up Main."

"Here they come!" a lookout shouted from atop a building. "And there's a mob of them!"

Louis and York separated, with York ducking behind a horse trough and Louis stepping back into the shallow protection of a store well. Both had drawn their guns.

Tie Medley and his bunch were leading the charge, followed by Studs Woodenhouse and his gang, then Paul Rycroft and Slim Bothwell and their followers. Bringing up the rear were Tustin, LaHogue, Shorty, Red, and Jake. Davidson, Dagget, Lapeer, Moore, and Brute were not in the bunch.

Louis yelled out, "You men on the roof, fire, goddamnit, fire your rifles!"

But they held their fire, and both Louis and York knew why: They had not been fired upon. It was the age-old myth of the fair fight; but any realist knows there is no such thing as a fair fight. There is just a winner and a loser.

Louis stepped out of the store well and took aim. His first shot knocked a rider from the saddle. York triggered off a round and a splash of crimson appeared on an outlaw's shirtfront, but he stayed in the saddle. A hard burst of returning fire from the outlaws sent Louis back into the store well and York dropping back behind the horse trough.

The outlaws took that time to ride up to the bank and toss a giant powder bomb into the bank; then they charged their horses into an alley. When the bomb went off, the blast blew all the windows out of the bank front and sent the doors sailing out into the street.

Smoke and dust clouded the street. The outlaws tossed another bomb at the rear of the bank building and the concussions could be felt all over the town. The outlaws rode their horses into the back of the bombed-out bank building, and while a handful worked at the safe, the others began blasting away from the shattered front of the building.

The suddenness and viciousness of the attack seemed to stun the sheriff, the chief, and the local volunteers. From the positions chosen by the lawmen, there was nothing for them to shoot at; everything was happening on their side of the street.

Pinned down and fighting alone, Louis lost his composure and shouted, "Will you yellow-bellied sons of bitches, goddamnit, fire your weapons!"

Of course the locals were not cowardly; not at all. They just were not accustomed to this type of thing. Things like this just didn't happen in their town.

But Louis's call did get their attention, which was all he wanted.

"Call me a yellow-bellied son of a bitch, will you?" Mayor George muttered, his ears still ringing from the bomb blasts. Before anyone could stop him, George charged out of the building and onto the sidewalk. Kneeling down, he cocked the Dragoon and squeezed the trigger.

The force of the weapon discharging knocked Hizzoner to the sidewalk. His round missed any outlaw in the bank, the slug traveling clear through the wall and into a hardware store, where it hit the ammunition case and set off several boxes of shotgun shells.

The outlaws in the bank thought they were coming under attack and began shooting in all directions.

George raised to his knees and let bang another round from the Dragoon.

The slug struck an outlaw in the chest and knocked him halfway across the room.

"Clear out!" Tie hollered. "We're blowin' the vault!"

Fifteen seconds later, it seemed the gates to Hell opened up in the little town in New Hampshire.

23

The force of the giant powder exploding sent half the roof flying off and blew one wall completely down. George Mahaffery ended up in Sheriff Poley's lap and the chief of police found himself sitting on a spittoon, with no one really knowing how they got in their present positions.

"I got money in that bank!" a volunteer suddenly realized.

"Hell, so do I!" another called from a rooftop.

"Get 'em boys!" another called.

Then they all, finally, opened up.

"They just blew the bank building," Smoke called.

"Place needed renovating anyway," John returned the call.

Smoke laughed. "You'll do, John. You'll do."

And John realized his son-in-law had just paid him one of the highest compliments a western man could give.

Smoke heard the pounding of hooves on the street and jerked up his Henry, easing back the hammer. He recognized Glen Moore. Bringing up the butt to his shoulder, Smoke shot the killer through the belly. Moore screamed as the pain struck him, but he managed to stay in the saddle. He galloped on down the street, turning into a side street.

Out of the corner of his eye, Smoke saw Brute Pitman cut in behind the house, galloping across the neatly tended lawn.

"Coming up your way, Sally!" Smoke called, then had no more time to wonder, for the lawn was filled with human scum.

Smoke began pulling and levering at almost point-blank range, Lapeer taking a half-dozen rounds in his chest. Behind him, Smoke could vaguely hear the sounds of breaking glass and then the booming of a shotgun. An outlaw Smoke did not know was knocked off the porch to his left, half his face blown away.

"Goddamned heathen!" Smoke heard John say. "Come on, you sorry scum!"

Smoke dropped the Henry and jerked out his six-guns just as he heard gunfire from the rear of the house. He heard Brute's roar of pain and the sounds of a horse running hard.

Splinters flew out of a porch post and dug into Smoke's cheek from a bullet. He dropped to one knee and leveled his .44's at Tustin, pulling the triggers. One slug struck the so-called minister in the throat and the other took him in the mouth.

Tustin's preaching days were over. He rolled from his saddle and hit the ground.

"We've beaten them off!" John yelled, excitement in his voice.

"You stay in the house and keep a sharp lookout, John," Smoke called. "Sally! You all right?"

"I'm fine, honey. But Martha and I got lead in that big ugly man."

Brute Pitman.

And Smoke knew his plan to ride into town must wait; he could not leave this house until Brute was dead and Rex and the others were accounted for.

Reloading his guns, Smoke stepped off the porch and began a careful circling of the house and grounds.

Louis took careful aim and ended the outlaw career of Studs Woodenhouse, the slug from Longmont's gun

226

striking the outlaw leader dead center between the eyes. A bit of fine shooting from that distance.

A rifleman from a second-floor window brought down two of Davidson's gang. Another volunteer ended the career of yet another. Several of the men had left their positions, at the calling of Sheriff Poley, and now the townspeople had the outlaws trapped inside the ruined bank.

One tried to make a break for it at the exact time Mayor George stepped out of the office, his Dragoon at the ready. The Dragoon spat fire and smoke and about a half pound of lead, the slug knocking the outlaw from his horse and dropping him dead on the cobblestones.

"Bastard!" George muttered.

Four rounds bouncing off the cobblestones sent the mayor scrambling back into the office.

Tie Medley exposed his head once too often and Sheriff Poley shot him between the eyes. The Hog, along with Shorty, Jake, and Red, slipped out through a hole blown in the wall and crept into the hardware store. There, they stuffed their pockets full of cartridges and began chopping a hole in the wall, breaking into a dress shop and then into an apothecary shop. They were far enough away from the bank building then to slip out, locate their horses, and get the hell out of that locale.

"Let's find this Reynolds place!" Shorty said. "I want Jensen."

"Let's go!"

Smoke came face to face with Brute Pitman at the rear corner of the house. The man's face was streaked with blood and there was a tiny bullet hole in his left shoulder, put there by Martha's pocket .32.

Smoke started pulling and cocking, each round striking Brute in the chest and belly. The big man sat down on his butt in the grass and stared at Smoke. While Smoke was punching out empty brass and reloading, Brute Pitman toppled over and died with his eyes and mouth open, taking with him and forever sealing the secret to his cache of gold.

Smoke holstered his own .44's and grabbed at Brute's six-guns, checking the loads. He filled both of them up with six and continued his prowling.

Sally and Martha watched as he passed by a rear window, blood staining one side of his face. Then they heard his .44's roar into action, and each listened to the ugly sounds of bullets striking into and tearing flesh.

Glen Moore lay on his back near the wood shed, his chest riddled with .44 slugs.

Smoke tossed Brute's guns onto the back porch and stepped inside the house.

"You hurt bad?" Sally asked.

"Scratched, that's all." He poured a cup of coffee and carried it with him through the house, stopping by John Reynolds's position in the foyer.

"It didn't go as King Rex planned." Smoke sipped his coffee. "I got a hunch he and Dagget have turned tail and run."

"Then it's over?"

"For now. But I think I know where the outlaws holed up before they hit us."

The gunfire had intensified from the town proper.

"Where?"

"That big house with the huge barn just outside of town."

"That's Jennings Miller's place. Yes. Come to think of it, I believe he went to visit one of his children the other day."

"When this is over, I'll get the sheriff and we'll take a ride over there. Does Dagget still have kin in this town?"

John grimaced. "Unfortunately, yes. The Mansfords. A very disagreeable bunch. They live just north of town. Why do you ask?"

"Probably never be able to prove it, but I'll bet they helped Dagget out in casing the town and telling them the best place to hide."

"I certainly wouldn't put it past them."

The firing had lessened considerably from the town.

"I'll wire the marshal's office first thing after the wires

are fixed."

A train whistle cut the waning gunfire.

"I'll ask them to give any reward money to the town. I reckon that bank's gonna be pretty well tore up."

The train whistle tooted shrilly.

John laughed.

Smoke cut his eyes. "What's so funny, John?"

The gunfire had stopped completely; an almost eerie silence lay over the town. The train tooted its whistle several more times.

"I wouldn't worry about the bank building, Son. Like I said, it needed a lot of work done on it anyway."

"Bank president and owners might not see it that way, John."

"I can assure you, Son, the major stockholder in that bank will see it my way."

"Are you the major stockholder, John?"

"No. My father gave his shares to his favorite grand-daughter when she turned twenty-one."

"And who is that?"

"Your wife, Sally."

24

Only two outlaws were hauled out of the bank building unscathed. Several more were wounded, and one of those would die in the local clinic.

Paul Rycroft and Slim Bothwell had managed to weasel out and could not be found.

Almost miraculously, no townspeople had even been seriously hurt in the wild shooting.

Rex Davidson and Dagget, so it appeared, were long gone from the town. The sheriff and his deputy went to the Mansford home and gave it a thorough search, talking with the family members at length. The family was sullen and uncooperative, but the sheriff could not charge anyone. After all, there was no law on the books against being a jackass.

The bodies of the dead were hauled off and the street swept and cleaned up in front of the ruined bank building. The townspeople began gathering around, oohing and aahing and pointing at this and that.

The sheriff had deputized two dozen extra men and sent them off to guard all roads and paths leading out of the town. People could come in, but you had damn well better be known if you wanted to get out.

The telegraph wires had been repaired—they had been deliberately cut by Davidson's men, so the prisoners had confessed—and they were once more humming. A special train had been ordered from Manchester and Concord, and the small town was rapidly filling up with reporters and photographers.

Pictures were taken of Mayor George Mahaffery, holding his Dragoon, and of the sheriff and his deputy and of the chief of police and his man. Smoke, Louis, and York tried to stay out of the spotlight as much as possible.

That ended abruptly when a small boy tugged at Smoke's jacket.

"Yes, son?" Smoke looked down at him.

"Four men at the end of the street, Mr. Smoke," the little boy said, his eyes wide with fear and excitement. "They said they'll meet you and your men in the street in fifteen minutes."

Smoke thanked him, gave him a dollar, and sent him off running. He motioned for the sheriff and for Louis and York.

"Clear the street, Sheriff. We've been challenged, Louis, York." Then he briefed his friends.

"Why, I'll just take a posse and clean them out!" Sheriff Poley said.

Smoke shook his head. "You'll walk into an ambush if you try that, Sheriff. None of us knows where the men are holed up. Just clear the street."

"Yeah," York said. "A showdown ain't agin the law where we come from."

Since they had first met, Martha and York had been keeping close company. Martha stepped out of the crowd and walked to York. She kissed him right on the mouth, right in front of God and everybody—and she was still dressed in men's britches!

"I'll be waiting," she whispered to him.

York blushed furiously and his grin couldn't have been dislodged with an axe.

Louis and Smoke stood back, smiling at the young woman and the young ranger. Then they checked their guns, Louis saying, "One more time, friend."

"I wish I could say it would be the last time."

"It won't be." Louis spun the cylinder of first his right hand gun, then the left hand .44, dropping them into leather. Smoke and York did the same, all conscious of hundreds of eyes on them.

The hundreds of people had moved into stores and ducked into alleyways. Reporters were scribbling as fast as they could and the photographers were ready behind their bulky equipment.

"There they stand," Louis said quietly, cutting his eyes up the street.

"Shorty, Red, Jake, The Hog," Smoke verbally checked them off. He glanced up and down the wide street. It was free of people.

"You boys ready?" York asked.

"Let's do it!" Louis replied grimly.

The citizens of the town and the visiting reporters and photographers had all read about the western-style shoot-outs. But not one among them had ever before witnessed one. The people watched as the outlaws lined up at the far end of the wide street and the lawmen lined up at the other. They began walking slowly toward each other.

"I should have killed you the first day I seen you, Jensen!" Jake called.

Smoke offered no reply.

"I ain't got but one regret about this thing," Jake wouldn't give it up. "I'd have loved to see you eat a pile of horse-shit!"

This time Smoke responded. "I'll just give you some lead, Jake. See how you like that."

"I'll take the Hog," York said.

"Shorty's mine," Louis never took his eyes off his intended target.

"Red and Jake belong to me," Smoke tallied it up. "They're all fast, boys. Some of us just might take some lead this go-around."

"It's not our time yet, Smoke," Louis spoke quietly. "We all have many more trails to ride before we cross that dark river."

"How do you know them things, Louis?" York asked.

Louis smiled in that strange and mysterious manner that was uniquely his. "My mother was a gypsy queen, York."

Smoke glanced quickly at him. "Louis, you tell the

biggest whackers this side of Preacher."

The gambler laughed and so did Smoke and York. Those watching and listening did so with open mouths, not understanding the laughter.

The reporters also noted the seemingly high humor as the three men walked toward hot lead and gunsmoke.

"It's a game to them," a reporter murmured. "Nothing more than a game."

"They're savages!" another said. "All of them. The so-called marshals included. They should all be put in cages and publicly displayed."

Martha tapped him on the shoulder. "Mister?"

The reporter turned around.

The young woman slugged him on the side of the jaw, knocking the man sprawling, on his butt, to the floor of the store.

Jordan Reynolds stood with his mouth open, staring in disbelief.

"Good girl," John said.

A man who looked to be near a hundred years old, dressed in an ill-fitting suit, smiled at Martha. He had gotten off the train that morning, accompanied by two other old men also dressed in clothing that did not seem right for them.

Sally looked at the old men and smiled, starting toward them. The old man who had smiled at Martha shook his head minutely.

The three old mountain men stepped back into the crowd and vanished, walking out the rear of the store.

The reporter was struggling to get to his feet.

"Who was that old man, Sally?" Martha asked.

"I don't know," Sally lied. Then she turned to once more watch her man face what many believed he was born to face.

There was fifty feet between them when the outlaws dragged iron. The street erupted in fire and smoke and fast guns and death.

The Hog went down with three of York's .44 slugs in his chest and belly. He struggled to rise and York ended it with a carefully aimed slug between the Hog's piggy eyes.

Shorty managed to clear leather and that was just about all he managed to do before Louis's guns roared and belched lead. Shorty fell forward on his face, his unfired guns shining in the crisp fall air.

Smoke took out Red first, drawing and firing so fast the man was unable to drag his .45 out of leather. Then Smoke felt the sting of a bullet graze his left shoulder as he cocked and fired, the slug taking Jake directly in the center of his chest. Smoke kept walking and firing as Jake refused to go down. Finally, with five slugs in him, the outlaw dropped to the street, closed his eyes, and died.

"What an ugly sight!" Smoke heard a man say.

He turned to the man, blood running down his arm from the wound in his shoulder. "No uglier than when he was alive," Smoke told him.

And the old mountain man called Preacher chuckled and turned to his friends. "Let's git gone, boys. It was worth the train ride just to see it!"

The reporter that Martha had busted on the jaw was leaning against another reporter, moral and physical support in his time of great stress. "I'll sue you!" he hollered at the young woman.

Martha held up her fists. "You wanna fight instead?"

"Savage bitch!" the man yelled at her.

Lawyer John Reynolds stepped up and belted the reporter on the snoot with a hard straight right. The reporter landed on his butt, a sprawl of arms and legs, blood running down his face from his busted beak.

John smiled and said, "Damn, but that felt good!"

25

BANK ROBBERY ATTEMPT FOILED BY WEST-ERN GUNSLINGERS screamed one headline.

SAVAGES MEET SAVAGE END IN PEACEFUL NEW HAMPSHIRE TOWN howled another front-page headline.

Smoke glanced at the headlines and then ignored the rest of the stories about him. He was getting antsy, restless; he was ready to get gone, back to the High Lonesome, back to the Sugarloaf.

"Is that reporter really going to sue you, Father?" Sally asked John.

The lawyer laughed. "He says he is."

"You want me to take care of it, John?" Smoke asked with a straight face.

"Oh, no, Son!" John quickly spoke up. "No, I think it will all work out."

Then Smoke smiled, and John realized his son-in-law was only having fun with him. John threw back his head and laughed.

"Son, you have made me realize what a stuffed shirt I had become. And I thank you for it."

Smoke opened his mouth and John waved him silent. "No, let me finish this. I've had to reassess my original opinion of you, Son. I've had to reevaluate many of the beliefs I thought were set in stone. Oh, I still believe very strongly in law and order. And lawyers," he added with a smile. "But I can understand you and men like you much better now."

York was out sparking Miss Martha, and Louis was arranging a private railroad car to transport them all back to Colorado. His way of saying thank you for my namesake.

"I'd like nothing better than to see the day when I can hang up my guns, John," Smoke said after a sip of strong cowboy coffee. "But out where I live, that's still many years down the road, I'm thinking."

"I'd like to visit your ranch someday."

"You'll be welcome anytime, sir."

John leaned forward. "You're leaving soon?"

"Probably day after tomorrow. Louis says he thinks he can have the car here then. About noon."

"And this Rex Davidson and Dagget; the others who got away?"

"We'll meet them down the road, I'm sure. But me and Sally, we're used to watching our backtrail. Used to keeping a gun handy. Don't worry, John, Abigal. If they try to take us on the Sugarloaf, that's where we'll bury them."

"I say," Jordan piped up. "Do you think your town could support another attorney? I've been thinking about it, and I think the West is in need of more good attorneys, don't you, Father?"

His father probably saved his son's life when he said, "Jordan, I need you here."

"Oh! Very well, Father. Perhaps someday."

"When pigs fly," John muttered.

"Beg pardon, sir?" Jordan asked.

"Nothing, Son. Nothing at all."

They pulled out right on schedule, but to Smoke's surprise, the town's band turned up at the depot and were blaring away as the train pulled out.

Louis had not arranged for one private car but for two, so the ladies could have some privacy and the babies could be tended to properly and have some quiet moments to sleep.

"Really, Louis," Sally told him. "I am perfectly capable of paying for these amenities myself."

"Nonsense. I won't hear of it." He looked around to make sure that Smoke and York were not watching or listening, then reached down and ticked his namesake under his chin.

"Goochy, goochy!" the gambler said.

Louis Arthur promptly grabbed hold of the gambler's finger and refused to let go.

They changed engines and crews many times before reaching St. Louis. There, all were tired and Louis insisted upon treating them to the finest hotel in town. A proper nanny was hired to take care of the twins, and Louis contacted the local Pinkerton agency and got several hard-looking and very capable-appearing men to guard the babies and their nanny.

Then they all went out on the town.

They spent two days in the city, the ladies shopping and the men tagging along, appearing to be quite bored with it all. It got very un-boring when York accidentally got lost in the largest and most expensive department store in town and wound up in one of the ladies' dressing rooms . . . with a rather matronly lady dressed only in her drawers.

Smoke and Louis thought the Indians were attacking from all the screaming that reverberated throughout the many-storied building.

After order was restored, York commented, "Gawd-damndest sight I ever did see. I thought I was in a room with a buffalo!"

The train chugged and rumbled across Missouri and into and onto the flat plains of Kansas. It had turned much colder, and snow was common now.

"I worry about taking the babies up into the high country, Smoke," Sally expressed her concern as the train rolled on into Colorado.

"Not to worry," Louis calmed her. "I can arrange for a special coach with a charcoal stove. Everything is going to be all right."

But Louis knew, as did Smoke and York, that the final leg of their journey was when they would be the most vulnerable.

But their worry was needless. Smoke had wired home, telling his friends when they would arrive in Denver. When they stepped out of the private cars, he knew that not even such a hate-filled man as Rex Davidson would dare attack them now.

Monte Carson and two of his men were there, as were Johnny North and Pearlie and a half dozen others from the High Lonesome; all of them men who at one time or another in their lives had been known as gunslingers.

York was going to head south to Arizona and officially turn in his badge and draw his time, then come spring he'd drift back up toward the Sugarloaf. And toward Martha.

This was the end of the line for Louis. He had many business appointments and decisions to make, and then he would head out, probably to France.

"Oh, I'll be back," he assured them all. "I have to check on my namesake every now and then, you know."

Smoke stuck out his hand and the gambler/gunfighter shook it. "Thanks, Louis."

"Anytime, Smoke. Just anytime at all. It isn't over, friend. So watch your back and look after Sally and the kids."

"I figure they'll come after me come spring, Louis."

"So do I. See you, Smoke."

And as he had done before, Louis Longmont turned without another word and walked out of their lives.

Christmas in the high country and it was shut-down-tight time, with snow piled up to the eaves. For the next several months, taking care of the cattle would be back-breakingly hard work for every man able to sit a saddle.

Water holes would have to be chopped out daily so the cattle could drink. Hay would have to be hauled to them so they would not starve. Line cabins would have to be checked and restocked with food so the hands could stay alive. Firewood had to be stacked high, with a lot of it stacked close to the house, for the temperature could drop to thirty below in a matter of a few hours.

This was not a country for the fainthearted or for those who did not thrive on hard brutal work. It was a hard land, and it took hard men to mold it and make it liveable.

It was a brutal time for the men and women in the high country, but it was also a peaceful time for them. It was a time when, after a day's back-breaking and exhausting work, a man could come home to a warm fire and a table laden with hot food. And after supper, a man and woman could sit snug in their home while the wind howled and sang outside, talking of spring while their kids did homework, read or, as in Smoke and Sally's case, laid on the floor, on a bearskin rug in front of the fire, playing with toys their father had carved and shaped and fitted and pegged together with his own strong hands. They could play with dolls their mother had patiently sewn during the long, cold, seemingly endless days of winter.

But as is foretold in the Bible, there is a time for everything, and along about the middle of March, the icy fingers of winter began to loosen their chilly grip on the high country of Colorado.

Smoke and Sally awakened to the steady drip-drop of water.

Martha, who had spent the winter with them and had been a godsend in helping take care of the babies, stuck her head inside their bedroom, her eyes round with wonder.

"Raining?" she asked.

Smoke grinned at her. He and Sally had both tossed off the heavy comforter some time during the night, when the temperature began its steady climb upward.

"Chinooks, Martha," he told her. "Sometimes it means spring is just around the corner. But as often as not, it's a false spring."

241

"I'll start breakfast," she said.

Smoke pulled on his clothes and belted his guns around him. He stepped outside and smiled at the warm winds. Oh, it was still mighty cool, the temperature in the forties, but it beat the devil out of temperatures forty below.

"Tell Sally I'll milk the cows, Martha. Breakfast ought to be ready when I'm—"

His eyes found the horse standing with head down near the barn. And he knew that horse. It belonged to York.

And York was lying in the muddy snow beside the animal.

Smoke jerked out his .44 and triggered two fast shots into the air. The bunkhouse emptied in fifteen seconds, with cowboys in various stages of undress, mostly in their longhandles, boots, and hats—with guns in their hands.

Sally jerked the front door open. "It's York, and I think he's hard hit . . ."

"Shot in the chest, boss!" a cowboy yelled. "He's bad, too!"

"You, Johnny!" Smoke yelled to a hand. "Get dressed and get Dr. Spalding out here. We can't risk moving York over these bumpy roads." The cowboy darted back inside the bunkhouse. Smoke turned to Sally. "Get some water on to boil and gather up some clean white cloths for bandages." He ran over to where York was sprawled.

Pearlie had placed a jacket under York's head. He met Smoke's eyes. "It don't look good. The only chance he's got is if it missed the lung."

"Get him into the house, boys."

As they moved him as gently as possible, York opened his eyes and looked at Smoke. "Dagget and Davidson and 'bout a dozen others, Smoke. They're here. Ambushed me 'bout fifteen miles down the way. Down near where them beaver got that big dam."

Then he passed out.

Johnny was just swinging into the saddle. "Johnny! Tell the sheriff to get a posse together. Meet me at Little Crick."

The cowboy left, foggy headed.

York was moved into the house, into the new room that had been added while Smoke and Sally were gone east.

Smoke turned to Pearlie. "This weather will probably hold for several days at least. The cattle can make it now. Leave the hands at the lineshacks. You'll come with me. Everybody else stays here, close to the house. And I mean nothing pulls them away. Pass the word."

Smoke walked back into the house and looked in on York. Sally and Martha had pulled off his boots, loosened his belt, and stripped his bloody shirt from him. They had cut off the upper part of his longhandles, exposing the ugly, savage wound in his chest.

Sally met her husband's eyes. "It's bad, Smoke, but not as bad as I first thought. The bullet went all the way through. There is no evidence of a lung being nicked; no pink froth. And his breathing is strong and so is his heart."

Smoke nodded, grabbing up a piece of bread and wrapping it around several thick slices of salt meat he picked from the skillet. "I'll get in gear and then Pearlie and me will pull out; join the posse at Little Crick. All the hands have been ordered to stay right here. It would take an army to bust through them."

Sally rose and kissed his lips. "I'll fix you a packet of food."

Smoke roped and saddled a tough mountain horse, a bigger-than-usual Appaloosa, sired by his old Appaloosa, Seven. He lashed down his bedroll behind the saddle and stuffed his saddlebags full of ammo and food and a couple of pairs of clean socks. He swung into the saddle just as Pearlie was swinging into his saddle. Smoke rode over to the front door of the house, where Sally was waiting.

Her eyes were dark with fury. "Finish it, Smoke,' she said.

He nodded and swung his horse's head—the horse was named Horse. He waited for Pearlie and the two of them rode slowly down the valley, out of the high country and down toward Little Crick.

By eight o'clock that morning, Smoke and Pearlie had

both shucked off their heavy coats and tied them behind their saddles, riding with only light jackets to protect them from the still-cool winds.

They had met Dr. Spalding on the road and told him what they knew about York's wound. The doctor had nodded his head and driven on.

An hour later they were at the beaver dam on Little Crick. Sheriff Monte Carson was waiting with the posse. Smoke swung down from the saddle and walked to where the sheriff was pointing.

"Easy trackin', Smoke. Two men have already gone on ahead. I told them not to get more'un a couple miles ahead of us."

"That's good advice, Monte. These are bad ones. How many you figure?"

"Ground's pretty chewed up, but I'd figure at least a dozen; maybe fifteen of them."

Smoke looked at the men of the posse. He knew them all and was friends with them all. There was Johnny North, at one time one of the most feared and respected of all gunslingers. There was the minister, a man of God but a crack shot with a rifle. Better hit the ground if he ever pulled out a six-shooter, for he couldn't hit the side of a mountain with a short gun. The editor of the paper was there, along with the town's lawyer, both of them heavily armed. There were ranchers and farmers and shopkeepers, and while not all were born men of the West, they had blended in and were solid western men.

Which meant that if you messed with them, they would shoot your butt off.

Smoke shared a few words with all of the men of the posse, making sure they all had ample food and bedrolls and plenty of ammo. It was a needless effort, for all had arrived fully prepared.

Then Smoke briefed them all about the nature of the men they were going to track.

When he had finished, all the men wore looks of pure disgust on their faces. Beaconfield and Garrett, both big ranchers in the area, had quietly noosed ropes while

Smoke was talking.

Monte noticed, of course, but said nothing. This was the rough-edged west, where horse thieves were still hanged on the spot, and there was a reason for that: Leave a man without a horse in this country, and that might mean the thief had condemned that man to death.

Tit for tat.

"Judge Proctor out of town?" Smoke asked.

"Gone to a big conference down in Denver," Monte told him.

Beaconfield and Garrett finished noosing the ropes and secured them behind their saddles. They were not uncaring men. No one had ever been turned away from their doors hungry or without proper clothing. Many times, these same men had given a riderless puncher a horse, telling him to pay whenever he could; if he couldn't, that was all right, too.

But western men simply could not abide men like Davidson or Dagget or them that chose to ride with them. The men of the posse lived in a hard land that demanded practicality, short conversations, and swift justice, oftentimes as not, at the point of a gun.

It would change as the years rolled on. But a lot of people would wonder if the change had been for the better.

A lot of people would be wondering the same thing a hundred years later.

Smoke swung into the saddle. "Let's go stomp on some snakes."

26

The posse caught up with the men who had ranged out front, tracking the outlaws.

"I can't figure them, Sheriff," one of the scouts said. "It's like they don't know they're headin' into a box canyon."

"Maybe they don't," Pearlie suggested.

One of the outriders shook his head. "If they keep on the way they're goin', we're gonna have 'em hemmed in proper in about an hour."

Garrett walked his horse on ahead. "Let's do it, boys. It's a right nice day for a hangin'."

The posse cautiously made their way. In half an hour, they knew that King Rex and Dagget were trapped inside Puma Canyon. There was just absolutely no other way out.

"Two men on foot," Monte ordered. "Rifles. And take it slow and easy up the canyon. Don't move until you've checked all around you and above you. We might have them trapped, but this is one hell of a good place for an ambush. You—"

"Hellooo, the posse!" the call came echoing down the long, narrow canyon. It was clearly audible, so Davidson and his men were not that far away.

Monte waved the two men back and shouted, "We hear you. Give yourselves up. You haven't got a chance."

"Oh, I think not, Sheriff. I think it's going to be a very interesting confrontation."

247

"Rex Davidson," Smoke said. "I will never forget that voice."

Monte turned to one of his deputies. "Harry, you and Bob ride down yonder about a half a mile. There's a way up to the skyline. You'll be able to shoot right down on top of them. Take off."

"This is tricky country," Beaconfield said. "Man can get hisself into a box here 'fore he knows. Took me several years to learn this country and damned if I still don't end up in a blind canyon ever now and then."

They all knew what he meant, for they all had, at one time or the other, done the same thing.

"Hellooo, the posse!" the call came again.

"We hear you! What do you want?" Monte yelled, his voice bouncing around the steep canyon walls.

"We seem to have boxed ourselves in. Perhaps we could behave as gentlemen and negotiate some sort of settlement. What do you say about that?"

"Bastard's crazy!" Monte said.

"You noticed," Smoke replied.

Raising his voice, Monte called, "Toss your guns to the ground and ride on out. One hand on the reins, the other hand in the air."

"That offer is totally unacceptable!"

"Then you're going to get lead or a rope. Take your choice!"

"Come on and get us then!" Dagget yelled, laying down the challenge.

"We got three choices," Garrett said, a grimness to his voice. "We can starve them out; but that'd take days. We could try to set this place on fire and burn them out; but I don't want no harm to come to their horses. Or we can go in and dig them out."

Smoke dismounted and led Horse back to a safe pocket at the mouth of the canyon. He stuffed his pockets with .44's and pulled his rifle from the boot.

The others followed suit, taking their horses out of the line of fire and any possible ricocheting bullet. Monte waved the men to his side.

"The only way any of us is gonna take lead this day is if we're stupid or downright unlucky. What we're gonna do is wait until Bob and Harry get into position and start layin' down some lead. Then we can start movin' in. So lets us have us a smoke and a drink of water and relax. Relaxin' is something them ol' boys in that box canyon ain't liable to be doin'."

The men squatted down and rolled and licked and shaped and lit. Beaconfield brought out a coffee pot, and Smoke made a small circle of rocks and started a hat-sized fire. The men waited for the coffee to boil.

With a smile on his lips, Smoke walked to the curve of the canyon and shouted, "We're gonna have us some coffee and food, Davidson. We'll be thinking about you boys all hunkered up there in the rocks doing without."

A rifle slug whined wickedly off the rock wall, tearing through the air to thud against the ground.

"This is the Jester, King Rex, Your Majesty!" Smoke shouted. "How about just you and me, your royal pain in the ass?"

"Swine!" Davidson screamed. "You traitor! You turned your back to me after all I'd done for you. I made you welcome in my town and you turned on me like a rattlesnake."

He is insane, Smoke thought. But crazy like that much-talked-about fox.

"That doesn't answer my question, Davidson. How about it? You and me in a face-off?"

"You trust that crud, Smoke?" Johnny North asked, edging close to Smoke.

"No. I just want to see what he'll do."

They all got that answer quickly. All the hemmed-in outlaws began pumping lead in Smoke's direction. But all they managed to do was waste a lot of lead and powder and hit a lot of air.

"So much for that," Smoke said, after the hard gunfire had ceased.

He had no sooner gotten the words out of his mouth when Harry and Bob opened up from the west side of the canyon wall. Several screams and howls of pain told the posse members the marksmanship of the men on the rim was true.

"That got their attention," Monte said with a grim smile.

They heard the clatter of a falling rifle and knew that at least one of the outlaws had been hard hit and probably killed.

"You have no honor, Jester!" Davidson screamed. "You're a foul person. You're trash, Jester."

"And you're a coward, Davidson!" Smoke called.

"How dare you call me a coward!"

"You hide behind the guns of a child rapist. You're afraid to fight your own battles."

"You talkin' about Dagget?" Johnny asked.

"Yeah."

Johnny grimaced and spat on the ground, as if trying to clear his mouth of a bad taste. "Them kind of people is pure filth. I want him, Smoke."

"He's all mine, Johnny. Personal reasons."

"You got him."

"Dagget!" Smoke yelled. "Do you have any bigger bolas than your cowardly boss?"

There was a long moment of silence. Dagget called out, "Name your poison, Jensen!"

"Face me, Dagget. One on one. I don't think you've got the guts to do it."

Another moment of silence. "How do we work it out, Jensen?"

"You call it, Dagget."

Another period of silence. Longer than the others. Smoke felt that Dagget was talking with Davidson and he soon found that his guess was correct.

"I reckon you boys got ropes already noosed and knotted for us, right, Jensen?" another voice called.

"I reckon."

"Who's that?" Monte asked.

"I think it's Paul Rycroft."

"I ain't lookin' to get hung!" Rycroft yelled.

Smoke said nothing.

"Jensen? Slim Bothwell here. Your snipers got us pegged out and pinned down. Cain't none of us move more'un two/three inches either way without gettin' drilled. It ain't no fittin' way for a man to go out. I got me an idea. You interested?"

"Keep talking, Slim."

"I step out down to the canyon floor. One of your men steps out. One of us, one of you. We do that until we're all facin' each other. Anybody tries anything funny, your men on the ridge can drop them already out. And since I'll be the first one out . . . well, you get the pitcher, don't you?"

Smoke looked back at the posse members. "They're asking for a showdown. But a lot of you men aren't gunslicks. I can't ask you to put your life on the line."

"A lot of them ol' boys in there ain't gunslicks, neither," Beaconfield said. "They're just trash. Let's go for it."

Every member of the posse concurred without hesitation. The minister, Ralph Morrow, was the second to agree.

"All right, Bothwell. You and Rycroft step out with me and Pearlie."

"That's a deal. Let's do 'er."

Each taking a deep breath, Smoke and Pearlie stepped out to face the two outlaws. Several hundred feet separated the men. The others on both sides quickly followed, the outlaws fully aware that if just one of them screwed up, the riflemen on the skyline of the canyon would take a terrible toll.

Davidson and Dagget were the last two down from the rocks. Davidson was giggling as he minced down to the canyon floor.

And Davidson and Dagget positioned themselves so they both were facing Smoke.

"And now we find out something I have always known," Davidson called to Smoke.

"What's that, stupid?" Smoke deliberately needled the man.

"Who's the better man, of course!" Davidson called.

"Hell, Davidson. I've known that since the first time I laid eyes on you. You couldn't shine my boots."

Davidson flushed and waved his hand. "Forward, troops!" he shouted. "Advance and wipe out the mongrels!"

"Loony as a monkey!" Garrett muttered.

"But dangerous as a rattlesnake," Smoke advised. "Let's go, boys."

The lines of men began to walk slowly toward each other, their boots marking their progress in the muddy, snowy canyon floor.

The men behind the rifles on the canyon skyline kept the muzzles of their guns trained on the outlaws.

No one called out any signals. No one spoke a word. All knew that when they were about sixty feet apart, it was time to open the dance. Rycroft's hands jerked at the pistol butts and Beaconfield drilled him dead center just as Bothwell grabbed for his guns. Minister Morrow lifted the muzzle of his Henry and shot the outlaw through the belly, levered in another round, and finished the job.

The canyon floor roared and boomed and filled with gunsmoke as the two sides hammered at each other.

Smoke pulled both .44's, his speed enabling him to get off the first and accurate shots.

One slug turned Dagget sideways and the other slug hit Davidson in the hip, striking the big bone and knocking the man to the ground.

Smoke felt the lash of a bullet impact with his left leg. He steadied himself and continued letting the hot lead fly. He saw Dagget go down just as Davidson leveled his six-gun and fired. The bullet clipped Smoke's right arm, stinging and drawing the blood. Smoke leveled his left-hand .44 and shot Davidson in the head, the bullet striking him just about his right eye.

Dagget was down on his knees, still fighting. Smoke walked toward the man, cocking and firing. He was close enough to see the slugs pop dirt from the man's shirt and jacket as they struck.

Dagget suddenly rose up to one knee and his fingers loosened their hold on his guns. He fell forward on his face just as Smoke slumped against a huge boulder, his left leg suddenly aching, unable to hold his weight.

Smoke punched out empties and reloaded as the firing wound down. He watched as Pearlie emptied both Colts into the chests of two men; Minister Morrow knocked yet another outlaw to the ground with fire and lead from his Henry.

And then the canyon floor fell silent.

Somewhere a man coughed and spat. Another man groaned in deep pain. Yet another man tried to get up from the line of fallen outlaws. He tried then gave it up, falling back into the boot-churned mud.

The outlaw line lay bloody and still.

"My wife told me to finish it this morning," Smoke said, his voice seeming unnaturally loud in the sudden stillness.

"Anything my wife tells me to do, I do it," Garrett spoke.

"Looks like we done it," Johnny summed it up.

27

Beaconfield and Garrett called in some of their hands and the outlaws were buried in a mass grave. Reverend Ralph Morrow spoke a few words over the gravesite.

Damn few words.

Smoke tied off the wound in his leg and the men swung into the saddles. This part of Colorado was peaceful again, for a time.

The men turned their horses and headed for home. No one looked back at the now-quiet-but-once-roaring-and-bloody canyon floor. No one would return to mark the massive grave. The men of the posse had left the outlaws' guns on top of the mound of fresh earth.

Marker enough.

York would make it, but it would be a long, slow healing time. But as Dr. Spalding pointed out, Martha would make a fine nurse.

York had been ambushed in the late afternoon, but he'd somehow managed to stay in the saddle and finally made the ranch. He had crawled into some hay by the barn and that had probably saved his life.

"We'll call our ranch the Circle BM," York told her.

Martha thought about that. "No," she said with a smile. "Let's call it the Circle YM. It . . . sounds a little bit better."

Spring came to the High Lonesome, and with the coming of the renewal of the cycle, a peaceful warm breeze blew across the meadows and the canyons and the homes of those who chose to brave the high country, to carve out their destiny, working the land, moving the cattle, raising their families, and trying their best to live their lives as decently and as kindly as the circumstances would permit them.

Martha would be hired as the new schoolmarm, and in the summer, she and York would wed. Her teaching would be interrupted every now and then, for they would have six children.

Six to add to Smoke and Sally's five.

Five?

Yes, but that's another story . . . along the trail of the last mountain man.